The Narrow Abodes

Marcus Hardy

The Narrow Abodes

Book One of the Eternally Forgotten Series

JustFiction Edition

Impressum / Imprint

Bibliografische Information der Deutschen Nationalbibliothek: Die Deutsche Nationalbibliothek verzeichnet diese Publikation in der Deutschen Nationalbibliografie; detaillierte bibliografische Daten sind im Internet über http://dnb.d-nb.de abrufbar.

Alle in diesem Buch genannten Marken und Produktnamen unterliegen warenzeichen-, marken- oder patentrechtlichem Schutz bzw. sind Warenzeichen oder eingetragene Warenzeichen der jeweiligen Inhaber. Die Wiedergabe von Marken, Produktnamen, Gebrauchsnamen, Handelsnamen, Warenbezeichnungen u.s.w. in diesem Werk berechtigt auch ohne besondere Kennzeichnung nicht zu der Annahme, dass solche Namen im Sinne der Warenzeichen- und Markenschutzgesetzgebung als frei zu betrachten wären und daher von jedermann benutzt werden dürften.

Bibliographic information published by the Deutsche Nationalbibliothek: The Deutsche Nationalbibliothek lists this publication in the Deutsche Nationalbibliografie; detailed bibliographic data are available in the Internet at http://dnb.d-nb.de.

Any brand names and product names mentioned in this book are subject to trademark, brand or patent protection and are trademarks or registered trademarks of their respective holders. The use of brand names, product names, common names, trade names, product descriptions etc. even without a particular marking in this works is in no way to be construed to mean that such names may be regarded as unrestricted in respect of trademark and brand protection legislation and could thus be used by anyone.

Coverbild / Cover image: www.ingimage.com

Verlag / Publisher:
JustFiction! Edition
ist ein Imprint der / is a trademark of
AV Akademikerverlag GmbH & Co. KG
Heinrich-Böcking-Str. 6-8, 66121 Saarbrücken, Deutschland / Germany
Email: info@justfiction-edition.com

Herstellung: siehe letzte Seite /
Printed at: see last page
ISBN: 978-3-8454-4759-9

1

Prelude

Ainsley had never been to her great grandfather's home, nor had she ever met him. He, according to her mother was a severely reclusive man, never leaving the house or having visitors. Which is why this trip was so odd. Ainsley had had relations with her great grandfather tangibly through her mother's stories of growing up with him. Her favorite was that of when he first came to live with her mother.

Abigail was not in a particularly good mood. Which was further worsened by the fact that it was her birthday. She had woken up expecting what she always received on her birthday. Vis-à-vis, an array of gifts surrounding her bed; it had always been one of her favorite family traditions and she was none too pleased to see nothing but a flacked wall staring back at her.

Bewildered, Abigail hopped out of her bed and started to search her small if not microscopic room. A room that was both illegal and ill advised, being built hanging over a six-story apartment building out of nothing but lumber, nails and any spare items they could find. The irregular room consisted of a makeshift single bed, which at one time or another had been used as a coffee table. A small *desk* that was smaller than most nightstands. And lastly, a rocking chair; in proportion to the room the chair looked like it was fit for a baby giant. The room had a submarine hatch overlooking a small park nestled in between the two adjoined complexes. Perplexingly enough, the park had no visible access and yet was well maintained, maintained to the point of metaphysics. The door to Abigail's room was oddly enough a narrow two door; which would suggest that in the past, the door served as entrance to a walk-in closet. From the door was a small awkward landing that leads to a curved downward staircase that headed down one flight.

Abigail descended these stairs looking obsessively for any trace of packaging. Upon reaching the landing, Abigail turned and walked the narrow passageway to the kitchen.

The kitchen was by far the most technologically advanced room in the apartment, with a garden hose for a faucet, an icebox instead of a fridge and an oval island, with cupboards lining the overhead.

Abigail's father Alden had an obsession with carpentry, an obsession formed out of a fear of moving. He'd rather build a home than move, and that is what he was attempting to do twelve blocks north and 7 west. Abigail didn't think it necessary to inform him that once the house was complete, they'd have to move into it.

Abigail's mother Arlene had no will power. At least she had none left, after raising not only her three children, but her younger siblings as well; she was burnt out. Spending most of her time sitting in front of the poorly ventilated fire pit knitting what ever was needed for the family. Anything from tea cozies to pants. Beyond that, she did little else, speaking rarely above a mumble and moving in a subtle scuttle.

Abigail's brothers Alan and Aaron were attached at the hip, no, not metaphorically speaking. They were literally and biologically attached at the hip, but what proved odd was they weren't identical. Alan had dirty blonde hair and a chiseled outward appearance, while Aaron had platinum blonde hair and was pudgy. Neither got along and would intentionally disagree just to spur arguments over heedless events. The only thing they cared for was medicine, so they may one day be able to separate each other by themselves.

Abigail, now eleven, took a seat at the extinguished fire pit and sulked. They had forgotten about her birthday. She was always impressed that her dysfunctional family could remember; it was only a matter of time before they slipped up. Leaning in her chair to look at the kitchen island around the makeshift divider wall, Abigail sighed to see that indeed no note had been left. Where did they go? Why wouldn't they take her as well? Maybe they all remembered in the middle of the night, so they all ran out to fetch her presents. Abigail smiled at the thought of her family running down the streets in the pajamas. Getting up from the chair, Abigail looked round for some form of entertainment. Her only solace was the radio sitting on the kitchen island. Walking over to it, Abigail picked it up and turned it on. Turning, Abigail moved over to her brothers' double bed, inside the old alcove that once was a fireplace, whilst she tuned the radio onto the news. "Well it's been a grueling five hours but the standoff is now over and no one is harmed, a truly brilliant end to a truly terrible situation" commented the radio host to Abigail's annoyance. She had just missed something juicy. "Well that's all for us from the morning news, see you all tomorrow" 'Nuts' thought Abigail as the commentator signed off and dead air ensued.

Abigail's emerging passion was writing, ever since she was seven and her father gave her a diary, Abigail had been writing down every thought that occurred. Unlike other writers whom shy away from personal details, Abigail embraced it, she particularly loved to write stories surrounding her family, especially whenever a normal day was ruined by one of their personal endeavors. Take for example when Alden had arranged for the whole family to go to the beach for the weekend. Abigail had been in raptures ever since he suggested it; unfortunately, it just so happened that on that day, the building inspector had come to judge whether or not the

apartment was legally viable. Of course, it wasn't and Alden had to board up
the stairwell to Abigail's room and nail down the floorboards that had, for a
time, been threatening injury. Therefore, by the time the inspector did arrive,
the apartment looked more conspicuous than an elephant in a playground.
But, like every official in this town, the situation came to a swift, albeit
expensive end.

Feeling she should go and write in her diary about this disappointing
day, Abigail stood and shuffled over to the narrow hallway. However, before
she could ascend the stairway to her room, the front door, which looked
suspiciously like two layers of drywall, barged open and Abigail's whole
family, including her closest friends and relatives danced through the doors
holding streamers and party batons.

"Happy Birthday!" they all shouted in unison. Abigail's eyes went as
wide as watermelons as the whole familial crew surrounded her. "Oh my
goodness! You remembered after all!" exclaimed Abigail. "Well of course
we remembered, you're the only one of us who cares about this material
bull." Commented Alan, who with a smirk turned to his twin to see his
displeased expression. Abigail however wasn't fazed; it was true she really
was the only family member who cared about nice things. Just a look around
the room would confirm this. Her father, dressed in an oversized, moth-eaten
brown sweater and matching velvet pants. Arlene was wearing the only
dress she had, a two sizes too small sundress, that perhaps, at one point, was
yellow, but now was just a pale off white, and tearing at the seams. The
twins were wearing one of their trademark "h-shirts" that where two shirts
stitched together thus giving them differing outfits. An intriguing side note
about there shirts was that they were reversible, which in this household was
necessary, because each family member, on average owned 3 outfits. With

the exception of Abigail who demanded, that because she was both the youngest and the only daughter, deserved nicer clothes. However, even with her demands, she was only rewarded with two extra outfits.

After the initial shock of her surprise party seceded, Abigail noticed that a man was standing in the doorway. He was tall, muscular, and appeared to be in his 60's. He had long well kept platinum hair that fell cleanly at his shoulders in a fine ponytail. Unlike Abigail, and her family, this man appeared to be highly organized and compulsive. He had a brand new vest and suede's on and an overcoat that seemed oddly out of character for him, it was dirty, and well worn. "Perhaps a gift from Alden?" thought Abigail. But all this failed to intrigue Abigail as much as the large, leather bound book possessively in this man's grasp.

"Abigail, this is Arthur, he's your grandfather." Explained Alden. With surprised excitement, Abigail did the first thing that jumped to mind, she hugged Arthur tightly, "Its wonderful to meet you Arthur!" happily said Abigail, to which Arthur heartily replied "Oh now, none of that, you'll call me Artie." "Artie?" thought Abigail, "what an unusual name".

The first few nights with Artie were rather uneventful. Abigail's parents set him up on the living room couch, which received a howl of moans from the twins who not only would technically be sharing a room with Artie, but would also loose their "research lab" as they called it, which was the couch and every hand-me-downed book imaginable on medicine.

After an uneventful week, Abigail was beginning to wonder just how long her grandfather would be staying. Her father informed her it would be for a short while. He was only forced out of his household because one of the buildings it was connected with had recently been involved in a hostage situation, which ended with the building catching fire. No one was hurt, but some structural damage was done and collapse was possible not only for the building in question, but also for Arthur's as well.

Since he moved in, Artie had not uttered more than two words to anyone. He always appeared to be in a faraway place, lost in his thoughts. In fact, he talked so little; the twins struck up a wager to see who would speak more, Arlene, or Arthur. But what upset Abigail the most was despite how laconic Artie was, he had not said a word to her since their initial meeting. Furthermore, he hadn't even glanced in her direction; it was almost like he was intentionally avoiding eye contact with her.

Half the time, Arthur spent staring into the abyss, whilst the other half, he spent incessantly reading his leather bound book. Now, Abigail always prided herself on being an intuitive girl, being able to read situations, emotions, people, and understand how they tick. Arthur was puzzling to her. From what she heard from her parents, he was a very gregarious man, and what piqued her interest most was he apparently was like that up until he moved in.

Finally, one day whilst everyone was silently sitting round the circular fire pit, Alden carving a horse for sport, Arlene falling asleep, the twins reading one of their textbooks, and Arthur once again reading the book, Abigail calmly asked, "Artie, what are you reading?" This caused everyone to stop what he or she was doing and look to Abigail, all but Arthur, who bluntly answered "a book". Irritated by his evasive answer, Abigail pressed on, "yes, but what about?" Finally, Arthur stopped reading and looked toward Abigail, he smiled warmly and stated "your too young to understand dear, maybe some day." Content with that answer, and the promise of answers in the upcoming future, Abigail dropped it and turned back to the fire.

After an hour or so, everyone headed to bed, all but Arthur who continued to read. Abigail, being the last to leave the living room, which housed Artie, turned to look at him, suspecting something off putting about him. Sighing, she turned, climbed through the window that acted as the doorway to her staircase and headed to bed. She decided, lying there in her bed that she would get to the bottom of Arthur and his mysterious text before the end. Satisfied with that resolve, Abigail dozed off to sleep.

The following morning, Abigail bounded down the stairwell and was halted to see her entire family save for Arthur who was nowhere to be found, standing round the oval table in the kitchen, they were all hunched over something. Curious Abigail walked up and loomed over the table, on it sat a post card with a cartoony picture of the Earth on it, and on the back it said, "I've business in the world. Be seeing you all. Arthur." Abigail joined her family in their perplexed state. She grabbed the card to see if anything else was written. Seeing nothing, she looked down upset. Then from across the table a hand came into her view, it was that of her father's. In his hand was a very old key with the number three on it. "What's this?" asked Abigail, "Don't know he left it for you." Responded Alden. Taking the key from her father, Abigail looked at it and read the attached note, which said "To: Abigail, someday you'll understand." Confused, Abigail looked to her father. "But, what does it open?" Impatiently asked Abigail, to which Alden just shrugged his shoulders.

And so, time passed, and Abigail never saw Arthur again, he stayed in touch, sending postcards here and there, all as baffling as the first. But what truly baffled Abigail was this key, and so, every night, she would sit in her room, staring at the key, and dream of what mystery it possessed.

Part One

I. Ainsley and the Abode

Ainsley sat on the bus, thinking about what her mom told her "bring back the book, bring it to me." This struck Ainsley as odd because, first off, her mom had never asked her for a favor ever, and secondly, her mom never read, anything, but here it was, her mom asking her to do this and Ainsley rising up from the bus. She emerged from the bus, looking up and down the street. Peering down at her scrap of paper, Ainsley read the address: Apt. 1, 73rd Westmont St. Gazing up from the scrap, Ainsley saw that she was standing between the addresses of 72nd and 74th Westmont St. Confused, Ainsley turned and looked beyond the departing bus to see that no 73rd Westmont St. was on the other side of the road either.

Flipping over the scrap of paper repeatedly, Ainsley found no salvation, no answer to this riddle of the mysteriously absent 73rd Westmont St.

As a man walked by, Ainsley stopped him and asked "Excuse me sir, do you know where 73rd Westmont St. is?" The man stared at her for a second, determining her authenticity, seeing she was genuinely curious, the man raised his umbrella upwards to the sky and said " 73rd Westmont is there! Milady." Confused, Ainsley raised her gaze upward in the direction the man suggested, blinded by the sun Ainsley took a second to let her eyes adjust, once done so, Ainsley saw what she was looking for, a tall lanky structure sitting isolated in between the rooftops of 72nd and 74th Westmont St.

Absolutely baffled, Ainsley turned to ask the man how she was to get to it, but was disappointed to see the man had long since moved on down the street. Standing there looking up at the mysterious building, Ainsley gauged what she should do, looking round, Ainsley spotted a fire escape round the corner, deciding that was her best bet, Ainsley began to climb the rusting fire escape, more of a hazard than escape. One misstep and you'd be finished. But being the wise, little girl that she was, Ainsley never faltered, she climbed the fire escape with no problems arising.

Standing on the rooftop of 72nd Westmont St. Ainsley looked at the much more daunting structure of 73rd Westmont St. From way down below, the building looked quite small and thin. However, up close it resembled a poorly crafted mansion, the grandeur of a royal home, but the unfortunate narrowness of a slum. Ainsley, thanks to her grandfather's passion for carpentry, judged the building to be about 7 small stories, though being such a bizarre structure to begin with, that estimate could not be confirmed.

Growing ever more curious of the bizarre structure, Ainsley moved closer to the building. She noticed it hand windowsills plastered all over it, yet no windows, almost like it once may have had windows, but was later replaced with wood similar to the material of the house. The color of the wood was quite queer, it looked a dark blue, but as she got closer, the blue turned ever blacker and the surface of the wood looked wet, or perhaps slimy, almost as if it had been dumped in a swamp at one time. And the smell would confirm this; it smelt of rot, pure and unadulterated rot. In fact, the smell became so strong, that Ainsley had to cover her face with her tame pink jacket.

Coming to the steps leading up to the warped door, Ainsley placed her hand on the rail and was disgusted to find her hand covered in a black substance, grossed out beyond belief, Ainsley quickly rubbed off the substance on her jeans and hurried up the steps.

Reaching for the doorknob, Ainsley remembered she was supposedly meeting her great grandfather, being this his house, so changing the course of her hand, she instead reached for the knocker, which was in the shape of a deer of some sort, with a handle bridged between the antlers. Knocking appropriately, Ainsley stepped back to present herself accordingly, looking herself over, Ainsley adjusted her shoulder length wavy brown hair, the only member of her family to have such hair color, everyone else had blonde curls. Looking down, Ainsley noticed the large black smudge now on her jeans, sighing, Ainsley quickly tried to rub it out, but to no avail, the large wooden door, swung open.

Entering, Ainsley was quickly thrust into darkness as the door automatically shut closed, though being slightly paranoid, Ainsley assumed someone was responsible for it. So, naturally Ainsley called out "Hello? Arthur? It's me Ainsley, your great granddaughter? My mom told me to come by today?" No response, thinking of the size of the house, and that maybe Arthur was not in earshot, Ainsley started to move across the floor, which creaked and squeaked uncontrollably, suggesting it was rotten to the core and ready to collapse. Feeling quite unsure of her footing, Ainsley reached out for the nearest wall, and was surprised to find her hands touching the wall on both sides. Slightly confused and blissfully pleased to realize that the interior walls were not of the same semblance as the exterior ones, Ainsley moved down the hallway searching for a doorway or stairs, all the while calling out her great grandfathers name. "Arthur?! It's me Ainsley! Are you home?!" Repeating this several times, Ainsley was just about to give up and was starting to wonder just how long this house was, it felt like she'd been walking for a few minutes, when she tripped over the beginning of the steps.

Falling onto them, Ainsley rubbed of the dust that collected on her hands and wherever else her body touched the stairs. But what quickly caught Ainsley's attention was the angle of the stairs, they were unlike the usual 45 degrees of most stairs, even unlike the unusual stairs of her grandfathers which were anywhere between 30 and 50 degrees. No, this stairs were at least 70 degrees upward, making them more similar to ladders. However unlike ladders, they had distinct steps, enough space for a firm footstep to be placed.

Amazed and becoming more impressed with the design of this house, Ainsley looked upwards towards the top of the steps and saw a small opening where some low light was being emitted. Figuring that is where Arthur was, Ainsley started to climb the vertical steps, and while doing so was growing ever more curious how her 107 year old great grandfather could live in such a house with such steps.

Emerging on the second floor of this narrow abode, Ainsley looked round in the low light and saw no one, but, unlike downstairs, she could make out the hallway, for that was all that was there, another hallway with another set of vertical steps at the end of them. Also unlike the downstairs hallway, Ainsley was able to make out the décor of the hallway, she couldn't quite place it, being only 13 years old, didn't know historical real estate design very well. But what it did remind her of was her friend Heather's billiard room, with deep red lining the upper half of the walls and deep brown wood lining the lower half. Walking along the carpeted floor, Ainsley was surprised to notice this floor better kept for than the base floor, almost as if the base floor had all been forgotten about. This floor, unlike the last had no creaking, or to be fair less than the last, and did not smell of rot so much, which was immensely appreciated.

As she walked down the hall, she noticed on the left side of it, at around mid way, a small chopped couch sticking out from the wall. Perplexed by this, Ainsley ignored it and moved on to the stairs, which she dutifully climbed.

Reaching the third floor, Ainsley quickly detected a pattern occurring, every floor she climbed, the better kept it was, this floor had soft lighting with green colored walls and a wooden base like the last, this floor did not creak at all and was blissfully odorless. It also contained what Ainsley could only assume to be a fridge and oven half sticking out of the wall.

And so it went every floor she climbed, the better the narrow abode became, and on every floor contained an unusual piece of furniture, the fourth floor contained a dinner table, the fifth a bed, the sixth, a full toilet and sink which Ainsley had to squeeze by to reach the end of the floor. However, at the end of the sixth floor, Ainsley was surprised and disappointed to see no vertical steps leading up. No, all that remained was a bookshelf with old books in it, save for one obvious absence in the middle shelf. Disheartened, Ainsley turned round and began to make her way back past the toilet. But just then, Ainsley had an unusual euphoria overcome her as she sensed something from above, looking up; she saw a large metal handle dangling just out of her reach.

Smiling to herself, Ainsley climbed onto the toilet seat then the tank behind it and pulled down the large metal handle.

II. The Seventh Floor

As Ainsley pulled down the metal handle, she was overwhelmed by the most disturbing smell imaginable, far worse than that of the base floor, far worse than a junkyard. No the smell Ainsley experienced could only be described as years upon years of stagnant air, air that had not been refreshed for an age. The smell was so bad, it caused Ainsley to fall backward and collapse on the comfy carpet of the sixth floor. Yet, despite how comfortable the carpet was, it still knocked Ainsley unconscious. As she began to loose consciousness, she saw, entering the new doorway formed from the opened hatch, a blurred man, looking down at her, his expression impossible to read in her state. With that, Ainsley passed out.

It wasn't until the scent of eggs and bacon catching her nostrils that Ainsley woke. Forgetting where she was, Ainsley rolled right off the halved bed onto the floor of the fifth level. Coming to her senses, Ainsley looked round and took in her surroundings, she never realized it before, but on the wall across from her, there was a old map of someplace she was unaware of, it looked like an island, and was labeled in obscure languages and dialects. Looking at if for a few moments seeing if she could make sense of it at all, Ainsley then followed her noise, which was following her stomach, to the third floor.

Landing on the floor, Ainsley was surprised to see a brisk young man moving about the kitchen with great haste, almost as if he were in some cooking contest. Not knowing whom this man was, Ainsley cautiously moved into the light and asked the man "Excuse me, sir?" With a jolt, the man who was holding a sizzling pan of eggs tossed the eggs in the air, having them land all over. "Oh child, look what you did, getting me in a fright" said the man. Confused, Ainsley replied "Child? Excuse me sir, who are you, I thought this was my Great Grandfathers house?" "Indeed, yes it is child, been in his family oh, longer than knowledge allows" Wisely replied the man. "Okay, well who are you?" sternly asked Ainsley who wasn't particularly liking this man's devil may care attitude. "Names Artie, but if you insist, call me Arthur" said the man extending his hand in greeting.

Perplexed, Ainsley took his hand and shook it. Staring at him in a new light as he went about cleaning up the eggs, Ainsley felt compelled to ask "But your old!" "I most certainly am, closing in on my 47th, vastly older than you child." This just furthered Ainsley's confusion as the man made no hint that he was pulling her leg.

Having finished with the clean up, the man casually cracked two more eggs and asked "how do you like your eggs, I was making them scrambled, is scrambled alright?" Ainsley dazedly nodded then resumed her questioning. "But, no you were supposed to be like 107 years old, not 47, you can't be my great grandfather!"

Not responding immediately, Artie finished cracking the eggs then turned at last to Ainsley and stared at her dead in the eye, even bending down slightly to get right in her face, and said "I think it be best if you went up to the attic, might help explain things better than I can". With that, the young Artie continued to work on the meal, and Ainsley turned round, and headed up to the seventh floor.

Reemerging on the sixth floor, Ainsley found it just as she left it, the ceiling hatch open, and looming. Moving closer to it, Ainsley prepares for the fowl smell by covering up her nose with her trusty pink jacket.

Climbing onto the toilet tank then grabbing the rail of the fall down stairwell, Ainsley pulls herself upwards into the attic.

Standing on the last step of the stairwell, Ainsley makes to step, but trips over the out standing floor of the attic. With a yelp, Ainsley crashes to the ground.

Having lost her grip on her jacket, Ainsley was forced to intake the horrid air of the attic, but was shocked when she was greeted with a blissfully profound scent, a beautiful smell that she could only describe as all the best smelling flowers in the world combined into one. Completely distracted by this wonderful scent, Ainsley stood and wandered round the low ceilinged attic. Of all the floors, this was by far the smallest, not just the low roof, but also the collapsed portions of the room that let in the morning sunlight. Having spent so long in artificial light, Ainsley flinched at getting a full dose of natural sunlight in her eyes. Finally having her eyes adjust, Ainsley notices a small lamp on in the corner of the room, turning to look at it fully; Ainsley also notices a leather chair turned away from her.

As Ainsley approached the chair, she chuckled to herself at the thought of it being the only full piece of furniture in the entire abode. Standing in front of the chair, Ainsley's curiosity got the better of her and she spun the chair round to reveal a skeletal form of a man whom she instantly assumed was her great grandfather Arthur. Screaming, Ainsley fell backward onto her rump. Arthur was obviously not alive, nor had been for some time, his skin, or what was left, was a pale blue, his muscles, non-existent, his hair was long, wiry and thin. But what caught Ainsley's attention, the thing that shocked her, was his face, it still resembled the face her mother Abigail had gazed at all those years earlier, color changed of course, but still the same.

Truly flabbergasted, and disturbed, Ainsley stood and moved once more to Arthur, leaning forward, she looked closer at his comparably younger face. His nose, wide and firm, his mouth, slack jawed and toothless, his eyes, that is when Ainsley noticed something, Arthur's eyes were completely black, glazed over, appearing almost like glass. Leaning in, Ainsley gently touched the face of her deceased super-senior citizen. Caressing it with full respect, Ainsley marveled at its leather feel, similar to that of a cow or, bull, she had never touched any of those creatures, but that is what popped into her head. Slowly removing her hand from his face, Ainsley screamed once more as the head sharply fell forward and dislodged itself from the neck. It then proceeded to roll of the body and onto the ground to settle once more by Arthur's feet.

Trembling now from all the sudden bursts of terror, Ainsley bent down to pick up the decrepit head, and placed it on Arthur's lap. But, upon doing so, Ainsley noticed something. Under the blanket snuggled tightly round the skeletal form of Arthur's legs, was something large and box like was sitting. Picking up the head once more and removing the blanket, Ainsley saw what only she and her mother dreamed about, the large leather-bound text.

Ainsley's eyes glazed over has she hastily swapped the head for the book and looked at it with wonder. 'I found it, mom is going to be thrilled!' thought Ainsley as she did a sweet waltz round the attic.

Then, with a jolt, Ainsley stopped, something occurred to her, something unsettling. If this was her great grandfather Arthur, who was that man cooking scrambled eggs and bacon downstairs?

III. The Truth About Artie

Ainsley descended the ladder-like stairways of her deceased great grandfather's home, heading straight for the imposter. She didn't know what to think, this truly had been a bizarre day, and horrifying, never in her wildest dreams did she expect to discover her great grand father dead, though in hindsight she shouldn't have been surprised, he was 107 after all.

Arriving on the third floor, 'Artie' was still busy cooking, or rather, re-cooking the scrambled eggs he clumsily spilt not ten minutes ago. He appeared to show no sign of awareness to Ainsley's presence. Growing impatient, Ainsley coughed loudly. "Oh! Dear child you almost made me spill my eggs again!" Cautiously chuckled Artie as he narrowly avoided spilling his meal. "What the hell was all that up there?!" Sternly asked Ainsley, she was not pleased at all with having to deal with all this; after all, she was twelve for crying out loud! And she was most definitely not pleased with being denied meeting the man that had such an affect on her mother's and tangibly her own childhood. "What was that? I thought that be obvious, that was Arthur, your great grandfather?" "Gee, thanks Sherlock, I meant who in the hell are you then?!", rebutted Ainsley to Artie's smartass remark.

"I'm Artie, I'm Arthur, I'm your great grand father," Ainsley, frustrated, shook her head, "you are not making any sense! You can't be my great grandfather! I just saw him! His head fell off! I mean come on, I may be twelve, but I can tell a faker when I see one, I mean you are like the same age as my dad!" "I would please ask that you do not raise your voice, this house doesn't handle well to stress, the reverberations of the frequency of your tone, may well cause it to collapse on our heads" chuckled Artie. "I don't care! Just tell me what's going on, don't lie to me, or, or I'll call the police!!" Ainsley felt proud of herself or holding herself together. "There is no need of that my dear, why don't you take a seat?" Ainsley, too frustrated to argue, walks over to the stairwell and sits, or more likely leans. Artie, calmly, and confidently walks over, he leans down, and stares Ainsley dead in the eye, "I am Arthur, your great grandfather, so to is the man in the attic, but he is dead, I am his replacement, his replica, I am him".

Ainsley, not one to swear, stares firmly at Artie, "Are you fucking kidding me?" Artie, chuckles, a chuckle Ainsley is quickly growing to loathe. "No child, I'm not kidding you, people like me, we don't kid. I have been reincarnated, reborn if you will, only not quite, I'm more like rewound to my youth." "You are not young" countered Ainsley bluntly. "Yes, this is true, in fact, adding up all the many years I've been alive, I'm more like 373 years old." Ainsley just stares blankly at Artie, not believing a word he says. "Here let me explain" "Please do," pleaded Ainsley.

"I am one of seven individuals across the world, who at this time in our lifetimes, is required to step down, and retire, resume our regular lives and pass on our duties to the next generation." "What duties?" curiously asked Ainsley, not knowing what the hell he was talking about. "I am part of the Sevardinal, a sacred set of seven bookkeepers who protect the secret of the Inland, and who dwell in the narrow abodes all over the world." "Whoa, wait what? Sevardinal? Abodes? What are you talking about?" It is clear that only now is Artie getting frustrated. "Jeez, do they not teach any of this to you in schools? No I guess not." Artie sighs "look child, this is what I want you to do, take what you hold so close to your heart" Artie points to the book, which draws Ainsley's stare as she looks down to see that she has her arms tightly locked around it, eerily similar to the way Artie did all those years ago when Abigail met him. "Take the book home with you tonight, give it a read… then return here to me, you'll understand better at what I'm talking about. Then I'll fill you in on the rest, I promise," with that Artie gestures for Ainsley to follow, and they descend the stairwells.

They arrive at the doorway; Ainsley quickly remembers the disgust of the first floor however, Artie doesn't seem to notice. Ainsley turns to leave without a word, book wrapped in arms, but just as she turns, Artie rests a hand on her shoulder. "I have one thing to ask of you though my dear…" Ainsley looks up slightly concerned. "You have to promise me not to show this book to anyone, let no one know what it is, and what it possesses, especially your mother, do you promise?" Ainsley, thinking to quickly forget this request, hastily nods. Seeing this, Artie, desperately grabs hold of Ainsley with both hands "Ainsley! You cannot share this with anyone; your life is at stake! Keep it to yourself trust me, please. Promise me!" Artie shakes Ainsley, slightly frightened, Ainsley panics "Yes I promise! Let me go!" Artie does as requested and releases his grip. Ainsley runs to the fire escape, without a look back to see her great grandfather watching her go.

IV. Opening The Book

Ainsley didn't know what to think, so much had happened so fast. What was she supposed to think, the words of some forty-something imposter who couldn't possibly be her great grandfather... right?

Ainsley snapped out of her thoughts to see the bus pull up ahead of her at the stop. Quickly running, Ainsley barely catches it. She lives on the other side of the city from her great grandfather's narrow mansion, on the outskirts of town, so that meant she had lots of time to think about what happened. Ainsley takes a seat.

'Okay, lets think this out Ainsley, you know, from what mom says that Artie was old, very old, old back then so surely too old now, so logically that guy in there can't be him. It must be the corpse upstairs. Crimineys, a corpse, how messed up is that? I saw a dead body today; I... saw a dead body, that's surely not normal Ainsley. Okay, don't talk to yourself, what do you do about the body, do you call it in? Yes, yes you must, that's the right thing to do. But, that guy said my life was at stake, no, only if you told anyone about the book, or was it the body? Oh man, what's wrong with me, I can't keep things straight!'

The bus stopped at 4th and Flower, and an old lady got on and sat next to Ainsley. The bus resumes motion. The old lady is holding a bouquet of flowers with a message addressed to Paul. Becoming distracted, Ainsley began to think of all the possibilities Paul could be to this woman, and she distinctly decided that given her age, and sad expression, it must be for her dying husband, who is currently residing in Unit 51 of the cardiac ward of the Rockyside Hospital. Satisfied with her own rationalization, Ainsley sighed a sigh of content, and in a mild after thought, humored herself at how

Paul would soon be located 100 meters across the street, and six feet under from Rockyside hospital in Rockyside Memorial.

Ainsley had always been told she had a very dark sense of humor, she never understood why people said that, she never saw anything funny in happiness, if your happy then you aren't laughing, and besides, one should laugh, its medically proven to increase your life by 4 years. And all in all, laughing was probably her own enjoyment, so if she can't even laugh at the things she finds funny, what does she have?

The bus stops at Memorial Drive and Rockyside Way. The old lady slowly rises to her feet and lumbers off the bus, heading for the hospital.

Ainsley rubbed her tempos, she was getting sidetracked she always did. She was losing her concentration on what really she, and anyone else with a sane brain on their head should think about, the dead body, the consequences of listening to this lunatic masquerading as her great grandfather, and why she wasn't flipping out.

Ainsley looked to her lap, and there lay in a sort of complacence, the book that both her and, practically her entire family wondered about for years. Given all that had happened in the last hour, this was the first time Ainsley got to actually look at it. The spine was badly damaged, it was barely connected, the only thing really holding it together was its thick leather straps that, presumably, were wound through holes in the pages, sort of like binders you get at school, but more ancient. It was bound in deep rich brown leather that unlike the binding had held up quite nicely, suggesting that despite that one incident with its spine, the book had been protected obsessively. This didn't surprise Ainsley. On the cover was in embossed emblem, not like anything Ainsley would have recognized from her limited time alive. It was two thick vertical lines that wove across one another similar to a DNA strand, but they only weaved once, at each point, in the positions of North, South, East, West, there were these strange insignia's, also embossed. They were clearly in a different language, but none that Ainsley was familiar with.

Moving on from the cover, Ainsley looked to open up the book, but couldn't. It was locked; on the side laid a thick lock with a tiny keyhole. Given the size of the book, which was considerate, at least 300 pages, but taking into account this book was ancient and done on handmade paper, it is still incredible, and given weather damage, the book looks larger than it actually would be nowadays. The keyhole looked very tiny, like even the smallest key wouldn't fit. Frustrated that she couldn't read it, Ainsley attempted to pry open the book, pulling at the two covers, Ainsley was disappointed that the old lock and the ancient book, did not budge.

The bus arrived at the end of the line, Discovery St and Bentworth Way. "End of the line!" yelled the bus driver.

Ainsley looked up, she couldn't believe it; she completely missed her stop! She was at least an hour from home now. Pleading with the driver, she managed to get him to take her as far as Westcott Ave, which was still twenty minutes away from home but better than nothing. Arriving at Westcott, Ainsley hopped off the bus, gripping the book hard in her one hand, and walked briskly.

By the time Ainsley arrived home, it was nearly past midnight, her mom was going to be pissed. Whatever it wasn't her fault; she was only doing what her mom asked her to do. Abigail, Ainsley's mom, told her early this morning to go to Arthur's house to retrieve this book. Her reasoning was that Arthur asked her to send Ainsley, which didn't make any sense to

Ainsley, she never met the man, and really, had no intention to, but with a bribe of 50 bucks and a new mp3 player, Ainsley was sold. And now, to Ainsley's chagrin, she was caught up in all this stuff, stuff way above her maturity level.

Ainsley quietly opened the front door to her modest little cottage-esque house. This was what Abigail's father, Alden, had finally completed and, seeing the state of it, none of Abigail's siblings wanted it, so Abigail took it, only on the blessing that it got her away from her family for once.

The main floor was designed almost identical to the old apartment building that Abigail and her brothers and mom and dad lived in. It was clear to Ainsley that Alden, Abigail's dad, lacked the creative flare to design his own home, so he just copied what he knew, it is also a possibility that this gave him some comfort, because then he never really had to move out.

The open main floor, was dark, no one was awake, thankfully, Ainsley, wandered through the dark, attempting to minimize her creaks and groans as she walked across the poorly built hardwood floors. She made her way to the windowsill stairway that led to the second floor. As she rounded the winding stairway, she could see light beginning to seep into her vision, it was clear that her mom was awake.

Without knowing why exactly, Ainsley took off her jacket, and draped it over the book. She never usually acted impulsively, but for some reason, this felt right, like something told her to do so. Ainsley stood on the top floor of her grandfather's home. It was a long hallway, with doors every so often on either side. They all lead to either bedrooms or bathrooms, and in her entire living here, Ainsley still mixed them up. The only thing she knew was that her mother's room was the one on the end, staring back at her, doorway illuminated in candlelight.

Creeping along, Ainsley started to pick up speed, thinking that if she were faster her footsteps would be lighter. She was wrong. But it did not matter, she made it to her room, and thinking fast tucked the book under her bed.

"Where is it?!" Asked Abigail as she suddenly stuck her head in, startling Ainsley, "Jeez mom, you scared me" "did you get it?" "Uh…" Ainsley, who suddenly realized that she never decided if she was going to do as 'Artie' asked her too, suddenly had that blind impulse to lie to her mother, a rare occurrence. "No, the building was condemned, no one was there. It was emptied out." Lied Ainsley, "Damn it! … Fuck!" "Mom?!" said Ainsley astonished, she had never heard her mom swear before, this obviously was a very big deal to her. "I'm sorry hun', that wasn't aimed at you" "It's okay, are you alright?" Abigail looked to a very concerned Ainsley, and smiled. "Yeah, don't worry about me, I'll be fine. Just head to bed okay?" "Sure mom… night" Abigail shut Ainsley's bedroom door, Ainsley could hear her mom make her way back to her room and shut the door.

With that, Ainsley whipped out the book from underneath her bed and sighed. She didn't like lying to her mom, but she just felt like it was the right thing to do. Looking at the book, and remembering her frustration, Ainsley sighed and looked around her room.

It was small, not small enough to call cramped, but small enough to not be comfortable to a twelve year old, none of the other rooms were much better, the only reason Ainsley took this room was because it was close to her mom's room and when she was little she would wake up in the middle of the night and crawl into her mom's bed. Another reason she liked this room was it was her mom's old room way back when she was young. And it still held all of her stuff.

Covered on the walls were pictures of nameless models of hot guys and newspaper clippings of seemingly random things, a train derailing, a house for sale in London. You name it, it was plastered somewhere on Ainsley's mom's old room.

Laying the book down on the bed, Ainsley stood and walked over to her mirror, she looked herself in the mirror. She had a heart shaped face with beautiful green eyes and, as before mentioned, shoulder length wavy brown hair. She was short, not short enough to comment on, but short enough for Ainsley to notice, she had always been told she was just waiting on a growth spurt, and that once she hit puberty, yes that's right, she hadn't had her period yet, she'd fly up in height. But despite her prepubescent state, Ainsley was most definitely beautiful, there was no denying that, and she had a fashion sense that was all her own yet, matched her completely. In compilation to her tame pink jacket, which she wore almost every day; she wore black skintight jeans and a poufy black dress. Her uncle's always commented that she was born in the wrong decade, and that she would have fit perfectly in the 80's, she didn't know what that meant. But she also knew that her peculiar fashion sense was because her mom refused to take her to an actual clothing store, instead settling for street merchants selling stolen or illegally made clothes, at dirt cheap prices.

Sighing to herself, Ainsley turned to look at a billboard out her window, it read: Happiness is the key! Just reach out and take it! This confused Ainsley at first, but then something clicked, and she remembered one of her mom's stories about Artie, about when he left, and what he left behind...

Ainsley ran to her desk's drawer and opened it frantically; she was presented with a flack of cards, from all over the world and all addressed from 'Artie'. Filing through them, Ainsley found the card she was looking for, the one with the tacky picture of the earth on it, turning it over she found it, the key, the key without the keyhole, taped to the back of the card.

'Could this possibly be it? Could this possibly be what opens that?' thought Ainsley as she looked over the book. Ainsley pulled the key off the card and walked over to the book. She cautiously sat down and lifts up the book with one hand and gently inserts the key… It fits.

Ainsley gasps, she turns the key, it unlocks; the book is unlocked! She was so excited, she wanted to run out and grab her mom; she made for the door, then stopped cold in her tracks. That feeling was back, she didn't understand, she wanted so desperately to show her mom, but she knew she couldn't. Before she knew it, she was sitting on her bed, holding the book in her hands.

She calms her self, and takes a deep breath. Ainsley opens the book.

V. No Direction Home

The sand was hot, and sparkling a vicious white, my feet, bare as the day I was born, seared under the heat. My eyes struggled to adapt to the harsh land, this was not like my fantasy; this was real, real, and very unforgiving. I was in the middle of nowhere; everywhere I looked was just overpowering white. It took me time to adjust. Upon doing so, I could see I was truly alone, and not where I was when I closed my eyes last. I look behind me to seek out some distinguishable landmark, anything to guide my way. Nothing, mountains, encircled me on every side of the horizon. Before, I could think anymore of my isolation, I spin myself around and walk whatever way my finger stops. I head south… I think.

Days, and days past, but somehow, despite all that I'd been taught, it past in an instant, and oddly enough, I never tired, I never grew hungry, it was as if I was in some sort of elaborate dream, from which I could never awake. The mountains, the only recognizable thing in this desert, seemed to get further and further away as I walked towards them. Causing me, already afraid and alone, to become frustrated beyond all belief.

I remember watching on the TV once that supposedly when you walked long enough, and with no direction home, you would start to do circles, because your dominant foot would take larger steps than the weaker one and as a result would cause you to slightly turn over a long enough distance. My dominant foot was my left, I learned this because when I was 6, I played on a girls soccer team, err well I played with girls on a girls soccer team, they played in the field outside my house for a while, and I would go and watch and play when I was allowed. Anyways, I remember this because the coach would always praise me and encourage me, I was told later it was because I was a lefty, and he told me lefty's always think a little differently and act in a certain way that righty's don't; they always lead with their left foot. I didn't understand what he meant then, but now, it's perfectly clear, I must be going in circles, and the reason I never get closer to the mountains is because my left foot curves me into the center; like a ginormous spiral, in and out, over and over.

Proud of myself for coming to this conclusion, I attempt to compensate by taking ridiculously larger steps with my right foot every so often, hoping that would straighten my course. It did not. And so, as another day set on what must be the western mountain ridge, I collapse to the hardened sand, now cooled by the setting sun, and close my eyes.

I lay there, and dare myself to dream of home, but the dreams don't come, nothing comes, nothing but black darkness, I open my eyes to darkness, it consumes my surroundings, just as the day's white light consumed my surroundings. I hear nothing, nothing but the faint sounds of wind in the distance. I'm scared, I would cry, but can't bring myself to do so; I can't bring myself to do anything, save for stare up into nothingness.

I can't remember things, in the dark, my memory becomes fuzzy, my family becomes disoriented, like it was a dream, the sounds of their voices, their smiles, everything, feels as if it didn't happen, and just like a dream, I forget. And so it went, every night spent in this endless desert, was another night of lost memories, and forgotten faces.

I'm walking, again, though by this time I do so just to keep my boredom from devouring me. I think mindlessly about random things, my bedroom, the smell of my sheets, the creeks of the handmade floors, things that once in my life would have been useless memories, thoughts that I once took for granted, but now, were all I had left. I couldn't even remember my name.

After that, nothing mattered anymore, my near dead nerves in my feet didn't bother me, my peeling skin from my severe sun burn's, on every bit of exposed skin didn't bother me, the perplexing quiz about why my memories left me and why I could not seem to escape this desert didn't bother me, all that mattered to me was this: "I am alone".

Bump!

I run into something, the experience is so fresh to me, yet old at the same time, my mind, wandering as it was is brought back to reality, as I look up at this structure, that of which I cannot see the top nor the edge of it. Almost like, it was endless.

At first I thought I had finally ran into the mountain side, but alas, that was not the case, what stood before me was stone, similar to that of those castles you see in the movies, but… newer, much newer and the blocks of which it was made of seemed to be smooth to the touch.

Exhilarated, at my discovery I run my hands all over the wall, taking in the new experience of touch, something I have not indulged in longer than I can remember. Feeling my excitement grow, I run along the structure, keeping my hands glued to it, for fear of it being a mirage. I keep running, and though at first I thought it was a never-ending wall, soon I was proven other wise. Running faster and faster, and breaking into a slightly crazed desperate giggle, I was soon touching nothing, my hands held up in a bizarre position reaching for a wall that was not there. I look back, and unlike before, where nothingness would inevitably wait for me, I was greeted with a curve in the wall.

I look along the structure, and see a ways down, a set of ascending stairs, wide stairs heading up, getting narrower and more steep as the went, leading into what appeared to be a chamber of some sort, suspended off the ground. I climb the stairs.

I feel light as a feather as I climb them, my empty head, with not a care in the world other than the primitive desire of curiosity. I do not look anywhere but up, up at the innocent looking stone booth, with its narrow doorway. As I climb however, I notice, that the narrow doorway isn't narrow. It's narrowing!

Out of my panic, I run up the stairs at a pace I did not think possible, and think I'm okay, but then as the stairs take a surprising degree of steepness, my left foot trips over the taller step. Quietly cursing my dominant foot, I limp up the steps and dive into the shutting doorway.

Then, upon landing on the cold floor, a feeling returns, and then another, and another, and before I know it, I'm bombarded with every thought, feeling experience and pain I ever had, and especially the ones I had but just wasn't aware of due to my lull in the desert.

Everything is hurting, everything, my eyes hurt, my nails hurt, my skin hurts, everything does. The pain paralyzes me, and as I lay there shivering, in the cold, surprisingly bright chamber, I begin to remember, all that I had forgotten. My eyes roll up into my skull and my body begins to seizure. The inside of my head flashed with millions of images and memories, and voices, the voices of my consciousness that had long screamed at my ignorant inner ear.

It is all too much to handle, and amongst all this pain and rediscovery, my mind manages to focus enough to comprehend one new thought: I really wish I never read that stupid book!

And just like that. My eyes refocus, my body calms, my mind quiet, I'm laying flat on the sixth floor of my great grandfather's narrow home, and I am perfectly unharmed, my sunburns gone, my wrecked clothes pristine, my hair, only slightly messed up due to my apparent stumble from the attic above. I ask myself if it was all a dream, if it really happened or I just went nuts. Then, just by chance, I look down to my shoes, perfectly fine, but they feel strange, I take them off, and white sand sprinkles out of them. I capture some of it in my hand. It was not a dream... it was real, very real.

"Still think I was making things up?" Asked Artie who appeared from nowhere somewhat startling young her. Getting to her feet, she is uneven, not being used to her own reinstated strength, she looks to Artie, still reveling what just happened to her, and trying to comprehend just what happened. "What happened to me?" Artie, smiles at Ainsley's question and extends his hand outward away, gesturing toward the half-couch. "Come, we have much to talk about".

VI. Inheritances

Ainsley and Artie move toward the half-couch, and as Artie goes to sit, the walls surrounding the couch magically sink further, revealing the missing back of the couch. Artie sits and Ainsley follows suit.

Artie looks knowingly into Ainsley's eyes, "I know you must be very confused by what you just experienced" Ainsley in response just lets out a guttural cough that one would assume means: You think? "It's not uncommon, it was your first visit, it gets easier every time you return, just out of curiosity, where did you end up?" Ainsley stares wild eyed at him, "What do you mean where did I end up?! What do you mean visit? I don't understand, why can't you just talk straight to me?!" "Calm yourself child, remember, these walls aren't as stable as they used to be" chuckles Artie amusing himself; Ainsley didn't see the humor.

"Look… 'Artie', I don't know what's going on, I can only comprehend what I see, and right now, I see a guy who is dead, but somehow still alive, I see a couch that vanishes in and out of walls, and according to you, I traveled somewhere! And speaking of travel, how'd I end up here!!! I was in my room last night!!!" proclaimed Ainsley with bewilderment. Artie smiles calmly and nods his head, "Yes, that may be confusing, but as for everything else, I don't know what you are talking about, you understand perfectly." Ainsley shakes her head frustrated and moves to leave, understanding his mistake; Artie quickly reaches out and gently grabs hold of Ainsley's arm. "Let go, I'm leaving, I don't need this, I'm a kid, and I should be hanging out with my friends, not entertaining some psychotic guy posing as my headless great grandfather." "I'm sorry, I was merely trying to calm your nerves, I see my sense of humor is out of date and not appropriate, please sit, I'll cooperate." Ainsley cautiously sits, keeping suspicious eye contact with Artie.

Artie, leans back in the couch, rubbing his hands together, as if he were trying to light a fire with the friction. "Alright, where to begin… well, to start, I think it's important that you understand that everything you know is not accurate, at least not fully, and that what I tell you may not make a whole lot of sense, but, well sometimes the truth is stranger than the fiction." Ainsley just calmly nods. "Alright, the place you visited tonight, has no name, there are many local names but to pronounce them here in this world is impossible, it comes out as static." Ainsley looks slightly confused. "Here, let me show you," Artie clears his throat: The place you visited is called SCCCCRRRRREEEEEAAAACH, the pitch of the word was so intense and otherworldly, it surely couldn't have come from a human's vocal cords, Ainsley had to cover her ears to prevent them from going deaf.

The screech stopped and Ainsley dropped her hands, feeling something wrong with them she looked down to them, blood, blood was pooled in them both, panicking Ainsley reached up and touched her ear drums, they were bleeding. "Oh, sorry dear, I should have warned you, my apology's" Artie rises, fetches some tissue paper, and hands it to Ainsley who rapidly dabs it at her ears. "You made my ears bleed!" "Yes… I am sorry, it's a common occurrence for trying to speak that worlds language here, usually dissuades people from attempting it. Don't worry; no damage will befall your ears, its purely cosmetic. Ainsley sighs a sigh of relief. "Good", Ainsley lets out a stressed chuckle, Artie smiles, and returns to his seat.

"But you see what I mean, things won't make sense, just for the sake of calling something, we will call this world the… Inland Island, for that is what it is, and Island, so vast, so grand, one could almost call it a continent, almost, one small catch, no one can see it, no one can find it. It exists, but now, only in memory, only in books once wrote a long, long time ago by individuals much like myself, in fact, the story of the Inland Island is still being written to this day, that is what I do you see, I'm a writer of sorts, I document it's world, I interact and participate in its history. To put it bluntly, I write history." Ainsley sits quietly, actually starting to believe Artie's wild tale.

"I am one of seven... seven individuals who have been since the dawn of time itself, we are the Sevardinal, and we are immortal. That is why you see me upstairs with my head on the floor, we die, that part of the myth is false, we live slightly longer than most, but will die, and a younger version of ourselves will emerge from the world to fill in our place, I have been reborn so called 3 times. And it is because of this that you are now here young Ainsley, you have been chosen..."

"Chosen?" asked Ainsley, now completely immersed in Artie's tale. "Chosen for what?" Artie smiles, "Chosen to replace me, to carry on the Sevardinal legacy for the next trinity year, that's three hundred years, just so you don't get confused"

Ainsley is dumbfounded, and at a loss for words "I, I can't be, I can't possibly. I mean come on I'm twelve! I'm way too young to do something this big!" "Ahh, but see young one, that is where you are mistaken, you already have done so much, your one visit, has completely changed the course of the Inland Island forever, your mere presence has sent waves throughout the land, the word is out, you are my successor" explained Artie. "But I didn't do anything! I just wandered around for a while, I didn't see anyone, I didn't interact with anything, it was just me, alone, how possibly could I have affected anything?"

Artie smiles, "Ainsley, you are forgetting one thing you did interact with…" Ainsley sits quietly, having no clue what he's talking about, "Well, it you want to be technical, you interacted with two things. Can you guess?" Ainsley just shakes her head and bumps her shoulders up in surrender.

"The book, the book Ainsley, you attempted to read the book…" Ainsley doesn't know what to say "I, I didn't mean to, I mean, I meant to, but I didn't know that all this would happen, I didn't mean to" Ainsley starts to hyperventilate, panicking that she made a big mistake, noticing her dismay, Artie encircles her with his arms in a comforting embrace. "It's alright child, you didn't do anything wrong, it was meant to happen, take comfort in knowing you had no choice in the matter. Everything happens for a reason, and it was you, not your mother, not your mother's siblings, all of whom wanted this," Artie gestures to the book. Ainsley starts to get teary eyed. "Come now, I know this is hard to hear, but there is no need in treating this as a bad thing, this is the greatest honor, more so than anytime in our history, because you see Ainsley, you are the first of us to be from here, and not born in our world."

"But why?" desperately asked Ainsley; not wanting any part in this whole affair.

"No clue, all of us are still baffled by it, but, all in all, it was meant to happen, you are here for a reason Ainsley, and the sheer fact that you didn't die in there, at your age, is in its own right, impressive."

"But I don't want to do this, I want no part in this, I don't want to live forever, or whatever, I don't want to revisit this world, one time was enough,

I just want to be a kid, play with my friends, fall in love, I want to be normal."

"But Ainsley, you are not normal, your entire family isn't, you have a peculiar set of traits that separate you from the rest of this world, and given how you were raised, you also possess a series of skills", "Like?" Asks a teary, but somewhat stabilizing Ainsley.

"You know how to build, compliments of your grandfather, you know how to heal, thanks to your uncles. Shall I continue?" Ainsley weakly nods, "You know how to remain silent, and keep secrets." "Who did I get that from?" quickly asked Ainsley. "Your grandmother." "What? Grandma? What did she do, she's so innocent?"

"Ah, that she is, I should know, raised her alone… do you know why she was so quiet?" Ainsley shakes her head. "She knew of my position, and of the Inland Island, however she herself could not comprehend it, and refused to believe it's existence, and because of that, when I visited the world, she thought I was neglecting her by leaving or ignoring her, and slowly it drove her slightly mad and left her near mute."

"Wow, really? That's so sad." Says Ainsley, Artie nods his head in acknowledgment, but shows sadness across his face. "Yes, it is, and I will forever grieve doing that to my own daughter, but my whole point is you too possess this important trait, secrecy."

"How do you know? How do you know I didn't go blabbing this to all my friends, to my mom?" challenged Ainsley. Artie wisely smiles, "two reasons, one, I myself have spent many years reading people and I can tell you did not, but secondly, and most importantly, you physically can't anymore."

"Huh? What do you mean I can't? Can't what? Keep secrets, lie?"

"No dear child, quite the opposite, you can and will keep this secret, you will because being my successor, you have been influenced, by me and the book."

" What do you mean?" Asked Ainsley, tired of being confused.

" Since the last time we saw one another, and you took the book home, did you have these impulses, these senses about people and scenario's, that prevented you from doing something?"

Ainsley looks away, and thinks, and shyly looks back. "Maybe"

"That's because your morals have been tweaked just slightly to allow you to protect this book and yourself for as long as you are a Sevardinal."

"So what you are saying is, not only do I live for like 300 years or something, I also have instincts that keep me and the book out of harm?"

"Yes, exactly, you understand perfectly." Artie exclaims joyfully.

Ainsley sits in thought for a long time, longer than she probably should of, it was just, this was a lot to take in. "So what does this all mean, what am I supposed to do?"

"I cannot tell you, no one tells you, its similar to the protective instinct you now possess, at random times in you life, maybe now, maybe years from now, you will suddenly have the urge to read this book, and all that I ask is… that you follow these urges. You have nothing to fear, no harm will come to you, so long as you listen to your heart, and your mind." Ainsley tentatively nods her head "right, so nothing will happen to me? Like I can't be hurt?" "Oh no dear, you can and most likely will be hurt, and you are also capable of death, all that happens in death is… well, to keep long story short, you are absent from life as long as you lived, meaning if you live for 13 years, you would be dead for 13 years, then reborn as you were when you died, that is the way of reincarnation in this world, if you die naturally however, you will be reborn in the form you were when you first became Sevardinal, do you understand?"

"Sure?" awkwardly answers Ainsley. "Good! Then there is nothing more to explain, I think I'll be off then, the house is yours to take care of." Artie stands and looks down to Ainsley. "Wait what? No you can't leave, I have so many more questions!" "All in due time my dear, all in due time, I promise you, as time goes on, you will understand, just as I did so many years ago, just trust yourself, trust your urges, especially the one to write in this book."

"But I don't write, I don't like to, I suck at it" explains Ainsley rapidly. "Ah… do you now? Well, believe me young one, when the time comes to write, it will come to you, you have no control over it, your body acts on its own. And you do have skills in writing, you know how I know?" Ainsley shakes her head. "Your mother has skills in it, and like with all your relatives, it's rubbed off on you." Artie smiles and moves over to a coat hangar that Ainsley was sure wasn't there before and picks up his fedora and trench coat, the same one Abigail saw all those many years ago. He places the fedora upon his head, slides the ragged coat over his slim build, and turns once more to look and young, wide-eyed Ainsley.

"Not to worry Ainsley, when you reach my age, and pass this gift onto someone else, maybe your grandchild, you'll look back at your life and think 'those were the best years of my life', and believe me child they will be." Artie slowly starts to move to the downward stairwell, still holding eye contact with Ainsley. "Come visit me sometime, I still have half my life to live out on the Inland Island, and I intend to make the best of it. So long child, until next time" and with that Artie turns and makes his way to the stairs "Oh and say hi to your mom for me". Artie lets out a deep chuckle, descends the stairs, and vanishes from sight. Leaving Ainsley alone in the narrow building she had now inherited.

VII. Urges

The bus ride home was a blur. Ainsley didn't know what to think. All this information being thrown at her at such a rapid rate, she didn't know what to make of it. She wished she could talk to someone; ask them their opinion about it. But, even if she wanted to, even if she was allowed to, which according to Artie, she no longer was. Who would she tell? It was hard enough to believe by herself, who knows what anyone else would think?

Sure, her family has been wondering for years what Arthur was all about, but surely none of them had an imagination as great as this to concoct such a tale. 'I mean it couldn't be real could it?' thought Ainsley as she slowly rose from her cold, awkwardly designed seat on the bus and made her way to the front to exit.

Watching the bus carry on down the road, Ainsley wished it were some other girl getting off the bus right now, confused beyond all belief, and unbelievably alone.

She started to walk the short distance across a deserted barley field towards her awkwardly designed two-story home, alight in the distance. She had a strong urge to take her time getting there.

Slowing her pace, Ainsley began to think out what exactly all that had happened in the last few days could be.

'Perhaps, I've gone mental or something? I mean that would explain the uber-realistic dream about being in the book. It would also explain why I'm actually thinking this could be real. I mean crazy people don't know they are crazy right? Oh god, listen to me… I'm talking to myself. I am so crazy. I should ask one of my uncles about what the definition of psychosis is?'

Ainsley arrived at the back door to her home; her usual entry seeing as it was the closest to the bus stop and the front door, if you could call it that, had the misfortune of being located across the street from a refining plant. Which she long ago got used to the smell of. Upon entering, all the lights were turned on, which, considering the dodgy wiring in this place, proved impressive and unusual. Usually only a few lights were on, giving the place a sort of twilight aura, the same feeling you get when you are huddled up by a fireplace on a cold night. In comparison to that, the harsh fluorescent overhead lighting, which exposed the truly horrid structuring of the building, came to be very unsettling.

Ainsley had a very bad feeling…

Ainsley crept further into the house. Entering the master room, as they all called it since before this clone of the apartment was built, Ainsley saw that no one was there, but the evidence that someone was, was alarming.

Everywhere Ainsley looked, chaos was to be found. Books splayed out all over the desk and floors, cupboards opened and emptied out onto the floor, clothes from upstairs lining the steps. Ainsley now knew, that something terrible was going on. 'Oh my god, have we been robbed?' thought Ainsley, but as it was before, her feelings told her that it wasn't true.

"Mom? Hello? Anyone home?!" Called out Ainsley, from upstairs, she heart rustling, someone was getting to their feet. The rustling didn't sound soothing, like that of her mom casually bounding downstairs to say hello. Ainsley felt this was different, she felt this was bad.

"Hello?" Called Ainsley once more, no one answered, all that was to be heard in the harshly lit house was the firm, slow steps of someone approaching. Ainsley approached the windowsill stairway, book clenched in her arms tightly.

She had the urge to run away, far away from here, and not look back. One of the strongest most intoxicating urges one could feel, it almost made her sick to her stomach. Ainsley's knuckles went white.

Beyond all her urges, Ainsley stood still, she did not move, scared to solidarity, or rigamortis, as her uncles would say. Ainsley just stayed there. Waiting for whoever was upstairs, to appear.

"Where is it…" came a dark, deep feminine voice from the stairway, no one was visible yet, but despite the ominous, and unusual tone, Ainsley knew it was her mom.

"Mom? Is that you?" Asked Ainsley relieved.

"WHERE.. is it?" repeated with venom dripping from every syllable.

"Huh? Are you okay mom?" While she spoke, almost against her will, Ainsley relieved her grip on the book and slowly slipped it behind her back.

Abigail appeared finally on the stairwell. She looked awful, her hair clearly unwashed and messily tossed up into a ponytail. Still in her sweats and tank top. She had a fine film of sweat covering every exposed bit of skin.

"Ainsley, ANSWER ME!!!" Screamed Abigail, clearly in hystEyes; Ainsley started to back away, now truly frightened, having never seen her mother behave this way. The urge to run was overwhelming. Every moment she resisted made her feel weaker and weaker.

"Mom, please don't yell at me…" weakly said Ainsley as she finally bumped into the island in the kitchen. She was trapped. "I don't know what you are talking about."

46

Then, all of the sudden, Abigail, closed the distance between the two and pinned her arms to either side of the island behind Ainsley.

"THE KEY! Where is my key Ainsley? Its not here so you must have it, and if you have it then that means you have something else too!"

Ainsley started to cry. "Please mom, I don't know what you are talking about, what key?"

Abigail grabbed hold of Ainsley and roughly began digging her long boney fingers into her pockets searching for the key. Ainsley just sobbed, wishing that this horrible version of her mother were just a nightmare she was having.

Not finding anything, Abigail stepped back and took a deep strained sigh. She looked over Ainsley, observing her. Then she noticed what both Ainsley and the book did not intend…

Ainsley's arms tucked behind her back.

Both Ainsley and her mother just stood there, staring into each other's eyes, seeing that something had changed, that they were no longer on the same side, that something horrible was about to happen, that would change their relationship forever, and their was nothing either of them could do about it, all that could be done was strike first.

"What's that you got behind your back, hmm?" Eerily asked Abigail.

Still sobbing, Ainsley was pulled out of her sorrows when beyond her control, the book, swung round from behind and struck Abigail square in the face. Knocking her to the floor, and concurrently knocked her out. Shocked at what just happened, Ainsley had no time to comment or see to her mother as the book then took off with her holding on for dear life.

Ainsley and the book exited through the back door. The same back door she was carried through when she was born, both her mother and now long gone father as happy as can be, welcoming baby Ainsley to the home of her childhood. A childhood that up to this week had been a perfectly normal one, but as Ainsley and the book took off into the darkness, so ended Ainsley's childhood though she did not know it yet.

The cold air chilled Ainsley's young, pale hands, as the book unrelentingly carried her further and further away from her home. As it did, Ainsley justified not letting go... 'I'll just go back tomorrow, I'm sure mom will be alright, I'm sure everything is going to be okay, I know it.'

Feeling confident in her reasoning, Ainsley focused ahead to the curiosities the fat, leather-bound text beheld, and forgot about her home. Not realizing, that it was the last time she was to set eyes upon it.

VIII. The Road

Ainsley had never been so tired in her entire life. She and the book had been walking for what seemed like hours. All that lay ahead of her was road all that lay behind her was road. She was on some deserted highway in the middle of nowhere, no artificial light to be had, no light at all; all that she had to light her way was the faint gloom of the moon.

The book had an unsettling strength to it, any resistance Ainsley gave against it, and the book returned ten fold. It was hopeless. Ainsley was beginning to understand that she had no control over her situation. She wanted so desperately to let go, of the book and run home to her unconscious mother, apologize for lying, apologize for taking the key without asking, apologize for it all. But she couldn't, the urges, they were in control, she was possessed. Her mind told her one thing, her body did something completely different.

Ainsley was convinced that even if she did release her grasp on the book, it wouldn't drop to the floor like anything would, no, she was convinced that the moment she released it, it would float there, as if nothing had happened. It was almost as if the book had a personality all of its own.

The autumn nights were cold, colder than she would have guessed, usually at this hour, Ainsley was fast asleep, on her makeshift bed with ear buds in each ear listening to soft soothing music. It was the only way she could sleep, ever since she was 7, Ainsley had a sleeping disorder, the doctors all told her that she was fine and that physically there was nothing wrong with her, that no chemical imbalance was occurring to deny her, her slumber. No, it was as one doctor rudely inferred: "All in her head".

'All in my head?? Wow, glad to see our taxpayers money is going to such good uses' thought Ainsley, it wasn't a doctor that ended up helping. No, in fact how Ainsley's sleeping disorder came to an end was all of her own discovery.

When Ainsley turned, 10 she had begged her mother to get her an mp3 player, she made the argument that it was only fair, she never got anything new, and she never complained about it. However, due to the fact that her mother worked as a freelance journalist for whoever would hire her, she had little to no money to spend on luxuries, even birthday presents. Ainsley knew this, but still every year she fought for something, anything that cost more that 20 dollars. But alas, she never got what she wished for. But this year, Ainsley had had enough, she wasn't going to take it anymore, by any means necessary, she was going to get her way.

Two weeks had past since her 10th birthday, and still mom wouldn't budge. So, in what would be Ainsley's one and only act of wickedness, she ran away.

Now granted, it wasn't far, just two blocks south to the local supermarket. But still for a 10 year old who had never wandered away on her own before, this was quite a feat.

Arriving at the supermarket, Ainsley, like a homing missile, walked directly to the electronics section. And without a word to any of the lurking salesmen, picked out a hot pink mp3 player, and walked straight to the door.

It happened so fast, and so easily, Ainsley instantly wondered why so many people got caught. But just as she exited the supermarket, the alarms went off.

Ainsley's heart froze, but luckily for her, her feet didn't, and before she realized it, she was hoping over a chain-link fence and was running full speed across an abandoned lot. Heading around the corner onto 12th street. Ainsley was relieved and both disappointed that no one was following her. Relieved in that she got away with it, and disappointed as well. She felt horrible, worse than when she got her ear infection 3 summers ago, worse than when she broke her wrist last winter, even worse than when Dawson's Creek ended! (And for the record, yes she knew that was an old show that ended years ago, but the television they had, only had rabbit ear antennae, which meant they got some weird programming.)

Staring down at the hot pink mp3 player, Ainsley instantly knew then, that there was a reason why people didn't do this, it wasn't the risk of getting caught, it was the feeling of getting away with it. And unfortunately for Ainsley, she was not one of the pathetic individuals who reveled in the experience.

Ainsley arrived home, the house was empty, surely mom was out looking for her, probably worried sick. Heading up to her room, Ainsley fell face first into her bed, colliding with the lumpy old pillow she was awarded to have. Taking a deep sigh, Ainsley set the stolen mp3 player down on the floor and tucked it away, decided right then, that she would return it first thing, tomorrow morning. Feeling good about her resolve, Ainsley decided she would try and get something to eat, so lifting herself off of the bed, something caught her eye; it was pink, hot pink to be exact, but it wasn't what she just hid away. No, it was a box, a wrapped box! It was a present!!

Ainsley couldn't believe it; her mother got her a present!

"Happy Birthday Ainsley" came Abigail's loving motherly voice from the doorway. Ainsley turned to see her mother standing there, all smiles, almost as if she were about to cry. In an instant, Ainsley got to her feet and took off towards her mom, practically tackling her.

"Oh my god, thank you so much mom!" exclaimed Ainsley truly overwhelmed with the surprise. Abigail just chuckled, too happy to respond, just enjoying seeing her only daughter happy for once.

That night, Ainsley slept like a newborn, and it was all thanks to her falling asleep listening to the hot pink mp3 player, no not the one the she stole, it was the one that came out of the pink wrapping paper.

Ainsley's feet, long since numbed to the core from walking such distances in her poorly designed, yet perhaps once fashionable slip on sneakers were starting to feel heavy. Like someone during her internal dialogues, had slipped on 40-pound weights per foot. She looked to her watch; it was now well past 5 in the morning, she left her house at 10, she had been walking for 7 hours straight!

A car's headlights splashed onto the back of Ainsley's pink jacket, causing her to wearily turn. She couldn't make out what kind of car it was, but it was coming fast. Just then, the book shot to the right, taking Ainsley with it, as they flew into the tall wheat fields. Landing with an 'oomph', Ainsley turned just in time to see that it was her mother, clearly balling her eyes out, flying by in her '94 Chevy.

Glad to see she wasn't still unconscious, but sad to see that she was so upset, Ainsley yearned to call out and chase after her. But unlike the time before, it wasn't the book that needed to keep her away, her body literally couldn't do it anymore, it was burnt out. She needed rest, and badly.

She pulled out her ear buds, and plugged them into her aging mp3 player and hit play, one of her many soothing tunes began to play. And as it did so, Ainsley's eyes began to close as she slowly fell asleep in the wheat field.

But as she slept, the book had other plans. The lock fell open.

IX. The Voice

Ainsley's head began to tremble; the soft, prickly wheat that she had
fashioned into a bed was gone. Ainsley reached round from where she laid,
her eyes still too groggy to make out what was happening. Her hand grabbed
hold of something hot, very hot, pulling it up so she could look at it with her
limited vision; Ainsley realized what it was. Sand. Amber tinged sand.
Snapping her eyes wide open, Ainsley then saw what was causing the beads
of clumped together sand to reverberate from her hand, a wall of horsemen,
in full gallop, coming straight at her.

In a state of shock, Ainsley quickly got to her feet and started off in
the other direction. But that too caused Ainsley to gasp. Coming kiddie
corner to the mounted men was a yet another mass of people, much further
away though, looking minute in the distance, like a wave of fire ants, but all
the same breathtaking in the sheer quantity of them. Taking her chances with
the apparent Army, Ainsley took flight, running as fast as her legs would
carry.

Though always admired in her family for her speed, Ainsley's
youthful vivacity was not enough to avoid the oncoming hoard of riders.
Peering back, to gauge their distance, Ainsley was surprised to see that it
was not in fact horses that these men rode. It looked as though it were
something more wildly. Like a deer or antelope, but much bigger, built like a
warhorse, but with the most amazing array of antlers she had ever beheld.
The antlers alone must've taken up half of the mass of the creatures.

Ainsley spent so long looking back at the mysterious creatures that she failed to see the small boulder resting in her way. And it didn't take long for her young little footsteps to trip right over it.

Hitting the hot sand with a thud, Ainsley looked back once more in terror as the immense creatures came bounding towards her. Too frightened now to stand up, or even crawl. Ainsley just lay there, as the riders were finally on top of her.

The sound, couldn't be compared, a thousand thunderclaps, happening all around her. Giant hoofs collapsing left, right and center. Ainsley's heart was beating faster than she could ever imagine, she had never been so scared in her entire life as she was in that moment. That moment which went on for an eternity. Ainsley dare not open her eyes, for fear of seeing the end of a hoof coming down on top of her. But none of this happened; the booming roll of galloping hooves subsided. The wave past by, and after a short bit, it was nothing but silence.

Ainsley opened her eyes, the first thing that she thought was that she was dead, but that wasn't true, no just like all other things, her gut told her otherwise. Turning and looking upward from her prone position, Ainsley saw off in the distance the clash between the riders and the army of men. At such a distance, it looked almost harmless, but alas, this was no harmless meeting, this was one of many battles these two clans had had over the trinity. This wasn't new this was a daily occurrence. But all this was yet to be discovered by the young, naïve Ainsley.

Getting to her feet, Ainsley could finally take her time to look around at where she was. It was familiar. 'I've been here before' thought Ainsley as she looked around. 'Where is the road, where is the wheat?' Ainsley then realized another thing that was missing. "Where is the book??" exclaimed Ainsley. Looking all around where she stood, she found nothing, no books, no road, and no wheat, just desert.

'Wait a minute, why do I care so much about that silly book? I mean I've only had it like a day and a half, sure it's a family heirloom and supposedly really important, but why should I care? I don't care, nope it was all just silly nonsense Artie was saying… right?' thought Ainsley, clearly struggling with the whole concept.

Not feeling comfortable standing still so near an apparent battle, and in the middle of nowhere, Ainsley decided to start walking away from the battle, in hopes of finding something other than hot blistering desert. "Alright, just breath Ainsley, work this out, you were walking along a road, not too far from your house, well how do I know that, I wasn't really paying attention as to how far I walked, whatever, I was walking along a road. It must've been near my house that would explain the wheat fields. Okay, so then the book dragged me off into the wheat; mom drove by then… Then, I fell asleep… so what am I doing in the middle of a desert!" Ainsley let out a frustrated sigh, not being able to solve her current situation, she usually was very talented at this, she took pride in not having a situation or problem she couldn't figure out on her own, very rarely did she ask for help, the only time she could remember was when her father left when she was born. She asked her mom why, and all her mom had to say was, "you're too young to understand, perhaps when you are older" She never did find out. In fact she often had a hard time remembering what her father looked like or what he was like, it had only been 5 years or so since he left, but still things were starting to slip away. But what upset Ainsley the most, what concerned her, was that she didn't even care. Did that make her a bad person? She hoped not, she always thought of herself as a very kind and loving person. But when it came to her father's unexpected leaving, she felt nothing. She often felt glad of this; it saved her a whole lot of grief that everyone assumed she would experience.

Looking up from the desert floor, Ainsley looked briefly around to see if anything of interest caught her eye, nothing. Just more desert, looking back she couldn't even see the battle anymore. Sighing, Ainsley looked back to the ground, walking at a leisurely pace, and fell into deep thought.

Ainsley thought about her mom, she didn't understand why she reacted the way she did, sure she should be a little peeved that she borrowed her key without telling her, but to react that way, it seemed, almost psychotic. Which was nothing like the mom Ainsley knew, the mom Ainsley knew was a very loving, humble soul, who did her best, given their limited means to make Ainsley's life enjoyable, up until that one moment, Ainsley had never seen her mom get mad, ever. She made note to ask her uncles if she ever got mad as a child. "What am I talking about? How do I even know I'm going to see my uncles, or mom? I mean either this is one of the most elaborate dreams I have ever had, or its as Artie said, and I'm now stuck in this mystical land dodging oversized deer!" *Well hold on, its not like this was the first time I've seen this place, I was here last time I opened the book too, surely that means that its real right?* "Heh, yeah or real insane" *Come on now, its not totally impossible, impossible only means something that cannot actually occur... EVER, and yet here we are, for a second time!* "Yeah, I guess, but we... wait, why did I think we? Oh my god, I really am losing it!" *No, your not Ainsley, I'm sorry, I should explained, you know how Arthur told you when your touched the book for the first time that it altered certain behaviors and personality traits?* "Yes?" responded Ainsley truly

57

confused by how she was having a conversation with an apparently separate subconscious. *Well he wasn't totally correct in saying that, none of your behaviors or personality traits have been changed. Just superseded when needed to.* Ainsley walked with a face that only could suggest baffled. "What? What are you talking about, you forget that you are talking to a 12 year old, listen to me I'm arguing with myself!" exclaimed Ainsley getting very frustrated with being confused all the time. *No, you aren't arguing with yourself, that's impossible, no, what you are doing is arguing with me.* Thought the voice.

"And who are you?" reasonably asked Ainsley. *Well, I guess the easiest way to explain it would be this, you know when people are like "the little voice in the back of my head told me to do it?" Well I'm that little voice, only I'm not just someone making stuff up, I'm the real deal.*

Ainsley walked in silence, trying to take all this in, and debating whether or not to believe it.

"So, you're a little voice in my head that can talk to me?" Sarcastically spoke Ainsley. *Yes, more or less, not so simple but yes* "So why couldn't I hear you before? I've been here before right, and what about all yesterday I couldn't hear you then? What about that, mister smarty-pants?" *First off, I'm no mister, I'm a missy, I'm your voice after all, that means I'm not going to be some 300-pound brute. Secondly, the reason you couldn't hear me before was because you didn't know at the time, but you were talking to me, you were just thinking it was you. And as for when you are out of here, in your world, anything I say falls mute, all I can do then is protect you by sending you urges, or feelings to guide you away from dangerous situations.*

"So that was you!! Oh, now that makes total sense, you were the one controlling the book??" *Yes, well no, not the book, I was controlling your arms, through the book, I can only control your actions when I'm in physical contact with you, any other time I can only send you feelings.*

"Wait so you are the book?" *Well no, not exactly, it gets really complicated, and I'm really not the person who should tell you all this, but basically I am in the book yes, but I am not the book itself. The book is a very old, and very strong source of power, whenever one of you comes into existence, it creates one of us to pair with you. So for all practical purposes, I'm the book, or at least its bridge between you and this world. You get it?*

"Sure? I guess? But if its not you who is supposed to tell me, then who is?" asked Ainsley, becoming more and more fascinated by this whole voice thing, and finding a new appreciation for that old book.

Well, Arthur was supposed to do a better job telling you, especially since you are the first not to be born from here, but it's never been his strong suit to talk clearly. "Heh, you think, the guy speaks in riddles" *Yes, unfortunately he does... Anyways, seeing as he didn't do a very good job of preparing you, I will have to get you to the northern coast, there we will find you someone who can properly train you in your duties, catch you up on 12 years of living here.*

"Okay, well then, lets go! How far is it to the northern coast?" excitedly asked Ainsley, now completely cured of her cynicism. *Well, on foot, it's about 7 months* timidly revealed the voice. "SEVEN MONTHS!!! It can't be, this place can't be that big! I mean come on that's ridiculous! We'll never make it, that's like, 200 days, give or take!!!" *What? No no no, forgive me, I should have specified, we do not operate on the same time system you do back home. We don't have 24 hour days, we only have 21 hour days, and our months are only 21 days, and our weeks are 3 days long, so that means for us we have 7 weeks in a month, our hours are 73 minutes long and our seconds only go up to 37, we don't have the numbers 8 or 9 here, so really its actually a much shorter time to the coast, certainly not 200 days, more like 140.*

Ainsley froze in her spot, flabbergasted by the barrage of information she just received. "Okay, I'm not even going to pretend like I can understand all of what you just told me, all I really heard was you saying its only 140 days? Are you kidding me? That's still ridiculous! I'm only twelve; I can't be wandering around some mystical land for 5 months! I have to get home, I have to get back to my mom, god my mom, she must be worried sick about me!" *Rest easy, time passes differently here, 5 months here passes in an instant back home, you won't be missed, you are still, too all inquiring eyes, fast asleep in a wheat field. Don't worry, and as far as your mom is concerned, you cannot stress over her.*

Slightly offended by this Ainsley retorted "Why not??" *Because in this regard Ainsley, she is not your ally, she stopped being your mother the moment you picked up that book, I know you can't possibly understand this, but believe me, your mother doesn't either, she may never understand this, but all you have to be concerned about is that your contact with your mom, in fact most of your family, has to be limited if not cut off.*

Ainsley began to breath heavy, she could feel her eyes well up with tears, something she wasn't accustomed to, and she fought back the urge to weep. But it was no use; tears already began to roll down her rosy little cheeks. "So, so, I can't see them? Any of them?" Hysterically asked Ainsley. *I'm sorry, I know this is difficult to understand, I wish I could explain it better, but I can't, just let me get to you to the coast and I promise you this will all be made right. You'll feel right as rain.* Encouraged the voice, but it fell on deaf ears, all Ainsley felt now was grief, and an overwhelming sense of isolation regardless of this new 'friend' she seemed to make in her subconscious.

Not responding, Ainsley begrudgingly began to walk, not really caring where she went, just so long as it was the way that would make her feel better.

X. The Follisenwit

Ainsley had been walking for hours, not saying a word, not hearing a word from the voice. She was enjoying the silence, it gave her time to feel upset, and without someone telling her she should feel better. Which at this time if someone did, she would squarely deny. It all felt so unfair, not being allowed to see her family ever again, she didn't understand, the voice didn't give any justification as to why she wasn't allowed to. Just that she wasn't, the same could be said about Artie, he too told her that she shouldn't mention the book to her mother. "But why, what was so bad about mom, my entire life she's been amazing, yet all of the sudden she is this evil person that I'm no longer allowed to see? I mean come on! What is with this place, why in the world would I want any part with it, all it is, is desert, desert and giant caribou running around with crazed riders on them! I mean it sounds crazy, it's stupid, and I don't want any part with this place. It's brought me nothing but trouble."

Ainsley? timidly asked the voice. "What! Can't you tell that I want to be left alone??" retorted Ainsley, *Yes, I can see that, but we really must start off toward the coast, I know you are mad, and upset, and I can understand that, but if you ever want to see your family again, you gotta listen to me. I'm only trying to help you I mean you no harm.* "Heh, that's funny, no harm, all you've done for me is torn me away from my family, I call that doing some harm!" *I know, its regrettable that it has to be this way, I'm sorry, but if we can just keep moving we can make things right!* encouraged the voice, in a tone that Ainsley could quickly see she would come to hate. "Whatever, you better be right… what do I call, you do you have a name?" asked Ainsley. Caught off guard, the voice responded, *Huh, me? Well, I don't know, you know no one has ever asked me before. I guess I could have one, if you so chose, I mean I am essentially a part of you, so if you feel it would make things easier, you can name me.* "Really? That's interesting, hmm, I'll have to think of that, I mean I just met you, I could be mean and call you something totally lame like Thelma or something" laughed Ainsley to herself, relieved for the opportunity to brighten her own mood. *Please don't, I may be the bearer of bad news some times but that doesn't mean I should be named something as un-suiting as Thelma.* Begged the voice. "Hah okay, well I'll have to think about it" *Okay, well take your time; I'm in no rush. But as you decide, can I please advise that we turn right* "Alright why?" *Because in case you didn't notice you are now reaching the side of a mountain,* confused, Ainsley looks up from her spot on the ground and is astonished to see a gigantic wall of mountains, spanning left and right as far as the eye can see, blocking any further forward movement. "Well that's great, now where do we go?" *Right, we go right Ainsley* "And why do we go right?" inquired Ainsley *We go right because I'm your guide around here and I know the lay of the land and in this particular part of this place, going left will lead you no where for miles while going right, you have a small pass through the mountains which will save us a month of wandering through this desert.* "Great, right it is then!" exclaimed Ainsley as she dutifully turn right and with new found energy, bounded along the steep mountainside.

The mountains in this place were dry; in fact the whole place seemed to be. Dry, and yet moist at the same time, it was strange, Ainsley never really looked closely at the rock and hardened sand she walked on before, during her last visit. But looking at it, running her hand along it she saw, alone the icy white surface a white glow parallel her hand. Everywhere she moved her hand along the dry surface of the mountainous rock, the white,

63

almost fluid glow followed. "What's happening to the rock?" asked Ainsley as she came to a complete stop and ran both her hands over the rock, taking the beautiful sight of the warm glow of the rock.

Nothing is happening to the rock Ainsley, that is all you. Plainly stated the voice. Ainsley, astonished, looked up as if to look at the voice, but of course not seeing anything. "Really?? How am I doing this??" excitedly asked Ainsley "Does this mean I have superpowers???" *No, well not technically, this isn't your world, there are no superpowers here, everyone here is pretty much like everyone you know back home, as are you, but because you are Sevardinal, you are granted certain… luxuries.* "Like being immortal and what not?" *Oh, so Artie did tell you something after all?* asked the voice. "Yeah well, I mean he wasn't completely vague, he told me I'd be a Sevardinal thingy for like 300 years or something and he told me I was immortal, sort of like I could live longer and die and be reborn sort of thing. Am I correct?" timidly ask Ainsley. *Yes, in a completely none technical way, but yes… did he tell you about the Follisenwit?* "…Huh??" asked Ainsley genuinely confused. Though no mouth to sigh out of, you could tell the voice was stressed with babysitting Ainsley and having to explain everything to her. 'He didn't tell you, oh Arthur, okay, a Follisenwit is a structure, and you've been in it before.' "When?" *The last time you were here, it was how you got home, and how you magically teleported from your bed to Arthur's, I mean your new home.* Ainsley paused for a second "that's what that was? That giant stairwell thing? That's a follisen.." *Wit, a Follisenwit, yes, there are seven of them. And they are the only known way back to your world. They are more commonly known as the Wind Chambers.* Explained the voice, doing its best to explain. "I see, so, so like, these wind chambers are like portals to Earth right?" *Yes, except its not Earth, you are*

64

still on Earth, think of them as a bridge through time. They are part of the magical fabric of the books each Sevardinal possesses, just like I am. No one outside of the Sevardinal knows of their existence or location. They are myths, part of legend, and that is how it must be. "I see, but okay, so they are time machines, kinda, that link up with the books?" Asked Ainsley as she slowly began to walk once more dragging her index finger alone the mountainside, leaving a dazzling glow behind her. *Generally yes, but they serve more purposes other than travelling to your home, they can also be used to travel between each of them, so we may travel more quickly across this land.* Ainsley stopped again, now frustrated. "Wait, your telling me these chambers teleport us all over this place, and we are walking?? Why are we walking?? Why don't we just go find the one I found last time??" *Try to understand Ainsley, these structures are not to be trifled with, they aren't for average use. You were lucky to make it out of the Follisenwit alive, let alone even make it in it. That's why you are here.*

"What do you mean *why you are here?*" cautiously asked Ainsley sensing she was about to be told something she didn't like. *I mean... I mean that if you didn't locate, and get inside and out of the Follisenwit, you would never have returned home, you would not have been chosen, you would just wander the desert forever, and eventually lose your mind, and become a vegetable, not actually, you know what I mean, a zombie, no soul left in you, no memories, no* "Wait!" interrupted Ainsley " No memories, is that why I couldn't remember anything when I was here last??" *Yes, that is why, you may not have known it, I doubt Arthur would have told you, but upon first entering the book, you go under a sort of initiation, or test if you will, to see if you are indeed the chosen one. And ultimately, the test is life or death.*

Ainsley began to feel the blood seep from her face, as it went white. "So, so I could have died last time?" *No not death, a punishment much worse, eternal existence with no consciousness; a lifeless life.*

Ainsley didn't feel like talking anymore.

XI. Venom's Pass

Night began to rise over the barren desert, and all went black, just as before. Ainsley hadn't talked in what seemed like hours. It had been a ridiculous week. One minute she's promised a new mp3 player, the next she's the newest member of some weird historian superman club, drawing white glow lines in rocks and, dodging death at every turn it seemed.

Ainsley walked without a hitch in her step, and the voice didn't intervene, didn't utter I mental word, just remained silent. And the weird thing was, Ainsley kinda wished it did say something, something that would make her feel better about this whole thing, cause right now she was depressed. And being only 12, Ainsley knew this wasn't your average sulkfest.

Stop. Sternly said the voice. Jolting Ainsley out of her thoughts.

We are here "Where, I don't see anything?" glumly asked Ainsley. *Turn and look at the mountain.* Ainsley did as she was told. Still not seeing anything other than solid rock as far as her limited vision could see, Ainsley was about to speak up when just like back home her hands became possessed and clapped together with a force that would shock most. Glued together, Ainsley watched as her hands struggled to pull apart from one another, slowly pulling apart, Ainsley witnessed that same white fluid glow appear from her hands, expanding, and filling in the empty space between her dividing hands. The light coming off of the glow was so vibrant and bright; it illuminated most of the mountainside. "What's happening??" frantically asked Ainsley, not receiving an answer this time. Looking forward, Ainsley finally spotted that though in the dark the mountainside looked solid it in fact wasn't, and there was indeed a small narrow path, steeply leading up in a zig zagging fashion up the vertical wall of the mountain.

Its okay, start walking up it, I got this, said the voice referring to the mystical makeshift flashlight the voice developed. Ainsley decided it was best not to ask questions and just walked. Having to be careful with her step, Ainsley had to take small steps, with her feet close together, due to the narrow foothold that was available to her.

While she climbed, Ainsley noted, that this part of the mountain ridge appeared to be the lowest part of it, which she figured was probably why it was chosen as the location of this secret pathway.

In what seemed like no time at all, Ainsley reached the top of the ridge, and found it to be fairly narrow, with a small landing no bigger than her room, enough to lay down in, but not much else. Looking down the other side, Ainsley saw no walkway, no path no steps. Looking to her right however, she did spot a similarly narrow walkway between the two summits of the conjoined mountains.

Ainsley was about to move on toward the path when the voice intervened. *We should stop* "Why?" asked Ainsley. *Its not safe to continue this journey at night.* Cautiously explained the voice.

And with that the white glowing flash between Ainsley's hands shot out and pinned itself to the floor of the small landing. *Come, let us rest.*

Ainsley was almost about to retort that she wasn't tired in the slightest, having felt fine for the long day she had endured in the ever intense sunlight, when a large yawn shook all the life out of her and, without another word, she laid down and past out.

When Ainsley awoke, she half hoped that she would wake up in her bed, and that all had been a bad dream, or at least back in the field where she could go home and see her mom, who must be worried sick about her. But no, she was still here, on top of the shallow mountaintop, listening to some sort of consciousness instructs her and teaches her about this mystical world.

Feeling a little better than she was last night, Ainsley asked, "You never did tell me what all the white glowy stuff is about. *Oh, didn't I? I must have more in common with Arthur than I thought.* Joked the voice earning a chuckle out of Ainsley, who was more than grateful for it. *Well I'm sorry, let me clear that up now. Because of your status as a—* "Sevardinal, I know" interrupted Ainsley. *Yes, because of that, you are given certain abilities that allow you to survive more defiantly in this cruel environment. Tools if you will, and these tools come in the form of that glow you saw. So basically, that glow is a Sevardinal's energy, seeping out of you into the rocks, which is why you can see it. With the proper training, you can learn to master how to use it and how to defend yourself, and, like I did for you last night; keep you out of the dark.*

Ainsley was flabbergasted; she had never heard anything in her life that was so undeniably... cool! "No way are you serious! So I can like make force fields, laser beams, flashlights???" excitedly asked Ainsley. *Yes, yes and yes. And much much more, and before you get your hopes up, I can't train you Ainsley, you need another Sevardinal to do that.* Ainsley was clearly disappointed. "Aw, why can't you, I wanna learn!!" whined Ainsley, falling into her old 12 year old mentality, whine until you receive. *I'm sorry, but I'm a part of you, as well as this world, so because of that, I can do all the things you would be able to do someday. Because it is my job to defend you and look after you when you cannot. I'm sorry.* Ainsley let out a huge sigh as she slowly began to rise from her prone position to a standing one. "Okay, well, congratulations, you actually gave me something to look forward to and motivate me to stay," confessed Ainsley, not enjoying the fact that this delirious world she was in was actually starting to interest her more and more. *Good! I'm glad to hear that, now we really must be on our way, a long journey still awaits us, and believe me Ainsley; this world doesn't all consist of this desert.* Ominously explained the voice.

Starting to walk down the narrow path, Ainsley let out a sigh, expelling any grief she had felt from last night, and began to sing an old song she used to sing when she was little, a song her mom taught her that always made her feel better when she was upset:

I once went on a journey,
And it led me to quite a tourney.
And while I sang and danced the night away,
All I could say was hooray!
I once went on a journey,
And it led me to a man named Bernie.
And while we sang and danced the night away,
All I could say was hooray!
I once went on a journey,
That had me end up on a gurney.
And while I sang and danced the night away,
All I could say was hooray!
I once went on a journey,
A journey that led me many places.
I once went on a journey,
A journey that introduced me to many faces.
I once went on a journey,
A journey that never ended.
A journey that I never wanted to end.
And while I sang and danced the night away,
All I could say was hooray!

As Ainsley sang her song, she didn't realize, in fact neither Ainsley nor the voice realized, that they were in fact being watched.

They were being tracked…

As Ainsley walked she noticed that the narrow path, which had been
in a steady downward tilt for the past hour and a bit, was beginning to
widen, and the tall mountain summits were becoming taller and taller, or
rather, Ainsley was going lower and lower, thus farther and farther away
from the summits. This brought a slight smile Ainsley's face, knowing that
she was finally going to get out of this desert.

It was sunset by the time Ainsley finally emerged from the narrow
pass. She stopped and took in a big gulp of air. Smelling the fresh air that
barraged her face upon exiting the pass, which only proved to be stale, and
rather fowl smelling. Ahead of Ainsley lay lush forests, as far as the eye
could see, Ainsley could already tell that the vegetation here, just like the
animals, wasn't something you saw normally at home. It looked far more
unique and beautiful. Ainsley was beginning to lose her self in the beauty of
it all, even without having to think twice. Ainsley began to move towards the
forest.

FFFWHAP!!!!

The sound of the dart was the last thing Ainsley heard before she hit
the ground, paralyzed, all she could do was bare witness to a figure dropping
down from an unknown vantage point. Landing several feet away, all
Ainsley could focus on, what instantly terrified her, was the face of the man,
if you could call him that; the face of her hunter. A pair of large black orbs,
and a round mouth with a set of razor sharp teeth clenched together. He had
no nose, or ears by the looks of it.

Just those eyes, and that mouth.

As Ainsley began to lose consciousness, she gave one final thought. "I miss mom."

XII. Eyes meet Hands

Eye woke up from his afternoon nap. If that's what you could call it, it was the first time he'd slept in two days. For the young Eye was struggling as of late with his regular sleeping schedule. And all of this had to do with the Vitalmony. The oldest and most sacred ceremony his tribe had. And he was to undertake it tonight. After six months of studying the theory and ritualistic runes that made up the guide for new Vitalmoner's, Eye was nowhere near ready. And this feared him more than words could describe.

Eye, was a young man, not unlike most, nothing spectacular about him, average height, jet black shoulder hair, and a rich caramel skin color, distinct to his tribe and his tribe alone. Eye was turning 21, a sacred number, the number of maturity much like elsewhere, but for differing reasons. For Eye, the reason this age was of such importance, was because this was the day that would decide his fate for the rest of his days, it would decide his destiny.

Rising from his prone position off of the excessively large leaf that he had made into a cushion in his limited sleeping area. Eye looked over the vast hut that he shared with the tribe. See unlike in other cultures, the Vitaly, as they are bluntly called, being their proper name is 37 syllables and usually comes out as gibberish to an untrained ear, they were not nomadic by nature. They had all the food and shelter they could ever desire surrounding them, but due to their small numbers and the large populace of creatures that could easily kill a lone tribesmen, they naturally developed a habit to share huts. Keeping 7 warriors on guard at all times, the village, would bunker down in the lodger, a large tent like structure, similar to that of a sweat lodge, but much larger, equaling a high school gym in certain villages, this particular one was much smaller only measuring 20 meters across, and having a total of 70 tribe members uncomfortably nestling together every night.

Taking light steps, Eye exited the lodger and took a deep inhale of air. Reveling in the sweet freshness of it, never disappointing the young Eye, it was indeed his favorite, if not only thing he enjoyed about his village, the air here always smelt superb. Looking round, through the morning mist of the mixed wood, Eye spotted his good friend and mentor Claw standing guard to the center guard, the most respected and dangerous position, for in this village, the creatures that preyed on the poor Vitaly, were all tree dwellers. And being that the sheer size of the trees in this forest was massive, so massive you could not see the top, there was almost always a heavy fog just below the top of the trees.

Climbing the latter up on top of the lodger and carefully walking across the small wooden platform to the center post, Eye quietly and respectfully approached Claw, knowing one should never sneak up on a guard. And in this moment, Eye recalled his earliest memory of his famed friend, and why, there relationship, compared to others, was much closer.

When Eye was younger, a mere 6 years of age, just shy of the first of many ceremonial ages the Vitaly celebrate, the first being at 7, the year in which the child earns their lifelong title. Prior to this they are just referred to as 'Poodo' or naïve one. It was on this, his seventh birthday, that Eye, or Poodo as he was currently called, and the other Poodii all hatched a plan to pull a prank on Tribe Leader Long Tooth. The plan was simple, wake up super early, and release a wire snake into Long Tooth's inner hut, within the lodger. Wire snakes were not unlike any other snake you'd find, the only difference with them was merely that they were just that, as thin as a wire, similar to that of a coat hanger, and instead of delivering a venomous blow to any of its prey or predator, it releases a profound and intense screech, one only the prey or predator can hear. So to the Vitaly, they were mainly used as a hunting tactic. They would hurl them at large prey thus paralyzing them with the deafening noise and once done, would strike the final blow to the animal. A useful tactic indeed, but the Poodo's had no intention of using it to hunt, only to play fool.

Sneaking out of the lodger, the Poodo's all followed Eye to the warrior hut, a short walk away, down a steep hill, near a small shallow stream, sometimes used to clean off the weaponry, and also to collect the Wire snakes, being they lived in and near the water's edge.

Eye, and the other Poodii all arrived at the hut. "Go check in the hut you guys!" excitedly ordered Eye, meanwhile he approached the stream and crouched down and looked to the calm water. Seeing his distorted reflection, Eye playfully swatted at the water, watching the wire snakes scurry away fearfully from the disturbance. This brought a smile to his face, enjoying the fearful nature of the creatures. As the water settled however, Eye was presented with a reflection unlike the one prior to his swat. A large black mass hung high above his head.

Eye knew instantly what it was. It was what every tribe member feared, what everyone solemnly referred to as "The Black Hand".

Eye's heart stopped, he was petrified with fear, having never seen one of these horrific creatures in person, Eye instantly wished he never did. Slowly reaching down to his heel, where he and all other Poodii, stored their one and only weapon, a small dagger, dull in design, used primarily for training purposes as well as to help the collectors cut down vegetation.

Listening with all intensity, eye knew only two things about the Black Hand; the first was it always let out a blood-draining screech when it pounced, and second, no one, no one survived once it did.

Eye, now with a firm grasp on his dagger, stood perfectly still, figuring he had somewhat an advantage of over the large black beast, letting it think he didn't know it was hunting him. Eye, summoning up all sorts of courage a spritely 7 year old shouldn't possess, turned rapidly and faced the beast. The Black Hand froze, taken aback but the sudden aggressiveness of its prey, Eye looked deep into the kaleidoscope eyes of the Black Hand, and it looked right back. Eye refused to blink fearing, and in his heart knowing, the moment he did it would be over in a flash. Holding his dagger steadily toward the large animal, Eye was now at a loss of what to do.

Seeing that its prey was attempting to defend itself, the Black Hand, which anyone who looked at it, and had knowledge of such things, would know it was a giant spider of sorts, started to slowly descend from its perched position. Taking its time, it slowly lowered itself to mere 3 feet away from the terrified Eye. Looking Eye square on, it took Eye only a moment to see in its black orbs that the giant spider had made up its mind.

And acting on impulse, Eye raged his hand forward, letting out a loud yell.

PFFT!

The blade made contact, and skidded off the rock hard body of the Black Hand. Taking its opportunity, the spider acted fast swatting the dagger far way and playfully pushing its prey to the ground. Detaching itself from its web line. The Black Hand crawled over Eye. At this moment, the rest of the Poodo's excitedly exited the hut carrying a cage with the wire snakes inside. They stopped dead in their tracks upon seeing the scene that lay in front of them. Eye made eye contact with them, fear creeping through his tough physique, he signaled for them to run, and that's what they did. They abandoned him.

Turning to his death dealer, the young Poodo, alone now, lay relaxed, accepting his fate. Acknowledging its prey's submission, the Black Hand wasted no time.

SCREEEEEEEECH!!!!!!!

Came the terrible noise of the end, Eye wanted to close his eyes, but couldn't, instead he bare witness to the giant spider's hardened shell suddenly open up and reveal a series of claws and black tongues which he could only assume were sticky, used to hold onto the pray as it mutilated the body.

Finally closing his lids, Eye listened to the terrible noise from the Black Hand, but amongst all the terror, he heard a different noise, that of a slithering kind. Looking briefly over, Eye spotted a Wire snake mindlessly weaving its way towards him. Thinking fast, Eye grabbed the little snake and flung it into the inner mouth of the Black Hand. And there, a short break in the screeching occurred as the shocked Black Hand defensively shut its outer casing and stumbled back. And then from within the casing, came another screech softer than the last, but undeniably that of a Wire snake.

Eye rose to a crouching position once more, eagerly watching the inner war between the Wire snake and the Black Hand. The Black Hand was clearly in distress, wobbling back and forth, using its forward legs to feel at its casing, desperately trying to reach the intruding foe. Being unable to do so, in a last ditch effort, perhaps out of revenge, the struggling Black Hand charged at Eye, and swiped at him with its foremost leg, and delivering a hard blow to his head, catching his left eye.

Eye let out a pained gasp as he fell back into the shallow stream grasping his head in agony.

And as that occurred, down the hill rapidly came several warriors, with the Poodo's at their rear; in the front was Claw, clearly alarmed, and seeing that Eye was down, he acted fast and withdrew his pike, and charged the flailing, disoriented spider, hopping onto its back, Claw twirled his pike and plunged the spearhead into the face of the black beast. Letting out that horrific screech once more, dying in agony, Claw twisted the blade and the screaming came to an end.

Eye lost his vision in his damaged eye, but because of his bravery and fast thinking, he was granted the title of 'Eye', which amongst his tribe was highly respected, being that their first tribe leader also shared this title.

"Ehem, how goes the watch brother Claw?" politely asked Eye to an unsurprised Claw. "Same as it is every day, shit until the dawn" chuckled Claw, aged, and in his 40's, turning to Eye. "What brings you out this morning brother Eye?" "I, I have fears about the Vitalmony tonight brother" I've studied all that I could but I fear I'm not ready, I've practiced all the moves, but nothing seems to stick." Confessed Eye, timidly keeping his sight to the ground.

"Ah brother Eye, worry not, this isn't a test of your memorization skills or even the elegance of your performance, it is about being yourself.

We don't want you faking whom you are and before you know it, you are doing some terrible job that is not suited for you. This isn't about looks. It's about soul. Just be yourself and you'll be fine. I remember being just as afraid, but it will prove... quite underwhelming when you get to it tonight, trust me."

Eye squinted his already thin eyelids, analyzing Claw for any hidden sarcasm. Claw had been known to exaggerate and mislead in his stories, so Eye was skeptical whenever he heard a story come from him, which was literally every time they talked. "I'm not sure brother, you are sure I have nothing to fear?"

"Well I wouldn't say that no" chuckled Claw. Eye's eyes shot open at this, "what do you mean, you just said—" "you misunderstood me brother, I merely said you had nothing to fear about the dance portion of the Vitalmony, but the trial, that could be something."

Eye stood there in silence for a moment, "So, so there is a trial?" he finally timidly asked. Now it was Claw's turn for his eyes to go wide. "What? You don't know about the trial? I thought you got through all the runes??" nervously asked Claw. Feeling slightly embarrassed and offended, Eye quickly countered, in a tone harsher than he intended "well it wasn't like I had anyone to help me translate it!"

Silence fell between them, Claw seeing that he had pinched a nerve quickly changed from his friendly, joking way, into his big brother tone. "Listen Eye, I know you above most have had a hard time with this, with your father, well him being away, we all should have helped you out. I apologize on everyone's behalf." Eye didn't respond, possibly not even listening clearly lost in memories too painful to bare. Feeling uncomfortable, Claw pushed on "The trial, which for your sake I hope turns out to be an easy one, is a challenge given to you once the quality of your character is deducted and examined." Eye listens, though keeps staring off into the distance, suggesting he was doing his best to suggest he didn't care. "What sort of challenges do they give?" he asked after a short pause.

"Oh all sorts of things, pick a goldsberry from the tallest tree, run to the forest barrier and back, cook the Tribe Leader a feast, kill a wild boar, you name it…" Eye finally turned to look at Claw, recognizing his cautious tone. "Claw, what aren't you telling me, I'm not a little kid anymore I deserve to know what I'm up against here" Claw let out a deep sigh and raised his hand to Eye's scrawny shoulder. "Okay, Eye, this trial does consist of potential challenges like I just suggested, but others, well, they are a little more dangerous." "How dangerous?" "Well I don't want to go giving you false fears but a rare few in the past have been, well they have been fatal."

Eye's heart began to pick up pace, instantly reminding him of his encounter with the Black Hand all those years ago. "Fatal for me? Or fatal for something I have to hunt?" carefully asked Eye. "Possibly for both, possibly for you, or possibly for whatever they have you hunt, if they have you hunt at all." "What is that supposed to mean?" asked Eye, coming across more panicked that he would have liked. "It means brother, that I can't tell you what its going to be like, I can't tell you what they are going to do, what they are going to make you do. All I can tell you is that if you survive it, you will be what everyone in this tribe yearns for…" "And what is that brother Claw?" asked Eye, confused by the last bit of Claw's words.

"It means you'll be a man Eye, it means your long role to adulthood will be complete, it means your life will be complete." Proudly proclaimed

Claw, clearly in a state of reminisces. Eye remained silent at this, he was unaware of what exactly Claw meant by 'your life will be complete'. "So, so after the Vitalmony, I'll have nothing to live for?" Cautiously asked Eye, not liking the sounds of his own words as he spoke them. Breaking his abyss-like gaze. Claw sternly looked to Claw, all business, and told, but came across as an order "You live for your tribe Eye, as we all do, your Vitalmony will decide what you will do with your life, and you will do it! Do you understand?"

Taken aback by the harshness coming from Claw, Eye recognized that this was nothing to ask further on. So, deciding it best to say nothing, Eye just respectfully nodded and backed away from the warrior, the warrior he respected most and treated as a surrogate father.

Carefully walking backwards across the narrow wooden plank, Eye finally turned and leapt down to the ground. Eye now felt more uneasy than he had when he woke, not only was he terrified for the Vitalmony because of potentially screwing it up, but now he was terrified of it for a new reason.

No more freedom.

XIII. The Vitalmony

That day like no other passed with excessive sloth. Eye neglected all his chores, choosing not to join his fellow Poodo's as they all went swatballing in the northeastern part of the forest. Instead, after his solemn talk with Claw, Eye climbed into the lodger and found his spot near the deepest part of the far wall and lay down. And he didn't rise for the rest of the day.

All anxiety towards the Vitalmony had vanished from Eye, all that remained now was his fear of what Claw's words meant. Eye had always been an independent spirit, though he tended to hide it from people, he never realized that this trait of his, this secret that he greedily kept to himself, would come to affect him so much. He had always thought that his independence was to be cherished and embraced by his tribesmen, but now he was not so sure, he had never thought of it being an offensive factor. But here on the dawn of his manhood, a good friend of his tells him that he will do, as he is told, and nothing else. And Eye can't help but feel trapped by this fate. Now yes, he could be told to do wondrous things that even himself with his rather extravagant imagination and ambition could perceive, but that doesn't bother him, he knows that if it was all bad, that more would be against it, now, what offends Eye is the fact that no matter what he's told to do, good, bad or otherwise neutral, it is not his decision to make.

In fact thinking back on his short life, Eye came to realize that all of his most important moments, excluding his encounter with the Black Hand that is, were in some form or another, a form of control and routine. Every ritual he's taken, wasn't optional, every hunt he tagged along on, wasn't by choice. Every friend he made even, wasn't by pure chance meeting, all his

82

friends, were a result of the elders ordering the parents to acquaint the children so they may grow a lifelong bond that would serve them later in their eventual duties as adults, whether it be hunter, gatherer, builder, etc.

Eye couldn't believe it; he was shocked by his own revelation. Shocked and revolted at the same time. He had never realized until this very moment, how unhappy and dissatisfied he truly was with his life in the village. But he really was. And that fear he had about the Vitalmony, it had festered into something far more potent and irresponsible… resentment.

As Eye lay alone in the lodger, he came to realize that he hated his village, and almost everyone in it, not hate in the way normal society perceives it, but hate the way his society functions, and how crippled he was. He had no choice, if he didn't go through with the Vitalmony, or any ceremony thereafter, he would be branded a "Fallop", coward, and would be fed to his old friend... The Black Hand. And Eye had no intention of fighting off so valiantly a beast just to be spoon fed it years later.

The sun had set, and the twinkling sunlight that dominated the overhead treetops was replaced by the warm glow of torchlight, as thousands, if not more, of torches were light. Providing a large cushion of warm light over the village. And as the torches began to light up the night sky, so did the soft drum of the tribal baseflap (drum like instrument).

Eye could foresee what was about to happen, soon someone would come for him, and "kindly" guide him down from the elevated perch of the lodger to the sacred pit, a massive bonfire, that never went out. They would guide him to his own enslavement. Eye would have none of that.

He had to leave.

Luckily for him, tonight's Vitalmony wasn't solely for him, a fellow Poodo, commonly known as Chin, was also turning 21 and seeing as they go in alphabetical order, he was to go first.

Rising from his soft leafy mat, Eye carefully approached the lodger entrance and peered out down the hill towards the dominating bonfire. He could hear the screeches and jeers, and cheers erupt as two warriors emerged from a distant hut dragging an overanxious Chin with them. The woots became manic, as Chin got closer to the massive flame. And as he got closer his struggling limbs became more rampant. But it was no use, the poor Chin was simply no match for the dual warriors towering over him and weighing at least 4 Chin's.

Silence befell the gathering tribe as Chin was finally released in front of the elders. He stood, shivering one would assume from nerves of the situation. Eye thought that perhaps Chin had also come to a similar conclusion he had, but merely happened upon it to late? At any rate however, Eye knew that whatever the reason for Chin's struggle, he was beyond Eye's help now. And as it just so happened, Chin provided Eye the perfect distraction to make his escape.

Gathering his limited personal items from underneath his mat in the lodger, Eye, cautiously exited the lodger and proceeded down the hill in the opposite direction from the Vitalmony.

Eye knew that before he left he needed to stock up on supplies, because he knew that when you are going on a journey, a journey that has no final destination, you could never have too little supplies. So quietly, Eye paused at the bottom of the hill, and peered around the steep corner of the hill to the mania that was occurring at Chin's Vitalmony. Eye couldn't make out much of it, but he could see that Chin had begun his ritualistic dance.

84

Many had told him this was the hardest part of the Vitalmony, you have to perform a very specific dance, and you have to sustain it as long as possible, in the old days you had to maintain it for 3 hours, but the elders found it harder and harder to maintain a decent population when they kept having to dispose of all the failing Poodo's. So the length was changed to an hour. And though his dance had just begun, Eye could see Chin was already struggling severely, attempting to remember the 73 different positions required. As he danced, every move he did correctly was responded by a glorious golden flash from the sacred pit, and every misstep he took resulted in a burst of searing hot green flame that more often than not scolded Chin, thus making it even harder to perform the dance properly.

Shaking his head in disgust at the almost barbaric nature of the ritual. Eye quietly turned from it and swiftly bolted down to the stream to where the supply hut was still located. Entering, Eye quickly grabbed a sack and started to pile food and small jugs of water, and a couple of wine. Then he grabbed another sack and filled it with every type of fruit and vegetable imaginable and several loaves of potato bread. Finally, Eye grabbed a long bow, a holster of arrows, a blowgun, and the necessary darts, and finally a dagger.

Skillfully loading all the differing sacks and weaponry on his sparsely dressed body, Eye lumbered out of the hut.

Taking one last look at the entire tribe enjoying Chin's Vitalmony, Eye let out a pained sigh, and turned from the village and walked out of the warm torchlight it provided. Eye disappeared into the black cold of the forest night.

XIV. The Suckers

Eye, was alone, really for the first time in his life. The beautiful and somewhat annoying thing about growing up in such a close-knit community was that you were never alone, ever, even when you so desperately wanted to be. Everyone slept together in the lodger, went to the bathroom together, ate together, hunted together, gathered together, you name it they did it together. It made sense, with so few in the tribe, and being probably one of the weakest, yet most perseverant tribes in the whole world, everyone had to rely on one another to survive.

The Vitaly were known for their hunting and tracking skills, being more than efficient killers, what they were truly renown for was their defensive prowess. Numerous other tribes had, over the centuries, attempted, and failed to take the small patch of land that the Vitaly so furiously protected. And since the Vitaly's inception, none has succeeded. The reason for this is because of what the Vitaly protect, what every other tribe yearns for, the Gripe Trees.

The Gripe Trees are the tallest and widest trees in the world, and possess strange properties that provide any whom drink from their sap unfortold power. Granted no one in over 300 years had successfully tapped a Gripe Tree so many speculate that this power is merely a myth spun by the Vitaly to explain why the Gripe Trees were so immense. However, needless to say, that hasn't stopped some of the more superstitious and greedy tribes from taking notice.

Spanning a miniscule 3 kilometers in diameter, the Gripe Woods were the only place in the world that the fabled trees were located, and considering their size relative to the area they dominated, there stood only 37 of them, making their value even more grand.

To any oppressor, the Gripe Wood would appear simple enough to conquer. Located in a bizarre bowl shaped valley, deep enough and steep enough to allow the Gripe Trees to stand no taller than their normal brethren from a horizon viewpoint, the Vitaly village is located in the middle of it, and only spans just under a kilometer of the 3 kilometer valley. So realistically, any conquering foe would merely have to over run the tiny village and the mysterious Gripe Wood would be theirs.

Unfortunately for any ambitious tribe, the Vitaly had no intention of going quietly. Using numerous tactics, none the same as the other, the Vitaly refuted all attempts on their land. Sometimes they would hide and let the enemy walk right in, then when they let their guard down, they would unleash a fiery barrage of arrows upon them. Other times they would capture several creatures, such as the Black Hand and a Rufomol (a giant mole like creature, with characteristics similar to our bull). Whatever the tactic, the attacks came to an end, being the last assault was before Eye was born.

Eye was struggling up the steep valley grasping onto moss-ridden rocks and soil that littered the valley floor. Panting heavily, Eye was cursing to himself for packing climbing equipment. Reaching a ledge in the ever-steepening valley, Eye lay down resting for a moment. Staring up at the majestic Gripe trees above, Eye suddenly came to the realization that this was the last time he'd ever look upon them.

Fighting back tears, Eye halted his panting and held his breath; he listened intently to the sounds of the forest, swearing for a moment he heard the sound of a rustling in the distance. Hearing nothing but the wind whipping through the leaves high above, Eye let out a heavy sigh.

TWIT!

Eye heard it, a sound that was now unmistakable after spending years around Claw and the other Warriors. A twig had just been broken. Something or someone was near.

No time was lost, Eye rose from his ledge and climbed with new life up the remainder of the valley, not looking back, not wishing to see what it was that followed, if anything.

Collapsing on the suddenly even ground, Eye wasted no time in quickly standing and shuffling off into the darkness. Wishing he could move faster, but being unable to due to the amount of food and supplies he had on his person, Eye was panicked by hearing yet another rustle come from behind. Not thinking food and supplies were worth losing his life, Eye dropped most of his food and water, carrying now only his bow and arrows.

Breathing harder than he ever thought possible, Eye dared to look back once, and that was all it took, Eye suddenly flew into the air, entangled in a webbing of some sort, made of thinner, more flexible tree roots, Eye was in a trap, set by a hunter of some tribe, and by the looks of the trap, it wasn't his own.

Eye struggled furiously; knowing being in the clutches of a rival tribe was a fate even worse than that of having abandoned his own Vitalmony. Seeing it was no use, eye let out an exasperated sigh and rested his head against the net. Looking down at his pack, Eye was sickened when he saw what was making all the rustling behind him.

A Pine Rabbit (a rabbit with long paralyzing spikes on its back and side), leapt toward his pack, and preceded to munch down on the potato loafs.

Eye couldn't help but stare in languish in his stupidity, here he was, doing something no one in his tribe had ever done, abandon his family and friends, leave the Gripe Woods behind for greater things other than village life, and he was trapped in a net, watching all his food be eaten by a measly Pine Rabbit. Eye shook his head, in disbelief about his resounding bad luck. Gripping his bow firmly in one hand, Eye withdrew an arrow and held it tightly in the other, preparing for a tribesmen to come out of the darkness to finish of their pray.

Looking all round, Eye was surprised to see no warrior emerge. Feeling very cautious, Eye tried as best he could to keep his guard up as long as possible, but as the night drew on, Eye slowly fell asleep, forgetting all about his plight, wishing it was all a dream.

Hey... HEY!!... WAKE UP!!!! Ainsley woke abruptly, wincing at the afternoon light as it assaulted her eyes. Letting out a groggy moan, Ainsley quickly realized two things; one was that she felt incredibly weak and nauseous and the other being, that she was being dragged.

Don't say anything, keep your eyes closed, he doesn't know you are awake. Cautiously ordered the voice. Still drowsy, Ainsley quietly spouted "What?" *SSSSHHH* harshly replied the voice. *Just think, I can hear your thoughts just as well as your voice, its not safe to speak right now. Just think okay?* Processing that for a moment, Ainsley finally thought 'okay, what's going on? Where are we?' *We are in the middle of the Maltyrn Forest, I don't know where exactly, and we are in great danger* warned the voice. 'What do you mean in danger? What happened?' asked Ainsley still unsure what happened.

It appears, that as we came out of the pass we were ambushed by this Sookann 'Huh? What's a Sookann?' *It's a hunter for the Sookassn, the most powerful and dangerous tribe in the whole forest* explained the voice.

Ainsley just lay there, being dragged, in disbelief, 'So your telling me not only is there this psycho, but there are more of him and as you put it, even more tribes??? Your kidding me??' *No I'm not, an no, not more like him, just two others, you see, to explain to you just how much trouble we are in and how unlucky we are, I have to explain a little bit about the Sookassn.*

'Explain away please' encouraged Ainsley loving to get straight answers for once.

Okay, well like I said, the Sookassn are the largest and most powerful tribe in Maltyrn, really in the entire world. They are so big they have several villages spread out all though the forest, three to be exact. Each village has just one Sookann, their hunter who is responsible for bringing all the food to the village, by any means.

'So what your telling me is that by chance we got captured by 1 of 3 Sookann?? Wow, what are the chances?' joked Ainsley, not to the voice's pleasure. *This is no laughing matter Ainsley; the Sookann isn't going to invite us back for tea a crumpets. The Sookann as well as the rest of his tribe are all cannibals. They eat humans!* "WHAT!" Blurted out Ainsley entirely by accident.

The Sookann halted its movement, standing perfectly still; it slowly turned only its head, to an impossible angle to glare menacingly at Ainsley.

Not thinking straight, Ainsley starred right back, haunted by the face of the Sookann. Its large pure black eyes, looking unusually large on the rather bony face of the Sookann, unblinkingly gave a sign of annoyance toward its pray being awake. Ainsley's gaze dropped to its mouth, unable to comprehend the words to describe the horror of it; an inverted drill came to mind, the large scale kind used to burrow tunnels for trains back home, just layers upon layers of teeth tightening ranks as it went deeper into the Sookann's throat. Then without notice, a fleshy tongue darted out of the Sookann's mouth, with a large spike on the end. It buried its tongue in the dirt just shy of Ainsley.

Ainsley let out a panicked yelp, having never been so scared in her life before that moment. The tongue retracted, and the Sookann, fully turned its body, keeping its gaze locked on Ainsley the whole time. Taking a deep inhale of breath, it was just about to release its tongue once more on Ainsley when out of nowhere it seemed.

FWWWWAP!!!

The sound of the arrow puncturing the arm of the Sookann would stay with Ainsley for the rest of her life, especially the nightmarish sound that followed.

SCCCCCCCRRRRRRRRRREEEEEEEEEEEEAAAAAAAAACCCH!

Breaking its gaze from Ainsley, the Sookann turned to eye down its surprise attacker.

"Leave her alone suckface!" taunted Eye, still trapped in his net, having quietly watched the scene unfold in front of him.

The Sookann let out a hiss, clearly angered by Eye's presence.

"Why don't you fight someone who can actually fight back for once?" yelled Eye as he withdrew another arrow and pulled back rapidly and fired. This one however the Sookann, almost playfully dodged.

Seeing this, all Eye's confidence drained, he went for another arrow but the Sookann was too quick, in the fraction of a second it took him to take out another arrow, the Sookann leapt onto a nearby tree and pounced onto the net Eye inhabited. "Uhoh" was all Eye could say before the Sookann's tongue lashed out and knocked Eye out.

Meanwhile, Ainsley, still weak from the dart that put her out earlier struggled to get up from where she lay.

Turning its head again in its inhuman way, the pale hairless Sookann let out another hiss as it simultaneously cut down Eye's net, keeping the knot at the top in tact, trapping the unconscious Eye, and leaping the 20 yards distance to pin Ainsley to the floor once more.

Crushing her Eye's closed, Ainsley waited for the end to come, but no such thing came, daring to wedge one eye open, Ainsley saw the Sookann staring at her, not moving an inch, drooling from its permanently open mouth.

Unsure what the Sookann was doing, Ainsley opened her other eye to get a proper look at it. It was only after doing this that she realized the Sookann was in agonizing pain, to the point of shock. Peering past its horrific face, Ainsley spotted the cause of the stillness from the Sookann. A large pike buried deep in its back, and a tall man holding it there.

Before Ainsley could process where the man came from he twisted his blade in the Sookann's back and finished it off. "Rest now, sucker of life" poetically spoke the man. And with that, he withdrew his pike and watched the fallen Sookann fall limp on top of Ainsley.

"Ahh, help, could you please get this off of me??" Begged Ainsley to the stranger. Without speaking he kicked the corpse off of Ainsley. She worked her way to her feet, struggling to keep a steady foothold. "Easy now, you were paralyzed with Pine Rabbit poison, a powerful sedative and muscle constrictive, we also use it. It will take a few minutes more for your strength to return." Explained the man.

Ainsley, being clearly distraught and angry asked "Excuse me if this comes across rude or anything but who the hell are you?"

Smiling gently, seeing her frustration, the man spoke clearly " My name is Claw, I am member of the Vitaly tribe of the Gripe Woods, I was tracking our young friend over here when I came across the two of you. Your welcome by the way." "Well thanks I guess, sorry, you are tracking that guy?" Asked Ainsley referring over to the unconscious Eye. "Yes, he too is a member of the Vitaly, or he was, he ran away last night and we've been trying to track him down." "We?" Looking down, almost embarrassed, Claw confessed "I, I have been trying to track him down." Ainsley says nothing to this. "It is my job to look after him and if I don't get him home soon, he'll never be allowed to return."

"Why is that?" curiously asked Ainsley. "He missed out on a very important ritual, one that would grant him his adulthood and his rightful place in the tribe. If he doesn't return soon, he'll forever be exiled."

"But why?" "It is the way of our tribe, as it has always been." Proudly spoke Claw, to which Ainsley shook her head "No, why must he go back, if he left he left for a reason, and if he didn't leave I probably wouldn't be alive right now, so clearly it happened for a reason." "Possibly, but his place is with his tribe." "Maybe, but why don't you let him decide?" Defended Ainsley, not really knowing why she was defending a complete stranger. Claw stood there in silence, having never thought of things in this way.

"Look, from the way I see it, the only reason he should return is because you want him to, sounds kinda selfish if you ask me."

Looking over to Eye, Claw let out a strained sigh "perhaps you are right, who are you young one?" "Names Ainsley, pleased to meet you"

Ainsley extended her hand to Claw's, he took it, they shook, and as their fingers touched, that brilliant white light illuminated their touch. Claw stood there in awe, having only ever heard of such things and never ever expecting to see it in real life. As they released each other's hand, Claw fell to his knees, worshiping Ainsley. "Err, what are you doing?" awkwardly asked Ainsley.

"You are Sevardinal! In all my years I had never thought I would ever catch a glimpse of one, let alone make its acquaintance. I am honored by your presence mam." Feeling awkward by this inappropriate formality, Ainsley grabbed ahold of Claw. "Please stand up, you are embarrassing me." "Sorry mam, a thousand apologies" nervously spoke Claw. "Don't worry about it." Exclaimed Ainsley, turning from Claw to look at the unconscious Eye, *We need for that boy to come with us* cut in the voice. 'Huh? Why?' asked Ainsley to the voice. *I'll tell you later, just for now convince him to let him come*

"So, what have you decided for the guy?" gestured Ainsley to Eye. "Who Eye?" asked Claw. Ainsley let out an unintentional giggle. "Eye? Are you serious?" not getting the joke Claw said, "Yes Eye, what's so funny

94

mam?" Seeing he didn't get the humor, Ainsley quickly dropped her smile and reworded her question. "Are you taking him home or letting him go?" Claw let out a sigh and looked down and away in thought "I feel it is as you say and I should let him go, but I can't let him be alone, I mean he's been gone one night and nearly got killed, I can't in good conscious leave him alone.." Seeing her opportunity, Ainsley quickly jumped in "I have an idea, why not let him come with me? I'm heading north to meet the rest of the Sevardinal for the first time and I could use a bodyguard?"

Claw stood there in thought for moment, before it was clear he made his decision. "Yes, you are right, that is the best idea, he will go with you up north as a protector of sorts. At any rate its too late now for him to return home with me and my killing of the Sookann will likely cause a minor war. So its best I get home. But before I do, please give this to Eye when he wakes, it was his fathers, and I know he'll want to have it." Claw hands Ainsley his bow. "I will, have a safe trip home Claw, it was lovely to meet you, thank you again for saving us." Politely spoke Ainsley, to which Claw just smiled and nodded his head. And without another word between them, Claw left, leaving Ainsley alone with Eye, a person she had never met, who was her new bodyguard.

Walking over to Eye, Ainsley looked to the treetops and saw that the sun was setting, and feeling absolutely exhausted from all the theatrics of the day, Ainsley decided it would be safe to rest up for the night, and wait for Eye to wake.

Slouching down against a tree, Ainsley kept a close eye on Eye and smiled to herself thinking before she fell asleep "He sure is cute."

XV. Eye?

Ainsley awoke with a jolt. Leaping forward from where she rest against the great oak, Ainsley looked all round for what caused her sudden, unwelcomed burst of consciousness. She didn't have to look far, kneeling directly in front of her, was that boy she saw, the one who tried to save her yesterday. He was awake now and starring right through her it seemed, almost as if he were in a trance.

"Don't be alarmed, my name is Eye, I'm here to protect you." Calmly spoke Eye, looking deep into Ainsley's eyes. Not taking note of this from being half asleep still, Ainsley brashly said "What?" Not changing his tone for a second, Eye calmly repeated, "My name is Eye, I'm here to protect you, I'm to be your bodyguard."

Recalling what she and Claw discussed yesterday about Eye helping her get up north, Ainsley sat now confused as to how the boy in question came into that knowledge. "Huh? I mean yes, that's what you'll be doing but I'm sorry how did you figure that out?" asked Ainsley. This caused Eye to finally break his calm demeanor and replace it with a face that Ainsley could only describe as perturbed. "I, I was told to do so…" confessed Eye. "By who" asked Ainsley intrigued?

"You… actually…" awkwardly spoke Eye, feeling out the properness of the sentence as he spoke it, but by the look on Ainsley's face, it didn't come out clearly. "What? No I didn't, you were knocked out by the time Claw arrived I couldn't have told.." Eye's glance shot straight up. "Claw was here??!!" "Yes, but just for a moment, he saved me, he saved both of us actually. And then he was going to take you home or something but you tried to save me first, and frankly, I'm not enjoying being kidnapped and stranded in the desert with only me to talk to, so I thought it might be nice to have some company." Explained Ainsley, fibbing just a little bit, attempting to make it seem like she wasn't psycho and had an alternate subconscious that spoke to her.

"I see, so wait then, you convinced Claw to let me go?" asked Eye in a state of disbelief and excitement, and only a hint of sadness. "Yeah sorta, I mean it didn't take much, I think he just wanted to see if you were okay, he refused to leave you alone unless you were with us. OH, that reminds me..." Ainsley quickly stands and looks round the moss covered forest bed for the bow, spotting it not too far to her left, Ainsley jovially bounds over to it and picks it up. She then turns and subtly walks toward Eye, as he begins to stand.

"Claw told me to give it to you, he said it was your..." "Father's, yes it was..." Eye carefully lifted the bow out of Ainsley's delicate hands and admired it with nothing short of astonishment. Ainsley had billions of questions to ask the boy, but saw that now was not the time, so she too admired the artistry of the bow. It was made of the only Gripe Tree to have fallen within the last half millennium, stained a deep rich earth brown, and engraved with the same markings, all from a foreign, ancient script, long since extinct.

"Its beautiful." Commented Ainsley, meaning every word, but saying it merely because she felt awkward in the silence with this boy she'd known only a day and a half. "Claw told me that the day I became a man, the day I did what was right, was the day I was worthy of this." Spoke Eye, clenching it firmly in his grasp, reveling in the euphoria of holding it. Ainsley smiled, recognizing the connection of him having it now. Looking up from his newly acquired treasure, Eye warmly smiled at Ainsley. "Thank you for giving this to me." "No problem." Ainsley smiled right back at Eye.

"My name's Ainsley." Ainsley extends her hand, taken aback by this bizarre behavior; Eye timidly extends his hand not wanting to screw up her ritual. She grabs his hand and shakes it gingerly, then quirks her face in puzzlement "What did you say your name was?" "My name is Eye, of the Vitaly tribe of the Gripe Woods" Proudly spoke Eye, though felt slightly guilty to keep to that claim.

"EYE?? Are you kidding me?? What kind of name is that??" blurted out Ainsley at finally hearing his name. Slightly offended, Eye proudly defended his namesake "My name is a very well respected title in my tribe, I am honored to carry it." Ainsley broke out laughing at Eye's attempt at seriousness. Not knowing what to do, Eye just stood there, thinking to himself. "This is going to be a long trip."

XVI. The Hunting Party

The pair had been walking north for what seemed like hours, but in fact unbeknownst to them, was actually days. Having never travelled this far north before, Eye, nor Ainsley were aware that they had entered the Northern Woods of Maltyrn, which, like most quadrants of Maltyrn, had certain mystical properties. Unlike the Gripe Woods at the Core of the Maltyrn Forests, the Northern Woods, commonly known as the Evernot Woods, were known for their deceptive tricks regarding time. Because whilst in Evernot, dependent on when you enter it, day or night, it will never cease to be that time of day. None know why it acts this way, some speculate that Elders of ancient yore cursed the woods, not because of any wrongdoing, but merely to disorient and keep away invading forces from the Mainland.

Reaching exhaustion, Ainsley, without a word to Eye, who was equally tired, but refused to be the first to admit it, collapsed and fell flat on her face. Hearing this Eye turned round and wearily looked at her.

"Come on now, we can't keep doing this, if you want to reach the Northern coast before your 70 you have to keep moving." Encouraged Eye as he wimped back over to Ainsley. Grabbing her by the arms, he lifted her up and threw her over his shoulders, like he was holding a child, which for all intensive purposes, he was.

"I'm sorry Eye, I know its only been a few hours, but I'm just SO tired, can we just please rest for a bit, I promise I'll be better after a nap, I promise…." Ainsley didn't even finish talking as she fell asleep on Eye's shoulder. Smiling at her cute childish nature, Eye trotted onward; never steering off the beaten path they were currently following.

Though Eye had not learned of the Evernot Woods, he had been taught of the Crossroads of Maltyrn. Highways of sorts, that traveller's whom needed to get somewhere fast, and didn't care for some danger could utilize. There were dozens of them crisscrossing all across Maltyrn, and the current one Eye and Ainsley dutifully walked, had not been used in many years.

Slowly drifting off into a sort of sleeping walk, Eye began to slowly drift off course, until finally, after half an hour of this behavior, he and his younger counterpart, were in the middle of the Evernot Woods, with no clear path to follow.

The reason the path, that Eye unfortunately had lost track of, was so rarely used was because of its locations misleading nature, for you see, travellers, like everywhere else in the world, used the stars as navigational guides, but in the shade of the Evernot trees, you saw no sky of any sort, well, none that was genuine that is. The leaves of the Evernot, held special properties, similar to our Chameleon, in that they would absorb a sort of "light image" of their surroundings and mimic it, so if it was daylight they would emulate the sky above them, if it were night, they would mock the starry night sky. But seeing as several leaves would mimic the same spots, the sky, though appearing authentic, was in fact, completely false. So unless you were travelling with a large party of skilled Windreaders, a rare and elusive Eastern Tribe of Maltyrn who navigated by the gust of the wind, you were pretty much entirely dependent on the crossroad through Evernot. However, many speculate that it had never been finished due to its location in Evernot, and the sheer size of the woods themselves. Scaling to cover about 60 percent of the entire Maltyrn forests. It was the largest body of supernatural Vegetation in the world.

Finally collapsing to the soft red soil of the Evernot wood, Eye and Ainsley lay side by side in peaceful slumber, unaware of what was to occur.

Several days past in what seemed like an instant while the couple slept in the Everlasting evening sun, completely unaware that while they slept, a rare and wondrous creature was approaching them.

Lightly skimping across the lightly leafed floor of the Evernot Woods cautiously walked a Giant Deer fawn. A baby Giant Deer, being only a few weeks old and standing already the size of a 2-year-old horse, the "Gawn", as they were commonly known, put its snout to the ground sniffing for fallen berries from the bark of the Evernot trees (another unique trait of theirs). And as it walked, it quite by accident walked right into the slumbering Ainsley causing both of them to leap back in surprise.

"Ahh!" Yelled Ainsley as she rolled away from the suspicious creature she had yet to eye for herself. "Eye wake up! Eye!" called out Ainsley as she panickly shook Eye awake. Turning over to see what she was complaining about, Eye shot upward as he spotted the Gawn. "Whoa!" yelped Eye as he fluidly grabbed his bow, withdrew an arrow and pulled back ready to fire at the potential foe.

"What is it?" Asked Ainsley still unsure of the creature but no longer scared, seeing how innocent it looked. "I'm not sure, but I don't trust it" foreboded Eye as he heldfast on his bow. Standing up Ainsley was not of the same opinion, looking at the cute narrow face of the surprisingly brave gawn, Ainsley's heart instantly melted at its overall cuteness. "Awe but come on its so cute!" Gushed Ainsley as she walked over to the gawn and began to stroke its shorthaired back. "If its cute that means one of two things in these woods, either it's using its cuteness as a disguise to get up close to its prey before it strikes, or it's an infant..." "A baby! Oh my god that is so what it is, look at it!" cut off Ainsley as she started to scratch under the scruff of the gawn's chin. Just then a rather large berry fell from high above and landed nearly on top of the two comingling beings. Seeing this, Ainsley picked it up and examined it before the gawn swiped it right out of her hands. "Awe! Did you see that? Its hungry!" gleamed Ainsley as she fell more in love with this delightful creature.

"No Ainsley, you don't understand, if this is a baby, then its got to have a..."

THUMP!

"A what?" asked Ainsley not hearing the loud thumping.

THUMP! THUMP! THUMP!!!!

"Get behind me!!! Yelled Eye as he turned his arrow from the gawn to the whishing leaves to its right. Not listening to him in time, Ainsley was shocked when from the thick foliage emerged the largest Giant deer in the world, litterly. Standing 20 feet in height and at least 40 in length, the Giant deer came to a flashing halt overtop its now dwarfed child. Wasting no time, it waved its huge antlers picking up Ainsley and flinging her 30 yards away.

"Ainsley!" Yelled out Eye as he let loose of the arrow and watched it fly directly at the Giant deer's head. But alas, the deer was too fast and quickly waved its head round once more and deflected the arrow with its rock hard antlers.

Pulling out another arrow rapidly, Eye swiftly released that one as well and landed a direct hit on the upper forward thigh of the grand beast. Letting out a massive snarl at the minor irritance, the Giant deer lowered its head in preparation of charging poor Eye.

Reaching back for another arrow, Eye was stunned to discover that he had no more. Panicked now at the urgency of finding a weapon, Eye quickly remembered that he still had his Poodo dagger, pulling it out from his upper thigh holster, Eye prepared himself for the enraged deer.

Letting out a terrifying shriek, the Giant deer began to pick up speed as it charged Eye. Diving out of the way, Eye was unable to dive far enough as the vast antlers of the beast clipped his ankle, shattering it.

"AHHHHHHH!!!" yelled out Eye as he lay on the blood red soil in agony. Coming to from being unconscious for most of the battle Ainsley saw Eye was in trouble, seeing the deflected Arrow laying nearby, Ainsley went to grab it.

"STOMP"

The bare foot of a Sookann split the arrow in half. Looking up at the haunting figure of the Sookann, Ainsley could tell that it was not the one they had killed, but yet another one, and yet it appeared almost identical to the last except for a change of clothes and a more prominent brow bestowing this one, a brow that was clearly furrowed at Ainsley's presence.

Looking up from Ainsley, the Sookann turned its attention to the massive creature as it came round from its long run out of its charge. Pulling a large irregular flute from it satchel, the Sookann raised it to its lips and blew into it harshly. That did two things, first, it drew the attention of the

Giant Deer, and secondly it cause da flurry of Sookassi, Sookassn workers, to come out of hiding and charge the slowed creature.

Leaving Ainsley's side, the Sookann joined the charge. This gave Ainsley time to get to her feet and witness as the Sookassn all leapt on to the Giant deer and began to drain it, not so much for sustenance, but more or less to weaken it. Being overwhelmed the Giant deer was unable to fend them all off, getting only a few lucky clippings of one or two of them with its antlers, the Giant deer was left with on choice only, taking off in full gallop, it took off into the woods, leaving behind its poor distraught gawn.

Rising to her feet, Ainsley quickly ran over to Eye, who was struggling to get to his feet. "Easy, don't stand on that." Said Ainsley, taking on a naturalistic motherly tone, ignoring her Eye put his full weight on it and let out an exasperated gasp as he fell to his knees.

Dropping to her knees as well. Ainsley went to pick Eye up once more. "Wait, go fetch that thing." Said Eye pointing to the lone gawn, looking lost. Ainsley couldn't help but be confused "But why? Its mom just tried to kill us!" "We don't have to worry about her any more." Knowingly foretold Eye as off in the distance you could faintly hear the pained screams of the mother deer fade away.

"The Sookassn will be back for it, we can't leave it here alone, it won't last long, and besides, I'm in no shape to walk." Explained Eye pointing to his useless ankle. "Okay" responded Ainsley as she stood and walked cautiously toward the frightened gawn. "Where did they come from anyways?" "I don't know, they are far from home, but for whatever reason, the Sookassn felt that this creature was of some importance to send out a hunting party." Replied Eye now managing to stand whilst leaning against a tree. "A hunting party? You call that hunting?" Asked Ainsley becoming ever more disgusted with the Sookassn. "No, that is not our way no, but the Sookassn are very different from any other tribe, some say that they are decedents of bats." Ainsley thought about this for a moment, "hmm that would make sense, what with their eyes and all, but bats don't drink-eat things, only fruit and bugs I thought?" asked Ainsley confused, to which Eye gave her a quirked look "I don't know which bats you refer to but the ones I know of ONLY feed off flesh, and travel in packs." This horrified Ainsley, seeing as bats used to be one of her favorite nighttime creatures.

Having been distracted by Eye's telling of this worlds bats, Ainsley had forgotten about the gawn which looked at her, still uneasy. "Ainsley please we must hurry!" reminded Eye. "Oh yeah right, come here baby, easy does it." Taking off her jacket which ever since the desert she had tied around her waist, Ainsley now wound it up and turned it into a makeshift rope. Slowly wrapping it around the gawn, Ainsley quickly, yet gently tied a knot and held firmly on the young deer, moving it over to the pained Eye, Ainsley positioned the gawn in such a way to make Eye's mounting as easily as possible.

Grabbing hold of Eye's damaged leg, Ainsley lifted it off the ground while he used the other one to jump up and onto the gawn's back. As Eye positioned himself in the bareback saddle of the gawn, Ainsley thought back to the terrifying beast that nearly killed her and Eye, this baby's mother, and instantly Ainsley remembered that she had seen these creatures before. "I've seen these things before, when I first got here… there were hundreds of them all with riders." Eye looked down at Ainsley curiously, not knowing what to say to that really. *The Sookassn, sell them off to the Ironworkers of the South* suddenly explained the Voice "What? Really?" responded Ainsley to the Voice thinking nothing of it, making Eye even more confused.

"Whom are you talking to?" asked Eye, slightly confused but instantly remembering who it must be, but having not revealed that he knew of Ainsley's true identity, he played coy. Taken by surprise and not knowing what to say Ainsley quickly responded with a simple "To… myself… yeah. That's it, myself." Eye chuckled at this, "Ainsley you don't have to lie to me you know, I know who you really are."

"Who told you!" yelled Ainsley slightly too loud. Still playing coy, Eye simply responded, "You did."

Hearing rustling in the direction of the ill-fated mother deer, Eye quickly extended his hand and, accepting it, Ainsley was effortlessly lifted onto the saddle. "We must leave, we'll discuss this later." And with that, Eye and Ainsley and their new ride, the orphaned gawn, took off into the everlasting evening horizon.

XVII. Slipping

The gawn trotted along at a slightly quickened pace, slower than it could potentially go, but all this was due to the extra weight it now bared, being in the form of Ainsley and Eye. Sitting one in front of the other, Ainsley tightly wrapped her scrawny little arms around Eye's bare chest as he attempted to control the gawn with the makeshift reigns that Ainsley fashioned in haste. Occasionally grasping his broken leg as it bounced against the mid region of the tiny giant deer, it was clear to Ainsley that he couldn't go on much longer.

"Perhaps I should take over?" timidly asked Ainsley, starting to feel evermore guilty for causing Eye's pain. "I'm fine." Coldly responded Eye clearly agitated by the whole situation, and the pain he's enduring. Waiting a few more moments to respond, Ainsley attempted a different tactic " well we've been riding for hours now, and I haven't heard anything, surely its safe to stop for a bit?" "No, we have to keep going we have to make the break before Sookassi do."

Ainsley, in what was becoming a regular facial expression, scrunched her face in confusion. "Sorry, what break?" This merely caused Eye to sigh deeply, the same sigh Ainsley remembered her mother doing whenever she had to explain things more than once to her when she was little. "The break, is the break of the woods, its where our boarders and boarders of The Badlands begin, and before you ask, The Badlands is another province, completely separate from this one." Ainsley sat there in silence listening to the mysterious ambiance of the Evernot.

'I'm not sure I like him that much, he sure is mean.' Thought Ainsley saddened by her situation. *What do you expect? He did break his ankle and he is your soul protector, that's a lot to bare* spoke the voice unannounced. 'Oh look who decided to talk to me after all this time' thought Ainsley annoyed with the voice. *I am sorry Ainsley, I did not mean to upset you, it wasn't safe for me to speak whilst the Sookassi were around, the last thing we need is them hunting you for anything other than food.* 'How about not hunting me at all?' quipped Ainsley. *Yes, well, it is in our nature to be hunted, you are Sevardinal after all* 'So you keep reminding me, and reminding me' moaned Ainsley to herself. *I am sorry you are having a hard time adjusting to all of this; I can understand it's a lot to take in.*

"A LOT TO TAKE IN!" outwardly spoke Ainsley forgetting that she was having an internal conversation with herself. Looking to the back of Eye's head, Ainsley could only imagine what thoughts were going through his head. "Sorry, talking to myself" apologized Ainsley, to which Eye just shrugged his shoulders. This caused Ainsley to let out a frustrated sigh of her own, not enjoying at all Eye's cold, albeit justified demeanor.

'I thought you were supposed to protect me?' meekly thought Ainsley, feeling quite vulnerable and embarrassed from her past-immediate outburst. *I have protected you you have not been harmed have you?* 'Well no, but what do you call being flung like 5000 yards by this things mom?!' *I call that unpredictable behavior and therefore I could not anticipate, Giant Deer are generally very gentle and loving creatures. Though I will relent, they have been getting far more aggressive recently.* Sorrowfully spoke the voice, causing intrigue from Ainsley. 'What do you mean?' *It's difficult to explain Ainsley, the Giant Deer's along with many other creatures, are being used for ill means. They are using them for war...* explained the voice. Ainsley scoffed at this, thinking it silly that the voice spoke so heavily of the matter.

'I know, we saw them remember? In the desert? Those warriors were riding them.' *Yes they were, but what you don't see is that those were just the males, the females, the children...*

'What?' thought Ainsley, now concerned, looking down at the adorable gawn.

'They are using them for weaponry Ainsley, they are killing them.' Ainsley's blood ran cold; she had never heard in her young life such a horrific deed. She began to feel light-headed, and before she could acknowledge what was happening, she was slipping out of the saddle, and rather than falling the uncomfortable distance to the mossy floor. Ainsley was suspended in mid air. Coming to a halt, Ainsley wearily looked up and saw that she had indeed fallen to the floor, and was now surrounded by Eye who, despite his shattered ankle was desperately trying to wake her.

'What's happening?' asked Ainsley directing her thoughts toward the voice. She received no response. Now frantically looking round, seeing that despite how much she struggled, her body was frozen in mid air, similar to the way those contemporary dancers would twirl and hover above the floor with the use of wires. "Eye?" Asked Ainsley trying desperately to get a reply. Rotating so she was staring up at the tree-sky, Ainsley was shocked to find that she was being swished away from where her body lay. Taking one more glance over her shoulder to the scene she left, Ainsley could have sworn her body was disappearing.

And as her body sped above the ground at amazing speeds, Ainsley happened to look down at her body, and, just like her phantom body on the tree-bed of Evernot, Ainsley too was slowly disappearing. Picking up speed, Ainsley barely had time to recognize where she was flying to before she was right on top of it, flying up and over the encircling mountains of the desert,

Ainsley was then flung, as if from a catapult into the immense structure she had once seen, in what seemed like a lifetime ago.

Ainsley hit the chamber wall with a thud.

Ainsley opened her eyes, still propelled forward from the momentum of the throw; she was caught by a rusty old seat belt.

"Take it easy their kid, you're okay, you were knocked out" reassuringly spoke the Officer in the front seat of what Ainsley now recognized as a police cruiser. "Where am I?" Asked Ainsley delirious from the sudden change in location. "We found you on the side of the highway, looks like you had been there all night, your mom has been worried sick." Spoke the officer, more talking monotone, not really putting any feeling into his words. It was clear this was something he wasn't unfamiliar with doing. "My mom?" spoke Ainsley, not clearly hearing anything else.

Ainsley slowly relaxed from her tensed position against the strained seat belt, and as she rested her head and back against the rather stiff back seat of the cruiser, Ainsley was suddenly overcome with a splitting headache, unlike anything she had ever experienced before. And as this intense migraine occurred, Ainsley's mind refilled with forgotten moments: Her and Artie's meeting, Her mother freaking out at her, her lone walk along the highway, then nothing, nothing but pitch black.

Ainsley had past out once more. Had she remained awake a little longer, she would have noticed that the leather bound journal, was nowhere to be seen.

Part Two

XVIII. "W" and "R"

The headlamps of the police cruiser slowly died away as the vehicle came to a stop in front of the station. Exiting the car, the two officers, one being rather portly and clearly the superior officer of the two gestured to his partner to get Ainsley out of the back. Still unconscious and unaware of her books absence.

Slowly opening the door, the young fit cop gently unbuckled Ainsley's seatbelt and carefully lifted her out of the car. Standing on the first steps of the police station, the larger, older officer carefully shuffled ahead to open the door for his labored partner. Letting him walk in first, turning sideways to accommodate Ainsley's slender figure draped awkwardly across his arms, he briefly nodded and vanished into the station, followed shortly thereafter by the slower, older counterpart.

The lobby was dank and cluttered, well used but not well maintained, being located in one of the oldest buildings in the city; there had been great turmoil when news broke of its potential demolition to make way for a state of the art Police Headquarters. Being made of a unique shade of sandstone, reddish in tones, many left wing liberals and university students locally, and from nearby towns all fought gallantly to preserve and maintain the aging structure as a cultural landmark, but unfortunately were unsuccessful as it was slated for demolition at the beginning of the new year.

Getting its start as the first hotel in the mid-northwest, the Wayne Right Hotel was heralded as one of the finest accommodations in the country, getting royalty, celebrity, and politian's alike all flocking to its grand reddish sandstone, and being bedazzled by the striking red oak doors, and fine dining available 24/7, a rarity back then. It was also the first hotel to feature a full sized grand theatre, capable of performing both dramatic and, as the years went on, Vaudevillian performances; making the Wayne Right Hotel a true marvel of its age.

Unfortunately, as the years went on, and other buildings went up and stocks went down, so did the Wayne Right, filing for bankruptcy a mere 21 years after its inception. The only thing that survived the depression, and the only thing that wasn't abandoned strangely enough, was the Grande Theatre. Which thanks to some generous donations from certain economic untouchables such as Chaplin and Keaton, both of whom got their start in similar Vaudevillian grandstands, and had since then grown a fondness for them.

But alas, despite their valiant efforts, and many others since then, the Wayne Right Theatre too was doomed to eventually suffer, not from the economic downturn, but and at the birth of celluloid.

All across the country, in small houses, and pubs, tents and travelling circus', society was waning from the slapstick of the past and marveling at the brilliant, and revolutionary dawn of the "flickers".

Though built around the same time as film was invented, the Wayne Right Grande Theatre was initially designed for Operatic and dramatic performances, for the likes of the wealthy aristocracy of the early 20th century. But, not knowing of the growing popularity of the new technology. The Grande Theatre missed its chance. And so, with the second revolution of the film world, vis-à-vis the "talkie's", the Wayne Right was too old, and improperly designed to house, or even entertain the notion of installing the 1-ton projector required to present a motion picture.

So despite is slightly longer stance than that of the rest of the country, Vaudeville too died in the Wayne Right, as did its glorious 2000 capacity, crimson and gold theatre.

The Wayne Right Hotel and Theatre were abandoned.

Too expensive to rent, too expensive to buy, and particularly bureaucratic from a corporate standpoint, seeing as the owners, rich as they were, vanished around the depression. Many speculate they put a bullet in their heads, either way, the Wayne Right had no paperwork, and no known owners, so unless the government annexed the property back from the private enterprise, it was to remain empty.

And so it did.

All the way up until the late 60's when, at long last, the government, in an attempt to reach out to the youth of the world, began a series of "projects" designed to breath life back into the downtown sector, which like the Wayne Right, had become rotten, and mistreated and forgotten about. And so, shortly thereafter, the Wayne Right Hotel and Theatre, had its long since burnt out and shattered lighted sign taken down, its insides scalped and emptied, its rotten red oak doors replaced with regular cedar, its peeling white and red striped wallpaper stripped and painted over with a calm green. And finally, the resilient, and proud Grande Theatre, which had stood the test of time, and won, finally relented, and was dismantled.

It was turned into a parking lot… For the police station inhibiting the once great Wayne Right Hotel and Theatre.

Ainsley slowly opened her eyes, the overhead fluorescent lighting was bitter and cold on her weak eyes, and instantly made her screw them shut in bitter distaste for the light. Daring to peak once more, Ainsley was relieved to see that the intensity was subsided, and she could see clearly now. The first thing she noticed was the far wall, adorned with hundreds of pictures, displaying numerous celebrities and socialites from decades past, Ainsley herself didn't recognize any of them, but could tell by the crowd around them in the picture, and their sheer presence on this wall must have incurred their significance.

Sitting at the center of this collage of photos was a gold plated sign stating "In Memory of..." and below it awkwardly standing out from the wall, a pair of giant lighted letters, reading them they were the letters "W" and "R", clearly several of the light bulbs had burnt out long ago, leaving the signs only partially light, making the memorial seem terribly neglected.

Ainsley could see underneath the signs another gold plated sign, squinting tightly to make out the tiny font, Ainsley slowly read the words to herself, deciphering as she went. "If, if you want things to say as they are..."

"Then things will have to change" came a voice that startled Ainsley out of her squint as she lightly jumped out of her lean; she swiftly turned to locate the voice. She was greeted with a tall, narrow man, who was clearly well kept, and by the wide smile spooled on his face, a kind man as well. His arms crossed behind his back, pulling his atypical police uniform tight against his torso, the apparent cop slowly started to approach Ainsley.

"It's a quote, from a poet; Giuseppe Tomasi di Lampedusa." Ainsley sat enthralled with this man, clearly well educated, and well spoken, each word he spoke dripped with confidence. "What does it mean?" Asked Ainsley not exactly sure of its significance.

Slightly lowering his smile, almost to a melancholy grin, he unclenched his hands from behind his back, and looked to the wall, particularly the partially lit letters, then lowered himself in front of Ainsley, making eye contact with her. He gently rested his strong arm on Ainsley's youthful shoulder, and said, "It means, nothing lasts forever"

And with that, his smile returned, he dropped his hand from Ainsley's shoulder and left it hovering in between them. "I'm Detective Rhapsody" looking down at his hand, Ainsley quickly remembered her manners and raised her hand to accept his, not being used to this formal, and surprisingly enjoyable adult themed respect, Ainsley couldn't help but smile. "Hi, I'm Ainsley" Detective Rhapsody gently shook Ainsley's hand smiling even more if that was possible for this exceedingly nice officer. "Ainsley, that sure is a pretty name, did your mom give you that name?" Ainsley, though aware that he was being slightly condescending, enjoyed the conversation none the less, having rarely an opportunity to talk to a grown up other than her mom. "No, my dad did, he's not around anymore." Ainsley said hoping he wouldn't ask any more on the subject.

Ainsley had barely known her father, he left when she was born. Ainsley had asked her mom repeatedly for more details, but Abigail refused to tell; only stating, "You'll understand someday, perhaps when you are older." This infuriated Ainsley, and made her feel silly; she didn't even know her father's name.

"Well, he sure picked a wonderful name for a wonderful girl" Ainsley wasn't used to being complimented and couldn't help but blush. "Tell me Ainsley, why on earth were you wandering around in the middle of nowhere?"

Ainsley's smile instantly disappeared, she now realized that this Detective was doing just that, detecting, he was trying to subtly interrogate her. Ainsley was confused by this seeing as, at least from what she had seen in movies and TV he should have been doing this in those white rooms with the two way mirror dominating the left wall. Breaking her muse, Ainsley quickly composed herself as she prepared to answer. "My mom, she, we had a fight."

Detective Rhapsody gently upshifted his head, as if in preparation to nod once Ainsley finished speaking, but no nod came, it just lingered tilted upward. "Ah, I see. So what was this fight about then? Must have been serious to garner you running away?"

It was at this point that Ainsley felt that familiar feeling overwhelm her, doing her best to look left and right without seeming suspicious, Ainsley then finally realized that she didn't have the book. Her heart began to pick up pace, as the words from Rhapsody's mouth began to fall into the background. Peering past him, Ainsley noticed, to the right side of the lobby, where the offices began, inside one of them, was the pair of seedy looking officers standing on either side of none other than Abigail. Ainsley's mom, who until last night, had been Ainsley's favorite person in the whole world, but now, her feelings were saying otherwise.

'They don't know where the book is? Do they?' Ainsley thought, aiming it at the voice, which just then Ainsley remembered couldn't speak to her here. Regardless though Ainsley figured the Voice could still hear. 'They think I hid it, I didn't hid it, wait you hid it didn't you?! While I slept!' Ainsley was proud of her self-discovery, but did her utmost best to restrain any physical expression in front of the ever-observant Detective.

"Ainsley? Do you hear me?" asked Rhapsody, noting that Ainsley was lost in thought. Snapping back to reality, Ainsley realized she hadn't heard a word the detective had asked her. "I'm sorry what?" "There are people here Ainsley, that mean you harm…" This instantly caused Ainsley quirk her face, taking that as permission to continue Rhapsody rested his hand on Ainsley's knee. "Listen carefully to me now, I'm here to help you, I know about the book."

Ainsley's eyes went wide, all attempts to hide her expressions gone. "You do?" asked Ainsley, both excited, and at the same time terrified, 'If he knows who else does?'

"Yes, you are not alone, I can't say much on the matter right now, we are being watched." With that Rhapsody subtly gestures toward the two policemen and Abigail who are all burning a hole in his back. Ainsley silently leans over his shoulder to see them once more, upon doing so though, the leave the office, clearly heading her way.

"They are coming…" quietly spoke Ainsley to Rhapsody, as they approached, Ainsley began to feel nauseous, and fleetingly thinking that this must mean she was in real danger.

"Okay listen to me, you will speak nothing of the book or your exploits therein; do you understand Ainsley? Nothing, no matter what they do, do you understand?" Ainsley just nodded at this, having no time respond as the trio was upon her and Rhapsody.

"What are you doing Rick? She's a little young for you isn't she?" scoffed the slimmer officer who brought Ainsley into the station. Giving Ainsley one more knowing glare, Rick Rhapsody rose and turned to the gang of people. "I was only giving her some emotional support, sleeping under the stars isn't very magical when you are alone, along a highway, in the middle of nowhere." "Whatever, we need the kid, we have some… questions for her." Spoke the portly officer, which, Ainsley could tell by his uniform, was a sergeant, or something higher ranking than both Rhapsody and the other officer. Abigail made no eye contact with Ainsley; instead she coldly stared down Rick. "Rhapsody, long time no see." Turning his gaze from the sergeant to Abigail, Rick, bluntly frowned, having no pleasure in seeing Abigail. "Abi, not long enough if you ask me" Abigail started to shake her head, beginning to tremble with anger. "You are such a fucking asshole you know that!" Both Ainsley and the other officers remained quiet, the officers seemed to be in on the rapport of Rick and Abigail, however Ainsley was at a complete loss for words. "I'm only an asshole to those who deserve it Abi." Abigail then went to lunge at Rick, only to have her two accompanying officers block her off. "Alright that's enough out of you Rhapsody, bugger off please, I do believe you are a detective, and lingering around the lobby doesn't exactly seem like where you are supposed to be. Rick looked round at all of them then turned to Ainsley.

"Well it was a pleasure meeting you Ainsley" he extended his hand once more to which Ainsley again grabbed and shook it. Ending abruptly, Rick turned once more, nodded to his superior officer and walked off into the building. It was only during his leaving, and as all eyes turned to follow him go, that Ainsley realized he left something in her hand.

A piece of paper.

Quickly pocketing the paper, Ainsley sat quietly, attempting to keep her nausea in tact as the three adults surrounded her.

XIX. Official Procedure

The girth of the five fingers clamped firmly on Ainsley's shirt collar felt cold and clammy as they walked and his skin lightly brushed against Her neck. The Sergeant, holding dutifully onto Ainsley, carrying her more than escorting her, and his two colleagues the run of the mill policeman and Ainsley's mother, who as the days went by, looked less and less like the woman she knew and loved.

Looking swiftly left and right, Ainsley, now surely to barf at any moment, was looking for any way out of this situation, any exits, anything that could spare her of this feeling. But unfortunately all she saw was the messy, fervent halls of the station; busy with officers, coming and going all looking like there issue that made them walk so swiftly was a matter of life and death. Ainsley could only wish that one of them wouldn't be holding her case file that read 'Suspected Homicide'.

The quartet turned at the T end of the hallway heading leftward towards the far office near the front of the building. It was sunny out; this was about the only thing Ainsley could make out from the frosted windows spanning the front of the building, all with thick grating splattered across them.

Stopping at the entrance to the office, Ainsley could see the name on the door reading 'Sergeant Fredrick Mallory: Missing Persons'. It was now Ainsley's turn to feel her hands become clammy.

"Alright Abi, we won't be too long, you can sit here, or help yourself to some coffee if you need." Spoke Mallory, in a much kinder sweeter voice reserved for glad handing only VIP's. Turning to look in the way of the quasi-cafeteria at the other end of the T end hallway, Abigail turned once more and feigned a smile, "Thank you Sergeant" and with that, she turned and headed away from her only child, alone with two suspect cops. Ainsley began to cry, not once had her mother glanced in her direction, no apology for her actions yesterday, nothing, just a 'Thank you Sergeant'.

"Alright kid, get in there" spoke the officer whom Ainsley still didn't have a name for. She silently complied as Mallory opened the door for both of them, following them in, he firmly shutting the door behind him.

The office was barren, nothing left on the walls, save for the permanently attached clipboard. The heavy wooden desk, empty; drawers taken out and away from the there rightful place and stacked against the far wall besides some boxes. Ainsley glanced to see what the boxes said, but was redirected into the stiff chair across from the desk instead.

Sergeant Mallory sat his immense figure in the wheeled chair behind the skeleton desk, the creaks from the chair were clear to Ainsley that it wasn't designed to hold a man of his size. Looking round Ainsley found that the other officer was circling her with a venomous smile plastered across his face, it gave her a feeling of being some beasts prey; perhaps she was.

Fredrick, leaned forward in his chair and flipped open his slim file on the petite Ainsley, glancing over its contents. "So... Ainsley is it?" Ainsley meekly nodded, becoming tinier and tinier in the large chair in which she sat. "Why'd you run away from your mom?" Ainsley went to answer but was startled to find the other officer leaning over her right shoulder cranking his neck to make slim eye contact with her. "She's been worried sick you know?"

Not enjoying the perverse stare the slim officer was giving her, Ainsley decided to engage Mallory. "I, we had a fight, I didn't mean to run away so far or anything, I was going to go home after I woke up and all..." This caused the two officers of the law to knowingly look at each other. Rising from his looming position, the officer walked leftward around Ainsley and leaned against the desk facing her, spreading his legs wide, and placing one of them forcefully between Ainsley's claiming the ledge of her seat for his foot.

"You were going to go home after you woke up? Really?" Ainsley nodded to the officer who clearly was the aggressor of the two. "So, after how many nights were you going to do this?" This caused Ainsley to crank her head to the side, much like the baffled face of a young puppy, not understanding the instruction of its master. "I'm sorry?"

"What my accomplice, the good Detective Charles is trying to ask you Ainsley is why if the fight wasn't such a big deal that you didn't go home after the first night?" politely inquired Sergeant Mallory to which Ainsley looked at both of them like they were off their rockers. "What? No I was going to, I had only been out for one night!" pleadingly explained Ainsley. Again, the two officers looked to each other, a gesture that Ainsley was quickly starting to resent.

"One night? Really?" retorted Charles with strong emphasis on the 'really' and a glare to match it. Ainsley was quickly realizing that this wasn't a friendly situation, and that she really had to start listening to her urges more often.

Feeling faint, Ainsley could only respond with a faint "yes.." This caused caused Mallory to rise from his desk and snap his fingers at Charles, who, knowing instantly what he was wanting, went for the stack of boxes behind Ainsley. Pulling out a calendar, he threw it over Ainsley's head into Mallory's waiting hands. Mallory flipped to the current month. "Tell me Ainsley, what day is it today?"

Ainsley looked to the Detective Charles, not understanding the relevance of the question. "Its, it's the 7th?" Silence fell between the three of them, as Mallory turned the calendar so Ainsley could see it, and then using his grubby index finger, pointed to the date Ainsley specified. "Detective, could you be so kind as to tell me today's date?" Coming from behind Ainsley, Charles proudly said "Its Sunday, March 8th."

And with that Mallory slammed his calendar onto the desk in front of Ainsley. "THE 8TH!!!" Breathing heavily, the Sergeant quickly composed himself and again signaled to Charles with his finger, and again, Charles knew exactly what he was requesting.

Charles drew the blinds shut.

Ainsley watched him as he went around the room, pulling at the little cheap toggles at the end of each string, resulting in Detective Mallory's office being completely phased out of the public eye. Ainsley knew this wasn't a good sign.

Walking from behind his desk, Mallory intimidatingly leaned over Ainsley, getting uncomfortably close to her face. Placing his hands on either side of Ainsley, claiming the arm rests as his own. Drawing in a breath, Fredrick leaned ever further and whispered ominously into Ainsley's ear. "So tell me, runaway, if you were only gone one night, how in your wildest dreams to you imagine to convince me you walked 700 kilometers in one measly night?"

Logically Ainsley knew there was no way even if she got a lift, it wasn't possible. Logically she knew that she was screwed, either way she explained it she would come out a liar or crazy. "I, I don't know... I just did." Ainsley relented, trying to remain vague in order to buy her some time. Truth was she knew exactly how she made it that far. Whatever powers the book held, as she had seen at Artie's narrow mess of a house, she could travel great distances in the real world while she is in the book, and given how long she was in the book for this time, it didn't surprise her that she ended up so far away.

Mallory released his grip from the chair and rose from his leaning position and looked down at Ainsley disapprovingly, much like a parent who just caught their child stealing. "You just did. That is your reasoning? Christ kid, if your going to lie at least lie well." Ainsley took offense to that, not only that he could see so easily through her lie, but also that he ridiculed it. "Hey, I didn't lie!" retorted Ainsley, forgetting in that instance to who she was talking.

With this Mallory began to walk the room. "Oh of course you didn't kid, not at all, you just made 700 kilometers in 7 hours, really impressive, you an Olympic runner? Or a superhero? Can you teleport yourself anywhere you so choose?" Ainsley smiled at the irony of that statement, because after the fact she sort of could.

"What you smiling about missy?" eerily spoke Detective Charles, who, like Mallory at the moment, were both behind Ainsley. This caused her smile to quickly vanish. Mallory smiled at Charles' keen senses, but as doing so, he pointed to his watch, to which Mallory nodded knowingly, recalling the limited time they had. "Well Miss Ainsley, I'm afraid we are running short on time, so the formalities must come to an end."

Ainsley was going to reply, questioning how forgoing formalities was legal given the situation to which they were in, but before she could say anything, she was lifted up and out of her chair and thrown to the floor. The rotting wood, of the floorboards, having at once perhaps been covered with rug, but since stripped away, felt rough and unforgiving to Ainsley as her braced hands, which instinctively broke her fall, got several deep splinters deep within the heels of her hands and a few on her lower wrist. Ainsley let out a little gasp at the sudden broach of violence from the officers of the law; whom now both stood tall above her.

Leaping onto her upper torso, Detective Charles, quickly cupped her mouth disabling her from screaming out for help from some straight cops. And while his gangly hand cupped her petite lips, he withdrew with his other hand, a switchblade. But although terrified for her life, Ainsley couldn't help but notice the strange insignia's on the hilt of the blade. Charles lowered the blade to Ainsley's throat. Ainsley took a deep inhale of breath, attempting to suck in her throat as much as possible away from the razor sharp edge of the knife. "Now listen girly, you scream, and you and my little friend here are going to become much better acquainted, you hear me?" threatened Detective Charles, never faltering oh his hold over Ainsley.

Ainsley nodded subtly, not wanting to risk slitting her own throat on the blade tightly nestled on her throat.

"I'm going to lift my hand now, easy does it." Whilst Charles carefully tormented Ainsley, the Sergeant just stood facing the blotted out exterior window, almost as if he could see beyond it.

With Charles' hand removed from Ainsley's mouth, she breathed much easier, letting out deep gasps, trying to catch her breath, having not realized she had been holding it. Sergeant Mallory turned and faced Ainsley.

"I'm going to come clear with you Ainsley, we, and by we, I mean myself and the good Mister Charles here, are not members of the police force here, hell anywhere for that matter." Ainsley's eyes went wide in disbelief, thus explaining why her unease upon first meeting was so strong.

"We represent, a very secretive, a very powerful, group of individuals who, for the lack of better wording, are collectors of sorts. And as of last month, you have come into their interests." "Me?" expelled Ainsley softly, disheartened by how bad her luck had turned in such a few short weeks.

"You! Indeed, well not YOU, in particular my dear girl, no one really cares about you, hence my colleague's pointy little friend lodged against your jugular there." Charles playfully waved the blade across Ainsley's eyesight while Mallory crouched down beside her. " No, we aren't here for you my girl, we are here for what you carry with you, or at least you are supposed to be carrying with you."

Ainsley's mind flashed images of the book, still not knowing consciously where the Voice hid it. "You do know what we speak of don't you Ainsley? It would explain your sudden relocation last night quite well." Ainsley was hesitant to tell, especially after remembering what Rick Rhapsody had told her. 'Don't tell them anything about the book, no matter what' and that was exactly what Ainsley intended to do; however, the knife against her throat was beginning to penetrate.

Ainsley began to have a panic attack, 'I don't want to die, I don't want to die, please don't kill me, I'm only 13 for crying out loud you can have the book, just don't kill me' thought Ainsley, attempting to hold back tears, but failing miserably.

"Awe, the baby is crying, what do you think boss, you think I should give her medicine?" spoke Charles as he pressed the switchblade while he spoke 'medicine'. Ainsley began to weep, drawing some form of sympathy from Mallory. "Knock it off." Carelessly spoke Mallory as he pushed

Charles off Ainsley who still lay frozen on the floor, bleeding from her deep splinters and the small cut on her throat. Mallory sighed, not out of sympathy, but merely out of inconvenience. He turned to Charles who was chuckling to himself at his handy work.

"Look what you've done, last thing we want is her crying and bleeding you imbecile." Charles just shrugged his bony shoulders and rose from the floor walking off, cleaning off his switchblade as he did. Mallory turned once more to the petrified Ainsley, who had not moved since Charles had dismounted her.

"Talk to me Ainsley, you know what I'm talking about, he's gone he won't hurt you, you can trust me." Ainsley shuddering, turned her head to look straight at Fredrick, who had a warm smile glued from ear to ear. Being emotionally unstable at the time, Ainsley couldn't help but desire some much need kindness, as she had not received any in weeks. So, bluntly, attempting to hold a steady voice, Ainsley confessed.

"I don't know where the book is."

This caught Mallory off guard, who moved his head back in surprise. Charles also turned from where he stood to look at Ainsley in astonishment; his expression was more of anger. "Why you lying little bitch!" roared Charles who went to lunge at Ainsley, blade in hand only to be stopped dead in his tracks by the much larger, more burly Mallory who, effortlessly tackled him to the ground and ripped the dagger away. "Keep your head you retard!" yelled Mallory at the downed Charles.

Turning back to Ainsley, Mallory could see she had risen to a sitting position on the floor. Standing, the Fredrick went over once more and crouched down beside Ainsley who stared blankly over at Charles who looked lost without his blade, not knowing what to do, with his hands, he stood awkwardly in the background.

"You don't know where it is?" repeated Mallory, clarifying he heard correctly, this received a shake of the head from Ainsley, who's tear stained cheeks were flushed from the overwhelming emotion of the situation. "I woke up and it was gone."

Mallory sighs, and looks over at Charles, "Well this is most unfortunate news; I guess that's all the questions we have?" Charles nods his head, and then begins to smile sinisterly. Fredrick turns back to Ainsley, who having heard this from Mallory, began to let her hope soar.

"So, does that mean I can go?" anxiously spoke Ainsley as she went to stand. Mallory's thick hand grabbed her shoulder, holding her in place. "Not so fast I'm afraid. We can't just let you go kid, you could be lying to us, and even if you aren't, you'll eventually find out where the book is. So we can't let you go, but we can't kill you either, not here at least." Ainsley's heart picked up pace again, fearing the worst. "You, you're going to kill me?" Charles laughs, "What do you think we are? Serial killers? You are worth more to us alive than dead."

Ainsley was not confused by the situation. "So…" Mallory cut her off. "We can't let you go, and we can't kill you. BUT we do have you on record for running away, and lying about it, and what's worse, I'm afraid we've determined you have lost touch with reality." "I don't understand?" "No? Child, you told us you travelled 700 kilometers in one night using a book, a book you can't even present to us as proof. I'm afraid you are not mentally stable enough to be let loose. Wouldn't you agree Mr. Charles?" Ainsley began to hyperventilate, not believing what she heard. "Definitely agree Mr. Mallory."

With that, Mallory raised his hands in a shrugging sort of way, and snapped his fingers once more, thus causing Charles to produce a document from Ainsley's file on the desk.

"You are to be sent to the Singing Loon's Correctional and Mental Institute for Troubled Youth's". Charles then tossed the document to Mallory who brushed through it and forged Ainsley's signature.

Ainsley couldn't believe it, this was like a nightmare, one from which she couldn't wake. Thinking fast, Ainsley thought up every bit of legal information she knew, "Wait! Don't you need my mom's verbal and written consent?" This caused Mallory to stop writing, and smile. "My dear, how do you think we found you? Who do you think come up with the idea for Singing Loon's? Not only has your mother consented, she lead us right to you."

Ainsley began to cry, not wanting to hear such horrible, un-motherly things done against her by her mother Abigail. Ainsley couldn't refute, all she could do was hysterically repeat. "No, no, no, no, no, no…"

And as she fell deeper and deeper into her hysteria, Fredrick Mallory signed her name, thus changing Ainsley's life with the flick of a pen.

XX. Singing Loons

The weight of Ainsley's lids made it almost impossible for her to keep them open for any period of time. But for the limited time she did, she could make out only brief moments of time. The back of a police cruiser. A gate. A sign with three white birds on it. A white jacket. Glasses, hanging low on a portly woman's face. A pen. Then... nothing.

That was all that Ainsley could remember of her arrival here at the Singing Loon's Correctional and Mental Institute for Troubled Youth's. A very peculiar facility at best, first being named with a wry ironic phrase such as "Singing Loon's" but moreover in that this place offered, at least in Ainsley's opinion, no help whatsoever.

Ainsley had been here for three years now, a long three years. And all she learned from her stay here was that she was never going to leave.

Ainsley awoke at the beginning of the classical music that they incessantly played over the speakers 14 hours each day, she never knew what the song was that they played, surely something from Mozart or Beethoven, but she couldn't be sure, all she knew as that hearing the same song repeatedly throughout the day made her hate with a fiery passion, classical music.

Throwing her covers away from her in an every growing disgust for them, Ainsley lazily raised her body and looked around the sleeping quarters of the ward. All was as it was every single day, bland. All the other wardfellows were rising just as she, giving a large array of expressions, some of anger, despair, annoyance, joy, mania, fear. Really anything, anyone else would do upon waking, only difference was these individuals, for whatever reason, were considered clinically insane, or as the nurses would state "Unsuitable for public interaction".

Ainsley was a member of ward 7, a harmless enough name, unless you knew what it represented, which in the case of Ainsley, she did. Ward 7 meant that you, above all other patients at Singing Loon's were the most mentally unstable, or dangerous, either to yourself or others. The doctors would claim that Ainsley was here for her delusions of imaginary lands and creatures, phantom books and the book collectors that sought them. Sure Ainsley admitted to herself that from the common person, who didn't know any better, that would seem crazy, but Ainsley knew better, she knew, that despite how creative she may be, she wasn't inventive enough to conceive such a universe of mystery and intrigue. The doctors disagreed.

Climbing out of bed, Ainsley grabbed a neon green hair band off her nightstand, or what she used as a nightstand, but was actually the gurney in which the nurses stored medical supplies in case of emergency. Wrapping her long, light brown, oily hair into a sloppy ponytail, Ainsley proceeded quickly out of the sleeping quarters, making sure to stay ahead of the maniacs she called ward mates.

Though diluted by the traditional white scrubs supplied to the insane, Ainsley had grown into a figure of beauty in the three years since her arrival. Being only 15 years of age, Ainsley could easily pass off as a 20 year old, not only by her gorgeous looks, but also thanks to her very complex, and intricate personality and intellect. When she was 13, Ainsley, as part of a statistical study being done by undergraduates of the nearby Sawchuck University, was given an IQ test to determine the hypothesis that many mentally unstable don't necessarily suffer of temporal lobe deformity, but merely an excessively over stimulated brain. So basically they wanted to reprove why all geniuses in the world had/have psychological problems, to which Ainsley thought was stupid, "Of course they have problems, they are so smart they can readily recognize their insanity!" Ainsley would often vent to non-responsive vegetative patients, not seeking conversation, but merely to expel stress.

In the end, the ambitious undergrads of SCU were overwhelmingly disappointed by the results of their examination. 97% of the patients tested came back with average; to below average levels of Intelligence Quotient, all save for one. Ainsley. Scoring a 143, Ainsley according to the generally accepted IQ charts, scored just high enough to garner the title of genius. This information however, was intentionally withheld from Ainsley, not as part of the study. Higher powers, people Ainsley had never met, nor personally insulted, kept her scores away from her, instead giving her bogus scores of 118, average. And to this day that was what Ainsley thought she was. Average.

Ainsley arrived in the common room for Ward 7 patients. A large enough room not unlike any other common room in any other psychiatric ward; complete with grating over the windows, and grated partitions between exits leading anywhere else other than Ward 7. A lone glass room, separating the nurse's desk from the patients; a barrier from the sane and insane. And, of course the scattered chairs and tables, all with puzzles and games littering them. However, unlike most modern institutions, Singing Loon's contained no televisions, at least not in Ward 7. The reasons around the ward were all very entertaining to Ainsley; the paranoid schizophrenics specified that it was due Aliens continuing to steal them for their experimentations on the kidnapped patients of Singing Loon's. Ainsley knew this to be ridiculous, considering all the patients they mentioned, were all past patients that were released or transferred. The suicide cases claimed it was because they enjoyed to torture and isolate the innocent. Ainsley believed this more than Aliens, but alas, this too was untrue. The reason was wholly unremarkable. Thanks to her late grandfather, and his obsession with architecture, Ainsley knew that due to this buildings obvious age, having dated back as far as the turn of the 19th century; and the facilities understaffed, underfunded plight, that the reason no televisions were present, was merely because they couldn't afford it, they couldn't afford the massive overhaul the common room, as well as many others would require to provide enough electricity to power the energy-hungry portals to the outside world.

Nonetheless, in the far back right corner of the open common room was an arranged set of couches around what, was clearly a wall mount for a potential TV to be hung. However, until that day, all the couches were used for were group discussion. Which, as a chime rang out over the overhead signified was just that time.

Ainsley, though somewhat disinterested with group discussions in general, had her interest piqued due to the fact that this group discussion occurred first thing, a rare occurrence. Usually GD's occurred at 10, 2 and 6, 10 patients at a time, which comfortably covered the 29 patients on the ward. They never occurred this early, unless, unless something was happening.

Nurse Binny walked onto the ward with a breeze in her step. Ainsley observed this and noted that this would make her day a misery. Mathilda Binny, the head nurse of Ward 7, was a stout woman, standing no taller than 4 feet 10 inches, making her substantially shorter than all her patients, even the younger ones. But what she lacked in size, she made up for in overbearing personality. Mathilda was one of those individuals whom, when you see them across the room, and make eye contact you instantly regret doing so and attempt to either shy away or brace yourself, because Binny was a talker. She cared not for conversations, if she herself were ever analyzed in an institution such as this; she would be classified as a narcissistic logomaniac, or in laymen's terms, a self-centered talkaholic. If you didn't respond within three seconds of being talked to, Mathilda would answer for you. And it was because of this, as Ainsley mused, was why Nurse Binny was assigned to the hardest ward, because under her rule, you either talked, or didn't exist. And to the insane, not existing was the fundamental fear that they all shared.

"Attention everyone, if I could please have you come together for a group meeting that would be stellar!" jovially jeered Binny, as not waiting for a response, made her way forward taking light steps in her blindingly white porcelain-like shoes toward the makeshift circle of couches. Dressed in atypical nursing attire, Binny, though none knew this other than her and the old gentlemen on 12th street she went to, had to get all her clothing alternated. Being both aggressively short, and yet plump made clothing for Mathilda somewhat of a challenge, one that must've snapped something deep in her brain, and made her coping mechanism unnecessary happiness.

"Chop chop people! You haven't gotten all day! Oh wait maybe you do!" Binny laughed at her own backhanded joke as she took a seat on the only chair in the circular arrangement of couches. She then patiently waited as the miserable patients all reluctantly gathered, early arrivals claiming all the seating, leaving Ainsley, who defiantly waited until she was the last, before walking over, keeping on the outskirts.

"Alright folks, we got two bits of exciting news today! No wait! Three! Three bits of exciting news! YAY!" Mathilda gestured for everyone to clap and cheer along with her. None clapped, other than the poor chronic's who were too delusional to note that nothing was cheer worthy, not yet anyway.

"Okay buds, first bit of good news! As all of you are aware we have been one of the last officially recognized Institutions not to have a proper set of televisions gracefully mounted across our wards, well guess what?" Some foolishly made to respond, only to have the head nurse cut them off. "Well we are getting 40 wondrous plasma TVs in the coming weeks! Yay!" This caused all the suicide cases, as well as most of the ward to start to cheer at the news. Nurse Binny attempted to speak over top the ruckus "This was all made possible thanks to a generous donation by a Mr. Rickard Rhapsody of the FTC. He will be arriving here with the shipment of trucks in the coming weeks and wanted to deliver them in person, how sweet!"

This bit of news was far more fascinating to Ainsley than the silly Televisions. 'Rickard Rhapsody? Rick Rhapsody? His full name perhaps? A pseudonym? At any rate, the fact that he was coming within the month excited Ainsley more than words could describe.

Long ago, when she had her brief and potent encounter with the then detective, he handed her a small piece of paper, which not until much later, did she remember to read. It read as follows:

> Ainsley,
> I know our encounter was brief and we didn't get to talk about much,
> let alone get to know each other very well. Don't worry, we will someday.
> Today however, I need to leave you with this bit of hope, because where you

are going, you will need it. Please know, that the book is safe and secure, I

was the one that lifted it from you before the others arrived and could seize it.

It is safe with me, I can reassure you, I know this isn't very reassuring because

of how little you know me, but trust me, please, I mean only to protect you, and,

possibly more importantly, the book. I know you are scared; you have a right to

be, it's a scary world for a kid like you, but don't worry, no matter what happens,

no matter what they tell you, what put you through, know that you have friends,

friends that care very dearly about you. I hope some day soon we can talk about

our mutual interest in ancient tomes more, but for now, just know, we will come

for you, one way or another.

Your friend eternal,

R.R.

Ainsley was so lost in her memory of her encounter with Rhapsody, and the letter thereafter, that she completely missed out on the second bit of good news, hearing only the tail end of it. "Let us all wish Mr. Schleck good luck and congratulations!" Everyone began applauding for the 62 year old obsessive-compulsive Ernst Schleck who, as far as Ainsley knew, had been here since it's opening in 1968, so indeed this was some surprising news to hear of his final leaving.

Studying his face, Ainsley noted, beneath the put on smile, a hint of sadness; perhaps his problem wasn't OCD but not wanting to leave his home of some 40 odd years.

Now fully awaiting the final bit of good news, not so much out of curiosity, but mainly so she could retreat to her favorite arm chair in the far leftmost corner near the window which pointed SW toward the entrance gate of the Singing Loon's Institute, and contemplate the significance of Rhapsody's sudden reappearance in her life.

Nurse Binny, with a smile from ear to ear, ceased clapping for Ernst and turned her attention briefly to her clipboard reading off her final note. "Okay everyone, the final bit of good news! You all ready? Of course you are, here it is, we will be having a new patient join us on 7, he's a transferee from the New York Institute for Mental Health, so he's coming from a very prestigious background." Again, Binny laughed at the very unfunny history of the mystery person. "His name is Patrick and he will be joining us next week. So when he gets here, be sure to welcome him with open arms!" Everyone nodded in an obligatory fashion, all except Ainsley who besides everyone else, was genuinely excited by this. Meeting new patients and learning their history had become one of her favorite pastimes, so she was relieved to have one last excursion into someone's history before her encounter with Rhapsody at the end of the month.

"That's it folks! Thanks for your attention! Regular group therapy is at 10 as usual, Benny I expect to see you there!" stated the Head nurse pointing her finger to the sheepish looking kleptomaniac, who quickly nodded then hurried off away from the awkward spotlight. So did Ainsley, now with lots to think on.

Walking the short distance to her favorite chair, Ainsley sat down and, lost in thought, stared out the window at the entrance, and imagined seeing Rick's taxi drive up the driveway, wishing today was then. But alas, all Ainsley was left with, was waiting.

XXI. The Notebook

Ainsley rubbed her soft delicate fingers across the cracked leather of her armchair. Feeling the sharp, crater-like texture of the once deep rich brown armrest put in perspective for Ainsley, how long she had been here.

She remembered her first night, still in a state of shock of the events of the past few weeks, especially the last 24 hours. Being cornered by those goons, Mallory and Charles, being abandoned by her mother, and apparently, betrayed as well. Ainsley didn't know which hurt her more.

The long drive to her new home, where she was now. She remembered falling into a state of comatose during the drive, losing herself in the falling leaves off the varying trees along the way, and thinking how similar they seemed of the trees of Maltyrn, and how her heart yearned to return there. Now seeing that though dangerous and mysterious. Those woods, that land, had more friends to her than this one ever would.

It was dusk before they turned into the bricked enclosure of Singing Loon's, Ainsley didn't bother to look toward her new home; she knew that she would become very familiar with it. Instead she turned around in her seat, and in her weakened state, watched as the gates closed in behind her. Trapped.

The out of date police cruiser, reminding Ainsley of one of the reruns of the old police dramas she used to watch over at her friend Heather's house after school sometimes, came to a halt outside the front entrance of the equally out of date building. Mallory, leaning farther into the car then thrusting himself out with the momentum of the swing, came waddling around the side abruptly opening the door on which Ainsley's head leaned.

Falling forward slightly, Ainsley, instantly grateful for putting on her seat belt, unbuckled and climbed out of the back seat.

Looking up past the smug grin of Mallory as he firmly took Ainsley's young arm, Ainsley began to admire the beautiful architecture of the flying buttresses that created an awning of sorts over the entrance, similar to what you see on modern hospitals, but much more elegant, and unpractical. As Ainsley was dragged inside, she thought to herself about how cruel it was that such places of beauty, had to contain such horrors.

The walk through the ceramic tiled hallway, white washed from its original tint, was for lack of a better word, unremarkable; Ainsley felt nothing but boredom, and anticipation; no, not out of excitement, but out of determination. She had decided that if she were to suffer, and be punished for reasons even the most creative lawyers couldn't prove, then she was going to take it head on.

Arriving at the front desk, of the relatively cramped lobby of the Institution, Ainsley was again distracted away from Mallory explaining to the triage nurse her reason for being here, by the glorious spiral staircase encircling the tall atrium like room. Starting at the right of the front desk, and winding up along the walls 8 stories high ending in a glass domed ceiling, allowing ample light to fill the narrow room. Ainsley, however, was disappointed to see, white grating brutishly attached to the rails.

"Excuse me miss?" spoke the triage nurse, causing Ainsley to snap her neck back down to ground level. "Yes?" replied Ainsley to the very warm motherly face of the triage nurse, reminding her hauntingly of her mother, back before she went insane.

"I need you to follow me now." Ainsley complied without comment, looking back over her shoulder at the massive Mallory as he smiled, affirming his victory, and waving a sarcastic wave to Ainsley as she ascended the beautiful stairway. Scowling back at him Ainsley swore then and there to herself, that that was not to be the last time she saw that man, and when she saw him again, it would be he, not her, that saw life through metal.

"What's your name?" asked Ainsley to the comely nurse, "Its Amelia, but please, call me Lia" politely replied Lia, speaking to Ainsley as a mother would her child asking a question about why the sky is blue. "Lia? I like Amelia better." Jokingly scoffed Ainsley causing Lia to chuckle, Ainsley as well, something she hadn't been able to do for ages it seemed.

"Well Ainsley, if you want, you can call me Amelia, but only you" playfully told Ainsley, almost as if it were a secret, instantly easing Ainsley further, allowing her to forget about her horrid situation. "That's okay, I was only kidding." "Oh okay, well the offer still stands". Both smiled at each other, as the conversation died out as they reached the second floor from the top.

Ainsley looked to the frosted glass sign reading 'WARD 7'. She had always like the number 7, even before the Voice told her of it significance. Not because of its lucky stigma, but merely because it was the first of many things she learned when she was a toddler, the first number, the first word 'seven'.

Forgetting herself, Ainsley hadn't realized that Lia had turned toward Ainsley and knelt down to her eye level, appearing very close to her. Lia looked worried, an expression that, in the short time since there meeting, Ainsley figured was a very unnatural expression on her face.

"Ainsley listen carefully, I have some very important things to tell you okay?" this caused Ainsley to worry, reminding her that though she found

141

one nice person at last, she was still in a very bad situation. Ainsley nodded. "Now, I don't know what you did to get up here, but you have to be careful, people don't generally leave the seventh floor." Ainsley quirked her brow, feeling a slight ache there from here constant confusion in Maltyrn; Lia read here facial expression. "Ainsley the seventh floor is strictly for the chronic's and the committed. For the vegetables and criminals, its not a safe place." "But why Lia?" footfalls were echoing from down the hall, notifying the pair of them that someone was coming, acting fast, Lia pulled Ainsley and herself into a nearby vacant office. They remained quiet as an apparent male nurse casually walked by undeterred. Lia turned once more back to Ainsley. "Its dangerous for two reasons, first, these criminals have done terrible things to end up here, murder, arson, rape, you name it, and they've done it. And I can instantly tell just by looking at you that you don't belong in there, so you are in danger. That's the first reason. The second is the chronic's, they didn't start off as chronically ill, in vegetative states, they started off as unruly patients that were deemed incurable and given the drip." Ainsley didn't like the sound of 'the drip'. "What's the drip?" Thorazine, a very powerful drug that will essentially leave you with a dumbfounded glare for the rest of your days."

Ainsley's heart began to quicken, she began to hyperventilate, causing Lia to regret being so blunt with Ainsley, whom always caused people to forget her tender youth. "I don't mean to frighten you, only prepare you." Ainsley attempted to catch her breath as she spoke "how, does, this, prepare me?" "That doesn't, this does" and with that, Lia handed Ainsley a thin notebook. Ainsley looked at it with intrigue and mysticism. "What is it?" "Just read it, and all will become clear, I promise."

Ainsley looked down once more at the notebook, well used, and breezed through it, seeing every page filled with tiny font, pictures, floor layouts, everything. Looking back up to Lia, she simply nodded, to which Lia returned the knowing look. Standing up together, Lia then proceeded to escort Ainsley down the hall toward the sleeping quarters.

As they walked, Ainsley attempted to keep her gaze downright, knowing from being bullied in school, that the best way to stay out of trouble was to not make eye contact. However, seeing as Lia accompanied her, Ainsley dared a few glances upward. All the patients were huddled around the glass partition, awaiting their nighttime medication; about half were required to be wheeled over, due to their drug-induced lobotomy. Ahead Ainsley saw another long corridor with two-door wide entrances on both sides and a doublewide pair of heavy swinging doors at the end. On either side were the bathrooms, complete with bath tubs, showers, in the style you see at local swimming pools, and a wall of sinks, all lined in tiny navy blue tiles, and on the other side, a similar case, feature lime green tiles instead. Clearly, looking back at the patients, Ainsley deducted this was to accommodate the unisex nature of the ward.

Pushing the heavy doors open for Ainsley to follow through, Lia closed them behind her. The room was empty, and like lots of the other featured rooms in the institution, it was beautiful. A massive, round room, similar in size to a large conservatory, only instead of a massive space-defying magnifying glass, it was equipped with at least 50 single spring mattresses, all complete with padded night stands and, a trunk at the end of each bed. And at the center, was yet another triage desk, circular to match the room. It was clear to Ainsley this desk was purely cosmetic, to prevent any of the more emotionally insecure patients to attempt anything during the night.

143

Whitewashed and iron grated like the rest of the ward, Ainsley was genuinely depressed to see that the massive glass dome ceiling, similar to the lobbies, was instead whitewashed as well; blotting out the sun, and in its stead, a grid of harsh fluorescents were hung high above making the blind skylight almost invisible behind them.

Lia led Ainsley over to a bed near one of the many similarly whitewashed windows and set Ainsley down on the bed. Pulling the notebook away from her, Lia gently placed in under her pillow. "Let no one see it. Our little secret" Ainsley was pleased to hear Lia's joyful tone return.

"Now, the others are going to be heading to bed soon, I recommend you head to bed right now, so as to not draw attention to yourself. Ainsley nodded, seeing the logic. "Good girl, don't worry, you'll be alright, I'll be around if you need anything okay?" Again Ainsley nodded, causing Lia to squeeze her leg encouragingly. Then without a word, Lia tucked Ainsley into bed, and walked out. Leaving Ainsley alone.

However, Ainsley could not sleep, so much had happened so fast. Given all the drama she had experience here and in the woods of Maltyrn, Ainsley was beginning to believe she was insane, how else could she explain why she and people only she knew, Artie, the Voice, Rick, and the goons Mallory and Charles knew about the book and the other world, and how her mom was part of some conspiracy to punish her by locking her up. It was preposterous, and yet, Ainsley knew deep in the abyss of her soul, that it was real, all of it; truth, indeed stranger than fiction. But above all else, Ainsley ended her night pondering just two things… When would she be leaving this place, and what was in Lia's notebook?

XXII. The First Night

It was late; the fluorescence above long since went black. Leaving the whitewashed sleeping quarters in pure darkness. The only light source to ever occur was when a triage nurse would unsympathetically barge into the room and man the triage desk for 15 minutes, keeping up appearances more or less, then leave just the same.

Ainsley had been itching to pull out and read the notebook, but she had no way to do so. They confiscated her mp3 player when the cops picked her up so she had lost her only reliable light source in the world.

It was times like this that Ainsley wished she was back in the other world, where she had cool powers like being able to light things with her touch, that would make reading super easy. However, she wasn't, she was trapped here, and had no clue where her book was. Which constantly plagued the back of her mind, which Ainsley naturally accepted as the Voice trying to talk to her.

Staring up into the darkness, Ainsley felt the slack leather bound notebook resting underneath her pillow, teasing her with its presence. Ainsley didn't know what it could possibly contain, all she knew was it had something to do with her protection

Slowly pulling it out from under her soft polyester pillow Ainsley, in the minute light coming through the whited out window behind her, examined the novel closely. It appeared to be not very old, but well used, the tips of pages frayed and torn. Edges curled and bent, the spine was strained way back, suggesting the previous owner had squished the book open, other than the soft black leather lazily attached as the cover, there wasn't really anything spectacular. Opening the book randomly to a page roughly halfway through, Ainsley tightly squinted her eyes trying to make out any of the many words crammed onto each an every page.

'Whoever wrote this thing, sure had a lot to say' thought Ainsley as she gently ran her hands across the words of the page, treating it as some ancient text long since lost to history; much like her other book…

Losing herself, Ainsley failed to realize in time the immediate entry of a male nurse who, unlike most of the staff, entered silently in an attempt to show compassion for the poor souls slumbering within.

"Excuse me missy, I'm afraid reading isn't an option right now." Spoke the nurse, now looming on the opposite side of the bed, appearing out of nowhere as far as Ainsley was concerned. Turning round quickly, Ainsley out of instinct more than logic, flung the notebook back under the pillow from whence she pulled it; the nurse wasn't fooled.

"Come on, I know you ain't sleepin' hand it over now." Sternly, yet silently spoke the man, speaking more like a teacher than a man of medicine.

Seeing no other alternative, and really not wanting to get on the staff's bad side, especially if what Lia had told her was true, Ainsley reluctantly handed over the book.

As she did, the nurse gave the smallest of grins, appreciating complicity over rebellion, which was a common strain on him, and his fellow nurses. "Thank you miss?" Not fully understanding at first, Ainsley quickly realized he was asking for her name, and feeling slightly cheated, having once more come into possession of a rare book, and losing it, Ainsley felt no guilt in coldly replying.

"Ainsley".

"Ainsley? That your first name?" quietly asked the nurse, gradually growing on Ainsley quickly developing nerves. Sighing, Ainsley finally rolled over and slightly sat up in her bed, putting emphasis in each maneuver trying to stress the absurdity of a nurse trying to have a conversation with a patient at night. "I don't have a last name, just Ainsley" "Really, that's weird ain't it?" replied the nurse seeming to be more idiotic by the second.

Rolling her eyes, Ainsley sat up fully in her bed and glared at the nurse, wanting desperately to get attention off her; she'd get enough of that from the doctors. "And your name?" spoke Ainsley, almost sarcastically. Caught off guard by this, the nurse bluntly jumbled out his name "who me, Im Imma I'm Jackson. Nurse Jackson".

Ainsley couldn't help but smile at Jackson, clearly a buffoon, young, pencil thin, garbed in the traditional all white uniform, sneakers included, which all perfectly contrast his impossibly black skin, making his eyes, even in the middle of darkness, stand out white as daylight.

"Why you only have a first name?" bluntly asked Jackson out of curiosity, a curiosity, that at Ainsley ripe age, had already come to hate. So in response, she bluntly whipped back "Why do you only have a last name?" Jackson was about to reply when the room was suddenly filled with harsh fluorescence of the overheads. All including Ainsley and Jackson crushed their eyes shut, attempting desperately to blot out the harshness of the unexpected light.

Standing at the light switch, stood a widely stanced elderly nurse; by the nametag it was clear she was the head nurse. Salt and pepper hair done up in a perfect bun underneath her firmly set nurses cap; Nurse Margaret Chu stood glaring fiercely at Jackson, looking more like a patient than a colleague. Ignoring the confused looks her way from the grumpily woken patients, Chu stormed across the the large room to stand face to chest with

Jackson; cranking her head upwards, Margaret, though short in stature, made up for it in presence.

"What in the hell are you doing to her Jackson!" She yelled, with volumes seldom seen the old. Fumbling once more, Jackson, clearly shrinking by the second, drooped his head staring at the floor, fixating on a particular broken tile in the otherwise perfect white ceramic floor. "I was, I just had to, I'm sorry, I didn't mean to…" "That's enough out of you now, please move!" dismissed Jackson, before noting the book in his hands. "WAIT!" Jackson froze, and slowly turned once more to Chu, "What is that?!" without a word, Jackson handed the book over to Chu. Silently flipping through it, she quizzingly looked once more to Jackson for answers "It was on the girl" explained Jackson, desperately wanting to leave the situation. Ainsley, though initially disliking the man, felt sorry for him. "Which one!?" starting to cower in the presence of Margaret, Jackson, simply pointed at Ainsley.

Suddenly feeling the hot gaze now on her, Ainsley too shrunk down in her bed, pulling her sheets to her chin. "That'll be all Mr. Jackson, if you would be so kind to report to Dr. Jenkins, I believe he'll want to hear about this straight away." Jackson suddenly began to cry hystEyeally, causing Ainsley to be confused, having thought punishment wouldn't be all that severe for talking to a patient. "Please boss, I don't want to, I don't need to seem him now do I?" pleaded Jackson, "Oh I think you do Mr. Jackson, you are in big trouble and he'll need to be informed." Sounding calm and collected now, Margaret Chu seemed to frighten the man now more than ever, causing the man to hunch over standing lower now than herself. "Go." Ordered Chu, turning her attention once more to Ainsley, trusting that Jackson would comply. And he did.

She quietly stepped toward the near side of Ainsley's bed, making no noise, quite the opposite of her first entrance. Standing over Ainsley, the cold withered face suddenly did a very unusual thing, it tilted upward in a warm smile. "I'm terribly sorry about all that, it is protocol that I meet all new patients before bedtime but, you just seemed to sneak right in and fall asleep, we didn't want to wake you. Apparently we should have. I'm sorry where are my manners, I'm Head Nurse Margaret Chu, I'm in charge of ward 7, meaning I'm in charge of taking care of you." Ainsley timidly went to ask a question, much like a first grader on the first day of school, "What was.." "All of that?" interrupted Chu, anticipating the question. Ainsley nodded then loosened her grip on her sheets dropping them slightly.

Gently taking a seat on the edge of the bed, Chu rested her hand on one Ainsley's propped up knees. "That gentleman was not one of our nurses, his name is Willy Jackson, he is one of our chronic sex offenders, we usually keep him separate from these sleeping quarters, apparently he got out." Ainsley didn't fully understand what it all meant, seeing this Chu elaborated. "We keep our most volatile patients in their own separate rooms, for both their and your protection, if they aren't locked up, they most definitely attempt to do awful things." Suddenly it all clicked, and Ainsley's eyes went wide. "So he was going to…" "Yes, he was, unfortunately he's done it before in the past, before we've been able to reach him, but since then we've put security measures in place. At any rate, I must apologize for all of this, certainly not how we want our newest patients to spend their first days." Margaret chuckled at this, Ainsley merely gave a blank stare, lost in the thought of what would have happened if Chu hadn't arrived.

Rising from the bed, Margaret quickly glanced over her shoulder to the doorway seeing two nurses waiting on her acknowledgment of their presence. "Ah, well, lots to do, 4 am is the start of my shift, so I must be off, these two nurses have been advised to stand guard for the rest of the night, so no other incidents occur. Tomorrow we'll go over basic ground rules and safety precautions you must know. Until then, have a good rest of your night. Turning, Ainsley followed the black leather long forgotten in the Head Nurse's grasp, strolling off out of the wide-open double doors, which closed dutifully behind her.

Ainsley slowly lowered herself back into her bed resting her head against the slippery fabric of her pillow, reeling over the evening's events. The sharp lights overhead, once again went black, leaving Ainsley alone again in the abyss of the early morning darkness. And the first thing Ainsley thought after this occurred was this "I'm not getting any sleep tonight."

XXIII. Spilling the Beans

"Are you listening to me Ainsley?" politely, yet obnoxiously asked Dr. William Jenkins PHD, Supervising Doctor of wards 1, 3 and 7, as it said on the frosted glass of his door as Ainsley entered for her fifth meeting that week.

Ainsley had been having a lousy first week at Singing Loon's, despite now being to afraid to sleep, thus getting no shut eye, she also suffered at terrible food, and medication that, at least physically, did nothing other than make her more tired, and more agitated than she was progressively becoming.

During her first meeting with Dr. Jenkins, Ainsley had been polite enough to listen as he layed out all the rules and regulations of ward 7, two hours later she left feeling genuinely depressed, and far more likely to need medical attention, as she wanted to kill herself.

"No, personal items, other than what we provide for you."
"No, visiting hours from friends and family except on holidays."
"No, interaction with any other patients outside of your ward."
"Always take the medication prescribed, punishment for not taking said medication is electrotherapy"
"Always obey the staff, no matter what the case."
"Always be on your best behavior."

Blah. Blah. Blah.

On and on it went, making Ainsley finally realize something she should have seen instantly. 'I shouldn't be here.'

"Ainsley? Can you please respond?" ostentatiously repeated Jenkins giving a slight smirk as he gawked at Ainsley. Looking up from her twiddling hands, Ainsley repeated what she had always repeated since her first encounter with Jenkins, "Where's my notebook?"

Jenkins sighed, as he slouched back in his chair, frustrated with the lack of progress he seemed to be making with the young, and stubborn Ainsley. Pushing his oversized seventies era glasses back up his fragile nose, the equally stubborn Jenkins leaned forward once more and rested his oversized withered hands on his desk. "I've told you before Ainsley, we cannot give you that book, even if it was yours, which its not." Ainsley sighed, sending fierce glares at her foe and childishly crossing her arms tightly. "Why not though? What's with that rule? It makes no sense!" "It makes perfect sense, as I've told you before, patients in this ward are not to be trusted with personal trinkets, its not conducive to the healing process." Ainsley just muttered under her breath beyond frustrated with this daily occurrence.

Not waiting for any form of reply, Dr. Jenkins continues "Besides, not only does your name not appear once in it, but furthermore it belonged to a former patient back when we allowed personal items, so even if we did make exceptions, which we don't, I can't return property that isn't yours, sorry. But that's it." This caught Ainsley's attention, not his repeated dismissal of the subject, but the small bit of new information he revealed.

"Who did it belong to??" excitedly begged Ainsley, forgetting for a moment who she was asking. "Sorry, confidential, I cannot release that information to anyone, not even my wife."

"Bullshit" quietly exclaimed Ainsley, not believing for one second that this doctor would not tell his wife, let alone friends at Christmas banquets, and lectures. Ainsley stood, knowing full well that their time wasn't up and

153

the act of standing was rebellion incarnate. Turning, before the doctor could say anything on the matter, Ainsley went for the door.

"I hope..."
This stopped Ainsley, sensing it wasn't going to be what she expected prior.
"I hope, that next time we meet you'll want to talk about why you actually are here."

Ainsley didn't know what overtook her then, but somehow, someway, the phrasing, or perhaps the wording the good doctor chose to use to explain his hopes for these meetings, triggered something in Ainsley that she'd been attempting to suppress from him of all people, truth.

Turning and slamming her hands firmly on the desk slightly startling the septuagenarian back into his seat, Ainsley lowered her face down getting eye level with him.

"Look! Its not my fault that I'm here, all I did was listen to my mom, 'go pick up a book Ainsley, it'll be easy' she says, and you know what that gets me? Thrust into this alternate reality place where cannibals run around trying to kill me along with giant 20-foot deer. I hear this voice yap on and on telling me all these things that don't make any sense but apparently make perfect sense here, and when I come back, I'm still being chased by masochistic book collectors dressed as policemen, and then my mom betrays me and throws me in here with rapists, and ignorant doctors like you!!!"

Ainsley was out of breath, so all she could do was observe and think, and she instantly could tell by the wide smirk across Jenkins wrinkled face, that what she just said was a big mistake.

154

It took them till dinner time that night to adjust Ainsley's dosage, instead of some mild antidepressants, they loaded her up on anti-psychotics, pills that had to be cut in half just so the could administer the appropriate dosage for a child, seeing as antipsychotics of this strength hadn't been created.

As she held the small paper cup in her hand, looking at the severed pill laying still at the bottom of it, Ainsley strangely didn't regret spilling the beans, though she knew any hope of getting out of here was now lost, she found a strange peace in venting like that. Having no one previously to do so to, it was nice to say everything out loud at once, and hear just how loony it did sound. She didn't blame Jenkins for thinking she was crazy, she was. She had to be.

It was just too impossible to be real.

Making peace with her insanity, Ainsley then looked up to the expectant nurse behind the desk, waiting impatiently for Ainsley to down her dosage. Letting out a sigh of relief, Ainsley threw her head back and dropped the large pill into the back of her throat, then flushed it down with the ice cold tap water provided.

Ainsley then let all thought vanish from her mind, slipping silently into blissful numbness. Forgetting all about books.

XXIV. Vanishing Act

She lay still, flush with the tall grass that enveloped her similar to a snow angel. Rick took a long drag of his cigarette as he stood above her, knowing his time was limited. "Sir, we mustn't linger, they will be here soon." Announced Rick's driver from his seat; keeping the engine of the polished Royal's Royce always running, anticipating a quick leave.

"I know, don't worry, I won't be a moment." Reassured Rick as he took his final drag of his now spent cigarette and flicked it behind him onto the gravel of the side road. Crouching down, Rick Rhapsody smiled slightly at the peaceful nature of the faraway Ainsley. Her face suggesting pure tranquility, while her, were harshly wrapped around the opened book, appearing blank to a laymen. But Rick wasn't a layman.

As he observed the open book, it slowly became clear to him the words mystically filling the page, no pen present, no physical effort made by anyone, this was but part of the work of this most special book.

Smiling, Rick wasted no time in swiftly snatching the book from Ainsley's defensive grip and shutting it with a thump. "Alright lets go!" he yelled, as he turned and made the quick walk to his car, climbing without hesitation into the back seat. "Drive".

Rick knew from past experience that to interrupt the REM cycle of a Sevardinal was highly disorienting and by no means recommended, for the sake of the individual. In some past cases, it's caused permanent brain damage. But he had no choice, word of Ainsley's location came at such late notice, he and his brethren at the FTC had to secure the book, even if it meant sacrificing the poor girl's mental state.

As they drove down the lone highway, meadows on both sides and Rockies off in the distance, Rick felt bad for just leaving her there. He was against the operative from the start, he thought it would have been much wiser to retrieve the girl and the book and look after them both, train her upright. But unfortunately, he was overruled; it was not his call, nor the FTC's place to train, or even raise Sevardinal. Their sole purpose in the world, was to aid and assist Sevardinal in any way they could, whether it be transportation, relocation, nourishment, really anything a Sevardinal could ask for, but above all other protocols, their number one priority was the safety, and maintenance of the Books.

There were seven books, seven Sevardinal, one destined to guard and use each book. They were spread out all across the world, just as in the world they wrote about. And all of them had a chapter of the FTC nearby to look after them and their treasures, especially when they were *away*.

However, recently, more and more of the chapters have fallen silent, no contact for months. And in the hierarchical structure of the FTC, this was a very bad sign.

Rick knew that breaking Ainsley's REM cycle would wake her shortly; he quietly prayed that she would wake before the SLC would arrive. Thus letting her escape. Though as he watched the police cruisers fly past them, he knew this was unlikely.

The SLC, or Silva Lombard Collective are an extremely wealthy, and highly influential corporation that deals strictly in the collection and possession of all literary works; a harmless goal, except for the lengths at which the SLC are willing to go, vis-à-vis theft and murder. Having once been one and the same, the FTC and SLC unfortunately had to separate due to the emergence of the seven magical tomes which both organizations refer to as *Sevio Dionisus* when all together.

Uncovered in 1933, and entirely by accident, the *Sevio Dionisus* was actually uncovered by another book, long since destroyed during the Second World War. The *Natel* as it was known, was also part of the *Sevio Dionisus* collection, however unlike the others which held powers beyond anyone's wildest dreams, the *Natel* merely held within its covers the names and locations of each and every Sevardinal and their respective edition dating all the way back to the days of the Greeks.

It was this book that one member of the FTC accidently uncovered while cleaning out their deceased grandparents attic in Siberia. Which in turn, after decrypting it, lead to the discovery of the Sevardinal. It was at this time that the leaders of the FTC came into conflict.

The founding members of the FTC were Lawrence Henderson, and his life long friend Silvia Lombard, growing up together in Cordes-sur-Ciel France, the friends had long since been passionate patrons of the arts, particularly books. And so upon exiting College the two founded the FTC as a way to expand upon their own knowledge of this world's history.

So the discovery of a potentially new and untouched portion of history being at their fingertips drove the pair apart. Lawrence was of the opinion that the Sevardinal were sacred and had the right to carry out their rituals as they always had, and that we should respect and learn from them. Meanwhile Silva only saw the opportunity to seize the volumes of knowledge and expose it to the world, and enjoy the fame and riches that came with it.

And to this day that is what both organizations stand for.

The FTC were altered slightly after the split mainly because the Sevardinal were so thankful that they chose not to expose them that they granted them the exclusive right to guard and protect the volumes, should anything happen. And as time went on, they became the Sevardinal's earthly bodyguards.

Locking the book shut, Rick let out a sigh feeling sicker the farther he went away from, in what he took as his responsibility, Ainsley.

Arriving at their North AmEyean Head Quarters, a simple used travel bookstore that rarely if ever actually saw business. Rick climbed out of the car and waved off the driver as he sped away leaving Rick standing at the curb holding the book graciously in his arms as he entered the shop and quickly proceeded to the basement.

Gripping the rusting rail as he hunched over to dip his head under the low over pass of the old stone step way downward to a thick steel door, appearing as if it were designed to survive a nuclear fallout. Grabbing the handle with his one free hand, Rick unlatched the handle and slowly pushed the door inward, into the dark candlelit room.

Setting the book down on the stainless steel tabletop, Rick looked round the small room at his brethren as they all encircled the table.

"Is that it sir?" asked a young initiate named Evan, Rick simply nodded and smiled as he mused at how excited they all seemed to be. Most FTC members had never actually seen what they swore to protect, let alone a Sevardinal, only the Bookkeepers and Jackals were ever allowed to see them. So today was quite the exception.

"Move to the side brother." Spoke a soft spoken, yet well respected voice from the back of the small room. Rolling over to stop at the table, the wheelchair bound Lawrence Henderson, let out a sigh of relief at seeing the volume. "Good work Rhapsody, I feared we were too late." "I fear we may still be sir." Anxiously spoke Rhapsody, "Oh please Rick, we've been over this, there is nothing we can do for the girl, she will just have to make out on her own, it is not our place to care for her." Quipped Henderson, knowing full right what Rick was getting at. "But sir, she is a Sevardinal, it is our sworn duty to protect her and the book. Now we have the book, so what are we just going to leave her out there to rot?" argued Rick. "We will not interfere, besides the SLC will be there by now and have possession of her. Now, if you want so badly to help her, go right ahead, but hear me Rhapsody, if you do anything to jeopardize the safety of this book, I will hold you personally responsible." Warned Lawrence trying his best to dissuade his old prodigy. "Dually noted." And with that Rick left as quickly as he arrived.

"Why can't we help her sir?" innocently asked Evan not really understanding the context of the argument he just witnessed. Turning to him, Lawrence simply stated, "You don't become a Sevardinal until you've faced real fear, and Rhapsody saving her won't help her."

Though not fully understanding, Evan thought it best to leave the subject at that.

Driving fast to the Wayne Right Police Head Quarters, where he knew secretly, the SLC had a sect stationed, and he knew given the police cruiser he spotted earlier, that would be where they would take her.

Pulling into the parking lot, Rick reached into the back of his car and pulled out a briefcase which he quickly opened and withdrew a glock and realistic badge and then proceeded inside.

The place was packed, not only with swarms of people, but boxes upon boxes of stuff, making the once grand building feel stuffy and claustrophobic. Making his way through the narrow maze of hallways that made up the bullpen of the main floor, Rick quickly recognized Mallory and Charles standing off in a side corridor, most likely discussing the best way to withdraw information from the young Ainsley. Seeing that indeed that there was no clear way of getting Ainsley out without being seen, Rick slumped his shoulders in defeat.

Watching Ainsley rise from her seat and look at the wall of pictures, Rick quickly thought up a back up plan. Pulling a piece of paper from his pocket, as well as a pen, Rick quickly wrote a message attempting to explain everything. Though in hindsight he would admit he came across very vague.

Folding it to fit snugly in the palm of his hand, Rick composed himself and then preceded to walk over to Ainsley... His daughter.

XXV. Growing Up

Ainsley awoke feeling no sense of grogginess as she usually did from her drug-induced slumbers. This was solely due to the fact that Ainsley, being the increasingly resourceful woman that by necessity she had to grow into, had devised a method that she could prohibit her nightly drug from entering her system as she slept. This method was simple, every night after gratuitously swallowing her large pill that even over the years still struggled to wiggle its way down her throat; Ainsley would silently retreat to the washroom and purge her stomach of all the bile that she had just accepted into her body. This worked most nights, but if something came up, or she was delayed in reaching the washroom, or if someone was in there who could tattle on her, she was forced to feel her mind fog over and fall into dreamless sleeps, things that she hated more than the very building itself.

Last night, she was successful, and Ainsley wouldn't have it any other way, she was determined to be acutely aware of her surroundings for the day, because today, her last venture into the past began. Today the new patient arrived.

'Patrick, the boy from New York' Ainsley thought to herself as she lazily wandered out into the empty common room and found her place at her favorite chair, peacefully and inexplicably isolated from the community of orphaned chairs donated by schools, or demolished homes. Sitting surrounded by the cages, as Ainsley called them for that's what they were, that housed the more dangerous, and mentally unstable (helpless) patients whose crimes were aloof even to them. Sharing such close proximity to them didn't bother Ainsley; it had once years ago when she first arrived, but since, she had learned that nothing really was to fear in these misunderstood souls.

Over time, Ainsley slowly got to know each and every one of them, until just last month, Ainsley proudly proclaimed that she officially knew everyone in her ward. A feat that wouldn't impress many, if any at all, but to Ainsley, it was this small game of detective work that kept her mind trained on something, kept her mind from drifting off to subjects that she knew were dangerous to think about. Mainly, books.

Ainsley had flirted dangerously with the notion that she was indeed insane, that all that she experienced was, as the doctors explained, and as her Uncles, if she ever saw them again, would describe as paranoid schizophrenia; and if Ainsley wasn't the one experiencing it, she would have had to agree. But she was experiencing it, it was happening, Rick Rhapsody was real, and if he was real so too must be those sinister book collectors, so must be the book they all sought so much, ultimately… so must be that world that she could only remember now in her dreams. As if it were never real.

After her most difficult time in this place occurred, the day she confessed to all of her fears, and suspicions and beliefs about books, and worlds that only she knew about, and people conspiring against her. Ainsley went through a very dreary couple years, she was as complacent as any other comatose patient you see sitting in a wheelchair, goofily slouching in it like the life had been sucked out of them. So true was of Ainsley for those years. She had accepted her insanity and felt this was a fair treatment for her, in her bed at nights, she would actually dare to think that these medications were helping her, that she was hear for good reason, when in fact. All these thoughts of insanity were exactly what were expected to happen, in fact requested to happen. For Singing Loons wasn't an ordinary psychiatric hospital, it had dark secrets that Ainsley couldn't possibly imagine, and wouldn't learn of until much later. In the meantime she submitted to the cold abyss that Ward 7 offered her.

It wasn't until one night; during her usual nightcap that Ainsley had an allergic reaction. Earlier in the night, she had been spoon-fed a piece of cake from a party being held for Nurse Chu's retirement. She inhaled the cake similar to a cow mindlessly grinding grass in its mouth, and though mindlessly swallowing the sweet strawberry flavored treat, both Ainsley and the staff were unaware that she was in fact allergic to strawberries. Growing up, Ainsley was always too poor to afford strawberries, and any fruits and vegetables they did get, they traded with the local farmers nearby, mostly potatoes and plums. Some tomato's, but mostly fruits that Ainsley, like most civilized people, wouldn't eat. So the sudden gag that overtook the suddenly startled Ainsley surprised the entire staff. Having just downed her medication, Ainsley suddenly, and for the first time in a long time, guided herself up and out of her chair and ran frantically down the hall turning by accident into the men's washroom and not seeing any available stalls, vacated her vomit in a urinal.

Ainsley, though relieved to have all that toxic stuffing out of her system only then noticed the usually pleasantly dimwitted Andy standing at the urinal beside her laughing off tone, finding the whole affair outright hilarious; Ainsley didn't agree. Slowly rising to her feet, she attempted to steady herself on her malused legs. Ainsley suddenly had a swarm of emotion, and feeling jolt her body, and the first thought that entered her mind was how similar this felt to when she left that world…

Nurses ran in fearing Ainsley had hurt herself, but were surprised to see her standing upright, surprised at how much she had grown. Being a meager 4 foot 6 inches when she arrived, Ainsley now graciously stood 5 foot 3 inches. Wiping the vomit from her suddenly plump lips, Ainsley looked at herself in the mirror and couldn't help but be shocked by what she saw. It was as if this was the first time she had seen herself in a decade. It felt similar to as if she were to suddenly see her father walk into the room, after such a long absence, Ainsley was sure she wouldn't remember what he looked like, but would know it was he. That was how she felt, she knew it was her she saw staring back, but it didn't look it. Apparently overnight, Ainsley had gone from an innocent kid, who wanted nothing from the world except to have fun and enjoy life to a young woman who had seen the worst and come out on the other side in tact, for the most part. Ainsley felt a tear fall from her face, ignoring the nurses who seeing she was alright started to guide the still manic Andy out of the washroom. "I'm back," mumbled Ainsley, realizing she didn't recognize her own voice, having not used it in two years.

The rest of the night passed in a flash, the nurses quickly returned and wiped Ainsley clean then sent her to bed, forgetting to re-induce her drugged out state, leaving her for the first time in a long time, laying in bed being fully aware of her surroundings.

Ainsley couldn't help but think about how long she must've been out of it, what she missed out on in the world; but more importantly, Ainsley remembered what she so desperately sought before, 'what ever happened to my books?'

The thought so sudden and so alarming, that Ainsley was certain she was about to have a heart attack. She had been instructed to guard that book with her life and she hadn't and she hadn't even been able to read Lia's book either. 'Lia' is she still here? Has she moved on to greater things, gotten out of this hellhole? Ainsley couldn't be sure. Ainsley couldn't be sure of anything anymore, she felt just as confused as she once did when all this stuff started to happen with the book.

"PSST!"

Ainsley shot up in her bed; seeking out the sound so loud it surely disrupted some of the patients sleep. It didn't however, and Ainsley found the sound belonged to the patient next to her, a girl, who must've been only 11 years old by the looks of it. Ainsley though barely able to make her out in the gloom of the darkened room, could see that she had bandages on her arms, 'suicide case, she won't be here long' though Ainsley, glad, considering this was no place for a girl her age, hell anyone any age.

Not knowing what exactly the girl wanted, Ainsley awkwardly asked "what?"

Pulling back her covers the other girl silently one-stepped over to Ainsley's bed sitting at the end of it. Without saying a word, the petite child stuck out her hand palm up and removed from under her less bloodied bandage a folded piece of paper, she then handed it to Ainsley. Picking it up, Ainsley lightly examined it before curiosity got the better of her. "What is it?" the girl just shrugged her shoulders then whispered "don't know, it was addressed to you though, I saw it fall out of your bed one night, you never went to retrieve it, you were out of it though, so I thought I'd hang on to it."

This caused Ainsley to smile, though she was unsure what it was; it warmed her heart to know that there was kindness within the walls of Singing Loon's. "What's your name?" asked Ainsley, wanting to know that strangely enough more than what the letter contained. "Heather" quietly spoke the little girl, Ainsley could see that though her overall demeanor was dampened by her obvious reason for being here, she was a kindhearted kid and very beautiful with long flowing brown locks running down her back to her waist, suggesting she'd never cut her hair before. Reminding Ainsley a lot of herself at that age. "Heather, I used to have a friend named Heather, though I will admit, she was hardly as pretty or as nice as you are" complimented Ainsley, feeling a pang of loss at realizing that through all this this was the first time she thought of her once best friend Heather, the girl she would spend most of her waking days with, and now, was a distant memory, much like Ainsley's life. However none of that mattered then, all Ainsley wanted was to see Heather smile, and her compliment almost accomplished that.

"You're just saying that." Said Heather coldly, though not aware that I could see the faint blush that crossed her face and the twitch of a smile begged to be allowed face time. "I'm serious, you shouldn't be afraid to be kind Heather, that will get you far in life." Spoke Ainsley taking on a motherly tone she never knew she had, feeling somewhat protective of this girl she'd just barely met, knowing that though she'd know her for a very limited time, she felt that right now, she could help her.

Heather didn't respond, but merely smiled and then retreated to her bed and turned away from Ainsley, clearly not used to friendliness. Smiling after her, Ainsley then recalled Heather's purpose for coming over, looking down at the letter, Ainsley again examined it again, and then it suddenly hit her.

'This was that letter that Rick gave me at the station!' Ainsley couldn't believe she'd forgotten about it. After all this time she was sure it must've been confiscated or destroyed, but miraculously it hadn't. Feeling overjoyed by this, not only that she was about to get a new bit of information, but also that this would confirm her sanity, at least in part, Ainsley giddy in her approach, opened the letter.

XXVI. The Historian's Son

The gleaming white medical van pulled up the driveway of Singing Loons, from her perch on the seventh floor of the institution, Ainsley could tell that this wasn't the typical case. Being followed in by a police cruiser and a finely crafted limousine, Ainsley instantly knew whoever this Patrick was, he was rich, or came from money.

Stepping out of the medical van, a feeble young man collapses into the waiting wheelchair prepared by the nurses. Ainsley couldn't make out much of him other than his traditional white-garbed patient shirt and trousers. Heading inside with the policeman following closely behind, Ainsley turned her attention to the particularly peculiar presence of the limousine. Pulling forward as the vehicles in front pull away from the entrance, Ainsley listens closely as it goes under the flying-buttressed entrance.

"Click."

Ainsley hears the opening of the door.

"SLAM"

And the abrupt closing of it.

Bolting from her seat, Ainsley makes for the long corridor that provides the singular entrance and exit of Ward 7, flying by the startled patients and equally startled nurses, Ainsley lightly crashes into the grated rail of the spiral stairwell. Peering downward she can see the entourage of newcomers all standing in the same place she once did way back when.

Ainsley can't make out what the police officer is saying to the triage nurse, but she guesses it has something to do with the explanation of whom the man in the wheelchair is and why he's here. Looking at him, getting a much better view of him Ainsley can see that he is limp in his chair, zoned out and not paying attention to the proceedings around him, his skin seemed to be an angry reddish color, peculiar to see. Leaning down, Ainsley now sees the face of the man whom she speculates must've been from the limo. A well dressed man, a given since how he arrived, this man appeared to be in his late 60s. What hair he had, was silver and slicked back in a very sensible way, reminding Ainsley of some sort of butler. However it was clear that this man was no butler. But the way he gently spoke to the despondent individual who apparently was named Patrick, Ainsley could only assume that he was the young man's father.

Patting Patrick on the back, the man gently wrapped his arms around him and gave him a delicate hug then without so much as a word, vanished from Ainsley's sight.

Having finished all the arrangements, the policeman gently traded off Patrick to the triage nurse who carted him away, presumably to the elevator. Running back now away from the stairwell, Ainsley went to take a seat in the circle of chairs and couches that was used as the main announcement center. Sitting down, Ainsley waited. This had become a tradition for her, whenever a new patient arrived, she' spot them from her seat facing the entrance, watch their admittance then run to Singing Loon's then would bound back to the circle and get a good seat before everyone else had any clue of what was occurring. The doctors noted this as a slight case of obsessive-compulsive behavior, Ainsley didn't care, and she had stopped listening to them a long time ago, and just mused at their new theory on her reasoning for being here. Even if they were right, it was only because she was in here that she picked it up. If she never came her, she'd have no use for it.

Heart racing from excitement, Ainsley looked expectantly at the glass in which Nurse Binny and some of her subordinates all graciously read the faxed information of their new patient, and just like clockwork, Nurse Binny went to the overhead.

"Attention folks! Attention, we've got an announcement, meeting in thirty seconds!"

And with that she clicked off and exited the glass room and approached the opening of the circle. All the patients on hand casually gathered, some sitting to the left and right of Ainsley, most standing not really caring enough to make it to a seat. Once everyone had arrived, Nurse Binny quietly whispered to a young blonde nurse at her side who silently complied and walked off to the elevator. "Alright folks! Big day, like some of you must remember, today is the day that we have a new friend joining our clan!" Mathilda Binny always spoke like everything, even the stuff that was downright depressing, was good news. "His name is Patrick McHoullagan, and ah, here he is!" Side stepping out of the way, most of the ward gasps at the horrid appearance of Patrick. Ainsley instantly knew now why he appeared so reddish in the stairwell. He was horribly burned, head to toe. No hair left on him, his skin had become tough and warped due to its terrible experience in flames. Glaring around the room with his one eye that wasn't hidden partially by melted over flesh, Patrick went to open his stiff mouth. "Its nice to meet you all." He spoke quietly, Ainsley could tell that alone hurt him to say. Receiving no response from the shocked ward, Nurse Binny quickly jumped in. "Well Patrick, its nice to meet you too, and I'm sure I and everyone here on 7 will get to know you much MUCH better." Mathilda glared at all of us, particularly Ainsley. She had never liked her incessant conversations with everyone about their pasts; she thought it was unwise to bring up anyone's past, let alone criminals. But Ainsley very much disagreed, despite what pleasures she got out of listening to everyone's intriguing pasts, she could see that even though for most it was tough to talk about, they seemed generally happier about it. Every time they all seemed happier after they got it out. But just looking at Patrick's tortured face, Ainsley could tell that getting him to talk about his past, would be nothing short of miraculous.

After the short meeting disbanded, and all the patients and staffing spread out to their usual places. Ainsley just sat there, rudely staring at Patrick who was left to his own devices. Which seemed odd to Ainsley cause it was clear he couldn't move on his own accord. "Could you stop staring at me please?" pleaded Patrick, aching as he spoke every syllable. Realizing her rudeness, Ainsley quickly broke her gaze and rose and walked over to the crippled Patrick. "Oh I'm so sorry, I do that sometimes, it has nothing to do with you, I'm sorry though." Patrick didn't deem this worthy of a response and just glared up at her with his slightly odd looking good eye. Now being closer, Ainsley could tell it was because his eyelashes were undeniably missing. Feeling pressured under his invasive stare, Ainsley lowered herself slightly and extended her hand to his one good hand. She received no such handshake. Feeling slightly put off by this, she retracted.

"I'm sorry, I suffer from severe nerve damage, and I have no control over most of my body." Confessed Patrick, seeing Ainsley's hurt predisposition. "Oh my goodness that's horrible!" spoke Ainsley, feeling very bad for thinking this was an ordinary person she spoke to. In hindsight she wondered why she ever thought he would be able to do such a thing.

"That's not what's horrible; you know what's horrible?" Ainsley shook her head quizzingly. "Living."

And so over then next couple hours, Ainsley learned more about the young man named Patrick. She learned that he came from mass amounts of wealth, which granted him the opportunity to attend any university he so chose, and go into any line of business if he ever wanted to. Basically granting him freedom from responsibility. Listening to this, made Ainsley extremely jealous, not of not having freedom from responsibility, being locked up here imprisoned her to it, no what bothered her was not having freedom.

"So how did you end up here?" Ainsley was trying to keep his recap short seeing that every moment he spoke was excruciating for him. "My father, he is a, or rather was a world famous Historian before he passed, he owned a massive collection of rare texts. One day when I went to visit him in his study, I found him keeled over, face flat in a book, one I had never seen." Ainsley instantly took interest in this, seeing as over her short life, mysterious happenings around books, caused by books had become somewhat of a metal, her being a magnet, attracting these strange occurrences to her. Her book, and all the strange events in Maltyrn, Lia's Notebook which has fallen of the face of the earth, the staff denying its very existence; and now this book… Ainsley quiets her thoughts seeing Patrick has halted his story seeing her far away thoughts.

"I'm sorry please continue." He does so without acknowledgement. "I pulled his face back from the book and found that his face was gone." "Gone?" queried Ainsley. "Gone, as in someone took an eraser to it, just blank skin, no eyes, no hair, no lips, nose nothing." This alarmed Ainsley, she had recalled once that the Voice warned that anyone attempting to read a

173

Sevardinals book was unable to; she was now thinking that perhaps this very book was one of those cases. Realizing this deserved some sort of response; Ainsley awkwardly said, "I'm so sorry."

This caught Patrick off guard, making him strain to raise his head to make eye contact with Ainsley. "You, you believe me?" he said, "of course I do, why wouldn't I?" Looking down once more, Patrick looked more miserable than ever. "Because no one ever does, even the crazies; the doctors claimed I was hallucinating." "Why would they say that?" Before he could answer, Nurse Binny returned to his side, chipper as ever. "Okay Patrick let me give a quick tour around the place, and then we'll set you up in your own room. Grabbing hold of the handles of his wheelchair, Ainsley just watched as he was drove off down the hall, looking back carelessly as he listened to the mindless garb of Mathilda. And as he disappeared into the men's washroom, Ainsley had two thoughts then and there, 'why does he get his own room, and why doesn't anyone believe him?'

A few days passed with no appearance from Patrick, he was set up in the cages along with all the other dangerous patients, but unlike everyone else's basic set up, his cage was fitted with curtains that swept all round blinding him from the world, and shutting Ainsley out. It wasn't fancy curtains, the kind you'd expect to see ripped from a hospital room, the kind that partitioned patients apart, in meager attempts of privacy. At night, during Ainsley's occasional trip to the wash room she could see the makeshift room light up from candlelight, similar to how a young child makes a fort at night. Every time she saw this, Ainsley had the strongest urge to wander over and see if she could make out what he was doing, and why a burn victim and obvious suicide case was allowed an open flame. But she never did. Instead she always wandered back to her bed in the grand circle that made up the general sleeping quarters.

Nights had become Ainsley's only solace in this place, she loved to listen to people; hear all their varying sleeping patterns, watch as some flail about in their sleep, while others appear as still as unwrapped mummies. And when that got boring, she'd wander the halls, discretely of course, learning over the years when the nurses took their breaks where she could easily wander with no worries and where it was most dangerous. The caged village as some of the patients referred it as, was on of those places. Being the most dangerous, not only to others but more importantly to themselves, these poor individuals were under constant watch every moment of every day; while they slept, ate, peed, pooped, showered, everything. There was no privacy for these people. Which is why Patrick's apparent grant to such privacy seemed so peculiar. Standing at the threshold of the long hallway containing the washrooms and general sleeping quarters and the common room, the furthermost she could wander without being questioned or forced to return to her room, Ainsley stood there and watched.

The silhouette of Patrick was very distinct, given his feeble stature, however unlike the last time she saw him Ainsley could've sworn he was leaning forward, almost as if he was writing something, which she initially thought was impossible for him.

Dying of curiosity, Ainsley was almost about to relent and once again return to her room when suddenly, almost as if timed, Patrick let out a pained scream and Ainsley watched as he fell out of his chair and landed hard on the floor, toppling whatever fire he was allowed to have. And just like that the gentle twilight it provided turned into a maniacal white flame, blinding out his figure. Ainsley was still in a state of shock as a barrage of nurses and doctors, seemingly appeared out of nowhere, coming from all over the ward, even from lower wards and converged on Patrick's cell. Swinging it open, the first man there, a male nurse, young looking with pointy, gelled hair braced himself as the flame almost threw him back like a wild beast taking a swipe at a person. This instantly reminded Ainsley of the Giant Deer she and Eye faced in the woods now so long ago.

Rushing into the flames, several nurses dragged Patrick out with a small flame on his leg a doctor quickly threw over his jacket onto it and doused it. Then, like clockwork, a stretcher emerged from the elevator, rolling frantically over to the scene at hand the group now assembled gently lifts Patrick onto the stretcher, Ainsley can't make out if he's breathing or not, but the doctors seem to think its serious cause they run full speed back to the elevator, taking him presumably down to the basement where there operating rooms and infirmary were located.

Now suddenly alone on the ward, having been completely ignored by the staff, Ainsley's need to know what he was doing gets the better of her and she runs to the cell. With the curtains now on flames, Ainsley peers in, blinded by how bright and hot the flames are in such close proximity to her face, Ainsley can only make out some black lump splayed out on the floor of the room, though not being able to figure out what I is, she quickly darts in, making a beeline directly for the mysterious object and grabs it. Standing in place, Ainsley looks round, losing sense of direction given the adrenaline pumping through her, she swivels round and for a brief moment swears she sees a man standing in the door. Tall and brooding, hooded in an old-fashioned black velvet hood, Ainsley couldn't make out his face or anything else for that matter. 'Death' Ainsley thought, 'Death has come for me'. Raising its hands, the figure slowly points to the object in Ainsley's hand.

Looking down, Ainsley sees now what it is that she's holding. A book; much like, but not exactly like the one she had been given charge of caring for and using to document the history of the other world; the place she had been told repeatedly did not exist, and that was a figment of her imagination.

Looking back up to the figure, Ainsley was shocked to see no one standing there. Not having time to wonder if it was a hallucination, or something more, Ainsley speeds out of the cage and quickly dives for cover in the woman's washroom. And just in time too. Because as she lay against the wall just inside the room, she could see nurses returning with firemen, all of who rapidly enter and begin to extinguish the flames as best they could. As she watched them spray the flames with chemical retardant, Ainsley noticed that none of the other patients were in their cages either. She didn't recall them being let out at the break of the fire. But they must've. Which made her beg the question. "How long was I standing there looking at that figure?"

Quietly tip toeing back to the sleeping quarters, which were buzzing with renewed life, in the wee hours of the morning. Ainsley silently walked in, hands gripped round the book, ignoring several more mild mannered patients asking her what happened. Sitting down on her bed, Ainsley suddenly felt a great sweeping euphoria of sleep take hold, and without a moment's notice passed out.

XXVII. Last Opportunities

The night was dreamless, though Ainsley wished it hadn't been. She wished she dreamt of all the possibilities the book held, what that figure she saw in the door way represented, and most importantly of all, who was this Patrick really?

Sitting casually in her oversized leather chair. Ainsley turned the chair from the window, seeing no interest out in the real world when in her little twisted fantasy of reality, so much chaos was occurring. Patients were running rampant, it was as if every patient had somehow skipped their medication and instead somehow been injected with mass quantities of caffeine. Patients were giddily running up and down the ward, racing one another, tackling the nurses who desperately chased them. Several of the female patients, who Ainsley knew had problems with boundaries exposed themselves and walked stark naked around the common room, repeatedly asking all that past by them grotesque things 'like what you see sugartits?' or 'you wish you had my knockers don't you doc?'

Ainsley knew by the seemingly overwhelming amount of white robbed officials around that many must've been called from their duties on lower levels to subdue the madness that had overtaken the ward. Starting to laugh to herself, Ainsley couldn't help but be amused by all this. It was times like this that she knew she wasn't psychotic, where mentally unstable patients saw a fire in the common room as a meteor crashing in their ward, and tiny aliens crawling up their arms, Ainsley saw the truth. Or at least what she presumed to be the truth. That Patrick accidentally or otherwise intentionally light his cell on fire. And in doing so, forgot the book.

Lovingly holding it in her smooth hands, Ainsley felt no fear holding it out on the floor, ever since Nurse Chu's departure, personal possessions had become more common, though things deemed too dangerous where still confiscated. Flipping it over constantly in her hands, Ainsley was almost certain that what she held now was a sibling of her own personal copy. Being charred black, Ainsley could see that though the hardened leather was now dark, that it had once been a deep mahogany. Unlike her own which seemed to be akin to her hair color, a lush deep golden brown. Baring almost an identical locking mechanism on the lid of the book Ainsley dutifully noted that the lock was indeed broken. Not by the fire it endured last night, it appeared untouched by the flames, with no soot, or warped metal. No, instead it looked to have been tampered with somehow, almost as if someone picked it open. Patrick's silhouette flashed through her mind, remembering thinking he was writing something, but now thinking he was the one responsible for this defacement of the one and only security feature of this ever special book.

Being very careful not to open it, Ainsley carefully wrapped it in her supplied ward 7 button up sweater and then eased down between the cushion and armrest of her faithful chair. Ainsley knew after years of living here, that this would indeed be the safest place for something of such value. Having made friends, or at least friendly acquaintances with all of the patients and most of the regular nurses, Ainsley knew, that they knew to leave her chair alone. So feeling safe in leaving behind her book, knowing it wouldn't suffer the fate of the last two books taken from her keeping, Ainsley rose from her chair, taking in the bedlam of ward 7 one more time before taking in a deep sigh and thinking to herself 'I have to know more about Patrick.'

Having overheard several out of breath nurses rapidly informing one another as to what happened last night and where Patrick was taken, Ainsley knew that her suspicions were correct, and he was moved to the basement; the infirmary.

Over the years, Ainsley had grown close to her first friendly acquaintance at Singing Loons, that being Lia. Growing in to a sort of bigger sister role, Lia would often sneak Ainsley out of 7 and take her on tours of the rest of the facility, which surprising even to Ainsley, was gigantic. Bigger than she could have possibly imagined. Upon her initial once over when she got out of the police cruiser all those years ago, Ainsley had spected the place at 7 stories, which was dead on, if you don't count the ground floor as a story. 7 stories, for 7 wards, and the main floor contained the common area, and occasional sleeping quarters for the staffing, as well as the storage area for most of the laundry and medical supplies. Each floor was just as unspectacular as the last, same identical floor design, same paint job, and same amount of stuffy patients. In fact if it weren't for the signage proudly displayed at the entrance to each ward, Ainsley was convinced she would be unable to decipher them.

After the first year, Lia was promoted to Head Nurse of ward 3, not the most gracious of promotions, but still gave her privileged information about the more advanced functions of the innocent sounding Singing Loons. Climbing into the elevator, Lia took Ainsley all the way down, further than Ainsley had ever been allowed to venture before, to the basement. Lia spoke of it as having nothing to do really with Singing Loons, that it dealt more with scientific and R and D as she put it, which Ainsley didn't understand at first, but later learned meant research and development. Pulling the grated enclose back from the much more dingy looking basement of Singing

Loons, Ainsley mindlessly stepped out only to see that she wasn't accompanied. Turning back, she saw Lia standing still in the elevator, looking uncertain, which for Lia, was unusual. She generally had such a rebellion to rules. "I'm not so sure this was a good idea I showed you this Ains..." nervously spoke Lia, "not even us Heads are allowed down here..."

"Why though? If it's apart of Singing Loons, shouldn't you be allowed to come and go as you please? Besides, you said the infirmary was down here, so it's got to be part of your guys turf right?" Lia only slightly nodded her head. Ainsley doubled back to Lia, and gently pulled on her arm, encouraging her accompaniment.

"What are you two doing down here??!!" Came a booming voice from down the dimly light hall. Turning Ainsley saw standing what appeared to be a soldier of some sort, fully suited in black body armor, somewhat resembling SWAT attire, but no abbreviations to state it as such. Though this soldier had no weapons visibly on him, Lia panicked and quickly pulled Ainsley back into the elevator and cranked it back to 7. "Who was that?"

Lia, who anxiously looked up at the old fashioned arrow of the elevator as it measured the floors approaching 7, simply stated, "R and D".

That was the last time Ainsley ever heard from Lia, at first she assumed that she was just busy with her duties on 3, but one day, missing her friend, Ainsley snuck into the elevator carrying a ditzy nurse humming away some irritable tune as she jotted down notes on her pad, Ainsley herself couldn't believe her aloofness to the world, seeing as she was crouched right beside her. Exiting on 3 she casually blended into the crowd of free moving patients. Having less severe psychological impairments and no criminal entanglements, Ward 3, was your typical voluntary psychiatric ward, most if

181

not all patients were self admitted, for numerous reasons, most being, depression, bi polar. Or what Ainsley quietly suspected, was merely to escape life, if not for a moment. She herself could relate.

Looking at the glass enclosed desk Ainsley saw no sign of Lia, whirling rounding place, she could seen no sign of her on the ward. Looking at the time, she knew that she should be here, lunch was over not 2 hours ago, and a group meeting was immanent. "People listen up! Group meeting 2 minutes!" Spoke a deep masculine voice, turning, Ainsley saw a strikingly good looking nurse standing beside her, demanding the attention of the room, with a solid look of determination on his face this nurse quickly detected he had eyes on him. "Can I help you miss?"

Caught off guard by the sudden question, Ainsley timidly asked, "Do you know where Lia is?" the man looked at Ainsley with confusion written all over his face. "I'm sorry, but I don't know who you are, or what floor your supposed to be on, but Lia has been removed from this facility."

Ainsley couldn't believe it. "What? Why?" "Its none your business, now if you'll excuse me, I have a meeting to head." It was only then, as the man turned away from Ainsley, that she noticed the badge on his chest reading 'HEAD NURSE'.

Ainsley never did discover what happened to her lone friend. But she suspected it had to do with that basement, and that guard. So now, with double the need and with just under 3 days until Rhapsody arrived, Ainsley saw this as her last opportunity to find out the mysteries of the Singing Loon's basement.

XXVIII. The Basement

She wasn't stopped on her way to the elevator, Patrick's accident, and resulting chaotic morning thereafter made sure of that. Calmly entering the relatively new elevator, Ainsley silently pushed the lowest floor and watched the doors close dutifully. As they closed she noticed she was being watched, no not by any official, but by the little girl all those years ago who gave her Rhapsody's letter, and ultimately, brought Ainsley back to life.

Heather, as she was simply called, hadn't been at Singing Loon's long, a mere month. But over that time she mostly kept to herself, the incident with her and Ainsley occurred in her last week. So Ainsley didn't get an opportunity to learn about her. All she knew was that she was a suicide case, and that this girl saw something in Ainsley that brought on a sole act of kindness that Ainsley figured wasn't common for this solemn girl.

And as quickly as there moment together came, it vanished, the girl with the letter, finally succeeded in her escape from the world, slitting her wrists in a shower stall in the middle of the night. Ainsley overheard one of the nurses crudely commenting "she went down the street, not across it." Which meant that Heather slit her wrists along the veins, rather than severing it. Resulting in a much wider opening in her flesh. She was dead before long before the night watch ever found her.

But even though she knew this, knew that Heather, the girl who if she had more time with, could have become a good friend of hers, just like her old best friend from back home was. Even though she knew she was long gone, here she stood, just as she was that night, sadly admiring Ainsley, almost as if she knew what would result in Ainsley's departure into the basement. But as the doors finally shut, Ainsley quickly dismissed this thought, and the thought of seeing Heather.

Watching the old arrow slowly skirt along the numbers leftward, and downward toward "B" Ainsley thought how heavily her mind had been warped by her stay within the walls of Singing Loons. When she entered, she was a bright, charismatic girl, with a dark sense of humor and perhaps a flare for imagination, but growing up in her family demanded it. But now, after years of drug endorsed emptiness, and an overwhelming sense of betrayal by all those who she thought cared about her. Rhapsody, who had promised in his letter that he would rescue her, that he would save her from her plight, no matter what, had yet to do so, yes, he was finally coming but 3 years late. Not only did this frustrate Ainsley beyond all belief, but it hurt her for reasons she couldn't fully understand, she barely knew the man, she didn't know if he was reliable or even safe to trust. But despite her hesitations, her gut told her she could trust him. And she learned to live by her gut. As well as her mom… Ainsley didn't know what to make of her actions, they seemed so heinous, so cruel and inhuman, Ainsley often avoided thinking of such things, not wanting to break down, especially knowing doing so would only result in extra dosages of medicine and more meetings with doctors, which she had weaned down to once a week.

Ainsley missed who she was. All she felt was hatred and loneliness.

The elevator door opened silently, snapping Ainsley back to reality. Sliding the old grating away revealing the grimy basement floor. It looked just as it had that day Lia showed her it. As if it had been untouched since then.

Stepping out into the dimly light hall. Ainsley suddenly got a cold shudder whip through her body, a bad sign. This always occurred when something bad was about to happen. It was the Voice's way of trying to defend Ainsley in its limited state. But, unlike the last three years, in which Ainsley religiously followed her gut, Ainsley chose, just this once that she couldn't listen to it. She had to know.

Walking down the hall, Ainsley could hear only the sporadic humming of the twitching green fluorescents overhead and the light pats of her feet on the damp tiled floor. Coming to the end of the hall, which strangely enough held no doors in it, Ainsley found herself perplexed by this. 'Why would they design a hallway that has no rooms adjoined to it? Surely in a hospital that would be a necessity, storage?' But as Ainsley looked round the corner she saw something that she was sure was an illusion.

Doors upon doors upon doors, down the longest hallway imaginable; going off into the horizon.

Ainsley just stood there, looking down the hallway, shocked. She couldn't believe it. She never imagined this place could be this big. It didn't seem possible, or logical. 'What's the purpose of all these? What are they for? Where do they lead to?' Forgetting for a moment all about Patrick and the infirmary, Ainsley approached the first door on the left hand side. Pale green and rotting, the door, identical to the rest, stood contrast against the bland white tiled wall. Grabbing the aged steel knob, Ainsley turns it and opens.

She doesn't know what to expect, patients, and medical supplies, even offices. But instead, what she finds, she can find no reason for in a hospital.

Books. Lots of books.

185

Stacked up high, some boxed, some placed carefully on shelves, but most just laying in a pile on the floor. Ainsley just looked on, unable to process why they were here. And these weren't medical journals, or scientific magazines, hell they weren't even regular magazines, which Ainsley could understand perhaps, for waiting rooms and such. But not this, these weren't typical bouts of literature; these were things that were for lack of a better word, priceless.

Picking up one book and carefully examining it, Ainsley suddenly realized she was holding a diary, not of anyone she personally knew, but someone named Alexander Dumas, dated 1834, very old, Ainsley knew that even if she didn't know who this was, it must've been very valuable. All of these must've been, which made her beg the question once more. 'What are all these books doing here?'

And so it went, opening door upon door, and seeing the same identical scene, books, books, and books. Over and over, never ending, after 10 doors left ajar, Ainsley knew that it was pointless to see anymore, she could predict what they held. Ainsley just couldn't fathom it.

'Possibly the world's largest collection of literature nestled away in the dank basement of a crummy psychiatric hospital, why?'

This then led Ainsley back to the hallway, stretching onward into eternity. And suddenly it hit Ainsley. 'This isn't just a hallway in a hospital… it's a tunnel.'

Taking off in a light sprint, Ainsley briskly runs down the hallway, not bothering anymore with the doors that surely hold more books. Feeling sicker as she runs, Ainsley takes in deep gasps of breath, overcoming the urge to vomit, and keeps going. It isn't long until the seemingly endless tunnel, begins to thin out. Revealing that she was indeed right. Because at the other end of the Singing Loon's basement hallway… was a frosted glass door, with the etchings "S.L.C" inscribed on it.

Carefully opening the door, Ainsley suddenly enters into a whole new world; separate from the world she's known for the past 3 years.

Beyond the glass door, lies a massively wide room, well heated, not too hot, and not too cold, with air that almost tasted of lavender. The lights were overpowering, similar to the lighting you'd see in supermarkets, leaving not one inch of the room in darkness. The walls were basic concrete, but well maintained, with massive ventilation shafts overhead, being the only noise coming from the room. All this alone was impressive, but what was even more impressive was the immaculate maze of bookshelves spanning from here to nowhere.

Ainsley had never thought of herself as a patron of culture, or literature, much preferring a good song, or game of street hockey when she could find a game. But as she looked on what must be the most breathtaking display of collective culture in the world, she couldn't help but stand there breathless.

It was beautiful. So beautiful Ainsley didn't notice the eyes watching her.

XXIX. The Man with the Kane

They stared out, from amongst the barrage of history and fiction; unwavering as they watched Ainsley. She was so taken by the glorious sight of the collection; she didn't think to check to see if coast is clear. If she had, she would have seen him, aged and withered, grasping to life's final thread, approaching ever so caustically.

"What are you doing here?" came the voice emerging from one of the many walls of the books, startling Ainsley into finding its source. Turning to the center of the voice, Ainsley was surprised to see a mouse of a man standing before her, standing barely above her waist, clinging desperately to an undersized cane. Raising his gaze to rest upon Ainsley's less startled face, he looked disapprovingly at her; similar to how Abigail would show her distain for Ainsley's horrific jokes that she would occasionally make.

Looking down at him, Ainsley couldn't help but think how out of character his voice was to his stature.

Growing impatient with Ainsley mindlessly staring down at him, the man repeated once more. "I said what are you doing here girly?"

Snapping out of her stupor, Ainsley quickly remembered why she initially came down here and responded, "Oh sorry, no I'm not, I was trying to find the infirmary? A friend of mine was taken there last night?" Searching the man's eyes, Ainsley could see a faint flicker of sadness cross them. "You speak of the crippled fireboy right?"

Ainsley let out slight gasp of relief, "Yes, have you seen him? Where is he?" Ainsley had to stop herself, realizing her obvious err of desperation. The man just crinkled his paper-thin face into a smile.

"He's dead."

Ainsley fell deaf for just a moment, listening to her heartbeat, recalling every limited memory she had of the poor man from New York. His downtrodden stare, his small fickle frame, his pained breath. Ainsley didn't realize how much of an affect Patrick had on her in such a short space of time.

"What?" she finally responded.

"You heard me, now if you please, you have overstayed your welcome." Tersely spoke the man, poking at Ainsley with his cane, attempting to push her back to the door. Ainsley didn't stop him from pushing.

"What happened?" Ainsley's asked, not honestly expecting anything. Sighing the man, attempting to hide his quickened breaths from being either out of shape or too old or both, brought his hand to his mouth and patted it with a handkerchief with the flame red letters 'L.S.' woven upon it.

"I put him out of his misery." Exclaimed the man. This stopped Ainsley, and she no longer let him push her to the door. A trembling began inside her, deep; igniting a wave of emotion Ainsley was certain she no longer was capable of expressing. And before she knew what she was thinking or, what the repercussions would be, Ainsley let her hand fly full across the old man, tackling him to the floor with a soft thud.

Just as shocked as Ainsley was at her actions, the man, trying desperately to prop himself up onto his cane, fiercely stared at Ainsley. "What's your problem lady?! He was dying there was nothing any of us could do for him, I set him free!"

Feeling nothing but rage and a subtle shock and at her actions, Ainsley got hung up on just one word that came out of the short man's mouth.

"Us?"

The man led Ainsley through the endless library, walking surprisingly fast for his age and stubby legs. Turning occasionally left and more often than not right, making Ainsley think that perhaps her suspicions of this place being a maze were correct. After what felt like a dizzying marathon of twists and turns, Ainsley and the little man emerge from the shelves at the far wall of the subterranean warehouse and look upon nothing but barren concrete.

Not waiting for Ainsley's guaranteed questioning, the man walks a few paces to the left to a small hole innocently punctured through the wall. Raising his cane, he gently inserts the gold tipped end into the hole and twists carefully.

And before the both of them, the walls began to moan, and ache as they stiffly started to separate to reveal a narrow pass. Feeling unsure of being so confined, Ainsley hesitated, as the man slowly entered the pass, not caring if she followed.

As he disappeared into the darkness of the wall, Ainsley, suddenly feeling very alone and vulnerable, anxiously forced her way into the passage.

It was dark; Ainsley couldn't even see directly in front of her face, it gave her the impression that this was what to be blind. Not being able to hear the foot falls of the man in front of her, Ainsley started to feel as if it were a mistake following him, maybe she should have listened to her gut, the voice that had tried so diligently to keep her out of harms way. Instead she was uncomfortably cramped, trying to navigate this ominous tunnel in an even more ominous basement.

Just as she had decided to turn back, light broke through on the other side, not strong light like the type found in both the hospital and the warehouse of books she just left, no a soft candle light peacefully flickered back upon Ainsley's face as she excitedly pushed her way through the final leg of the passage.

Emerging on the other side, she first located the man, seeing him busying himself with what appeared to be tea. Seeing that first off he wasn't imaginary and also that he wasn't attempting to lead Ainsley into an ambush, Ainsley relaxed slightly, and took in her surroundings.

The overhead was low, barely tall enough to accommodate Ainsley's normal height, but just barely. The walls weren't like the concrete of the warehouse; they were earthy, made of what looked like solidified, or fossilized soil. Hardened over centuries, to create a small little cave, accessible only by this man's cane. In the cave with them was a petite four-poster bed, obviously designed specifically for the short man, looking almost comical in both size and location. Besides that, which dominated the room, there was a small wooden table and two stools that quaintly matched, as well as a makeshift fire oven bored out of the wall. But what caught Ainsley amongst all the truly peculiar furnishings was the minute bookshelf nestled kiddy corner to the bed.

Walking over to it, Ainsley leaned down and pulled out book at random, examining it; she noticed it held the same similar bizarre markings as her old book did.

Turning holding two cups of tea, the man loomed over Ainsley, clearly not pleased with her intrusion.

"Put that back now!" spat the man, roughly placing the tea down on top of the shelf and snatching the book away from Ainsley, and submerging it once more in its resting place, almost as if Ainsley had unearthed a dead relative of the mans.

Backing away from the man as he busied himself with resetting the book, Ainsley bumped her back into the bed, realizing just how small this space truly was.

Turning to face Ainsley once more, the man, who Ainsley was quickly, coming to see was a very sour individual, glared at her. "Don't you ever touch anything without permission!" Feeling slightly frightened, Ainsley just nodded and attempted to not look awkward, sweating under the man's gaze.

Seeing this, the man, eased his temper and began to observe Ainsley. Focusing on her face, he saw nothing special, her long brown hair, reaching far down her back, in dire need of maintenance. Her bodice, supple and truly breathtaking in appearance, but neglected, and appearing a ghoulish pale color. Finally his gaze rested upon Ainsley's hands, and it was here than his eyes bolted open.

Darting forward without explanation, the man quickly enveloped Ainsley's delicate fingers, and rolled them over again and again in his hands, attempting to feel as much of her skin as possible.

Beyond confused by this act, Ainsley contented her self with just watching him, hoping for a reason to present itself.

Dragging her over to the lone candle, the man held each and every of her fingers up to the light, looking at them as if they were cells of film. Finally releasing her, the man excitedly looks up at her once more, all notions of hatred or contempt gone from his face, instead, what Ainsley saw was a man beyond happy.

"What's your name child?" he kindly asked. "Its Ainsley…" responded Ainsley not sure why now the man took an interest in her. "I bet that's the only name you got ain't it?" said the man knowingly.

Ainsley was speechless, never had someone guessed that she only had a first name. She attempted to respond, but was too slow to it.

"And I bet, you like to read don't you? Old books, none of that rubbish they publish today, you like these kind of books?" said the man referencing his bookshelf filled with ancient literary wonders. Ainsley couldn't figure which of the millions of questions she had should come first, so instead thought of the simplest one. "Who, who are you?"

Smiling, and walking once more over to Ainsley, the man rested his arthritis-ridden hands, which Ainsley only now realized were covered with tattoos similar to that of her books, and knowingly looked up at Ainsley and said.

"No child, the question you should be asking is… who are you?"

XXX. Q &A

'Who am I?' the thought looped over and over in Ainsley's head, she was unsure of what exactly this old man meant by those words, but for some reason, she couldn't get it out. "Who am I?" Ainsley uttered aloud, seeing if it made more sense vocalized, but it didn't.

Coming back to the moment at hand, Ainsley looked back down at the man who held the most winning smile imaginable, as if he'd just solved the world's hardest puzzle. "Come child, please sit. So I may better explain." Spoke the man offering his hand to her; accepting Ainsley carefully sat on the nearest stool to her.

Venturing over to the shelf where he left his cups of tea, the man quickly returned holding them, slightly cooled, and set them down on the rickety table.

All was quiet for a moment, as he took a sip, almost as if he needed that sip to conjure up all that needed to be said. Then setting it back down, the man finally looked to Ainsley.

"So tell me, Ainsley, have you come into possession of any books recently?" nonchalantly asked the man, almost as if he were asking about the weather. Feeling slightly guarded given her experience in the past with such questions, Ainsley hesitated, considering the man. "Maybe" she said, hoping that would be enough. It was. "Ah, I see, and tell me, did you by chance inherit a house?" Ainsley was speechless, "How could you know that?" she gasped, instantly regretting saying as such. But no harm was to come the man merely chuckled, enjoying his line of questioning too much.

"Ah but Ainsley, I know many things you couldn't possibly dream of knowing… but perhaps for the sake of catching you up some, maybe it be best if I tell you what I know about you. Sound good?" asked the man, seeking permission, a luxury Ainsley wasn't used to. She nods tentatively.

"Alright then, I know this much; you are a relative, or close friend of a past Sevardinal, by the looks of you I'd say relative, which means since you are here, in this building of all buildings, as a patients I presume, that means you now are Sevardinal, and have fallen on hard times... how am I doing so far?" asked the man, staring up and away, lost in his predictions. Ainsley merely nodded, incapable of speech, hanging on every syllable spewing out of the man.

"So if all this is true, then that must mean you are the owner and guardian of one of the *Sevio Dionisus*..." Ainsley instantly snaps out of her trance; "Huh, the Sevio what?" she asked. "The *Sevio Dionisus*, a collection of 8, well 7 books, dating back long before the first documented book was published. Many consider them a fable, or unreal, due to their scarcity and lack of knowledge about them, only few have the privilege of that knowledge. If you are indeed an owner of one of these books, that means you've been to the land beyond then?!" excitedly proclaimed the man, looking expectantly to Ainsley for an answer. Feeling no longer like this man was a threat, seeing as he apparently knew everything she did, perhaps much more, Ainsley simply uttered, "Yes, I have been... twice."

This caused the man to retract in apparent disgust. "What? Only twice, what kind of Sevardinal are you girl? I mean I can see you've been detained here for a spat, but only twice? Surely you are mistaken?" "No, I, I went in once, not knowing I would, then once while I was sleeping. But I, I was interrupted men came for me. You see I was on the run and..." rambled Ainsley. "Hold on, you mean to tell me you've only been there twice, please tell me you've met with the council?" asked the man worriedly. Feeling a sudden jolt of guilt, and what's more worse, not knowing why, Ainsley just shook her head. This caused the man to fall silent, in disbelief.

"Unbelievable, the FTC has really lost their touch then…" said the man to himself more than anyone.

Sitting there, looking at the man, who was doing just what Artie was doing way back when, Ainsley suddenly tired of feeling stupid, and out of the know, and took command. "Look, I'm sick and tired you people doing this shit, saying you are going to explain things then fucking getting sidetracked and giving me half facts, or neglecting to tell me anything at all. I'm sick of it! Now I'm going to do the asking now!" Ainsley paused to gauge the man's reaction, seeing that he wasn't about to retaliate; Ainsley felt empowered in her resolve and continued. "Now tell me, who the hell are you? What is this place? Why are you here? That will be good for starters."

Smiling, the man kept his eyes locked on Ainsley's, almost as if he was testing her, see if she would crack, but the sheer act of his test, only maddened Ainsley more. "Alright Ainsley, alright, you are right, I'll tell you what you want to hear. My name is Leonardo Sevardina, this place is but one of thousands of safe houses for the SLC's or rather Sarah Lombard Collective's mass quantities of collected artifacts, as well as an adjoining prison of sorts for their enemies. I am one of those enemies."

Ainsley took a moment to digest the information. She then recalled something Leonardo mentioned back in the warehouse, about how there was nothing any of *us* could do. She now understood what he meant. "So what does that make me? What is Singing Loons then?"

"Singing Loons, is as you think it is, a psychiatric ward, but entwined in it, and without anyone's knowledge, except for a few key people, is a system that allows for the SLC to dispose of their political, cultural, and spiritual enemies. Its quite ingenious really, they dispatch us here as loons, and really, how can any of us explain otherwise? I mean look where we are? In a cave, attached to a massive room filled with books, underneath a mediocre psychiatric hospital? Sounds crazy to me. So I think you can figure what you are."

Secretly, Ainsley knew there had to be something more to Singing Loons, it felt very counter productive, even for a psych ward. But she never imagined her punishment was a common occurrence, that dozens, perhaps hundreds of people who, somehow, wronged the SLC, were subjected to ridicule and scrutiny, to defend themselves with what little proof they had, and to do so in a place where any action you make is a sign of some mental deformity. Leonardo was right it was genius, terrible but genius.

"I see... so, so what landed you in here? I mean what did you do?" asked Ainsley thinking of all the possible answers he could give. She did not expect the one she received. Dropping his perma-smile, just for a brief moment, Leonardo looked down to his tea, seeing his reflection whimper back at him. Sighing, he finally begins to speak. "That's not an easy story to tell child. It requires a very open mind, one most aren't capable of keeping..." Ainsley didn't respond, instead she reached out and gripped one of Leonardo's hands reassuringly, encouraging him to proceed.

"Very well... The first thing you have to know about me Ainsley is this... I'm old." Ainsley chuckled; thinking that much was obvious. "No, you don't understand, I'm not like the rest of you, not even you Sevardinal, I'm beyond old, so old I've given up keeping track of it in years..."

This confused Ainsley, causing her to ask the obvious question, "What do you keep track of it in?" Pulling his hand away from Ainsley's, Leonardo finally made eye contact with her. Taking a deep intake of breath, Leonardo simply said "Centuries."

Ainsley was gob smacked, she couldn't believe it, actually, she couldn't, and surely he must've been lying or severely exaggerating. But as she looked into his eyes, she could see something buried deep within, a sorrow, and an unquenchable thirst for the end, a longing for a way out. And it was only in his soft, faded blue eyes, that Ainsley knew he wasn't lying.

"So, how old are you then?" she calmly asked. Surprised to not be mocked, or laughed at, Leonardo couldn't help but break into a smile. "Well, in my case, I'm 70, century-years. So I'm actually roughly 7000, give or take a few decades." Leonardo let out a chuckle at his own surprise over his age. Ainsley couldn't say anything more than, "Wow."

Then they both broke out laughing. Both realizing simultaneously, yet hidden from one another, just how pleasant it was to spend time with someone who didn't initially think you were crazy.

The flames quietly cackled as a small grate lazily sat on top of it, frying a pair of fresh water salmon. Ainsley had lost track of time inside the cave of Leonardo Sevardina, unbeknownst to her, she had actually spent the entire day with him, and having done so, she had learned much more about the man. He himself was locked up because of his peculiar ability to withstand age, and for his intricate knowledge of *the land beyond* as he called it. A place he had actually been to when it existed way back when. It was where he was born; in the fourth trinity year of its existence; time that the Sevardinal knew as *The Witherney*. He informed Ainsley that each volume of the *Sevio Dionisus* was named something similar to *The Witherney*. They were known, in order as: *The Fools Wish, The Forgotten Throne, The Sevardinal, The Witherney, Violentus, Echelon,* and finally *Contraband*.

Seven in total, seven volumes, seven eras.

Pulling the hot grate from the fire, Leonardo, set it heavily down on the table and began to dissect the toasted fish, divvying them up into equal potions for himself and his guest. As they ate the juicy fish, Ainsley, for the first time in a long time, at ease, was overcome with billions of questions.

"So I'm Sevardinal right?" she asks. "Right?" "So what trinity year am I in charge of, I mean what era am I documenting?" Taking time to finish his chewing before responding, Leonardo bluntly says "Well describe your book to me, I can tell you then." Thinking hard, Ainsley recalls all her memories of the book. "I was large, very large, dark brown leather, with weird symbols splayed all over it, its spine was made up of thick leather straps, and it had a lock on it…" Speaking in a matter of fact tone, Leonardo says, "Those weird symbols you speak of are part of the *Sivianci* the divine language that gives you and your brethren power, its what allows you to speak with your dual consciousness', as well as each other, once you learn to use it properly. Its what also, governs the functionality of each volume. Many FTC and SLC scholars speculate that if these markings were razed from the tomes, the books would be destroyed. And there is some evidence in this in the *Natal*, the long lost record book of the Sevardinal Lineage." This piqued Ainsley's interest. "The *Natal*?" "Yes, it was the eight and final volume in the *Sevio Dionisus*, it held within it, each and every Sevardinal that was ever to be. From the land beyond's inception to its end of days." Explained Leonardo. "What happened to it then?" excitedly asked Ainsley, enthralled. Sighing, and looking down once more, playing with his food, Leonardo, fell silent for a moment. "That is a long story child, a story I'm afraid will have to wait until another time. All you need to know about it now is its gone. Oh, and as for which volume you possess, it's the third one; *The Sevardinal*. You should consider yourself lucky that is a very important era. Surely you know of the land beyond's global dependency on the numbers 3 and 7?" Ainsley just nods dismissively, as if to mutely express that she knew very well about it. "Well, same goes for the Sevardinal, I don't know what exactly occurs in that time frame, that's your job to find out." Leonardo chuckles, Ainsley says nothing, so he continues. "But what I do know is very important, and cataclysmic events occur in both the third and seventh trinity years. We can guess what happens in the seventh, the end of days. But not much is known about the third, or why the Sevardinal felt it above all other volumes, deserved the name *The Sevardinal*. But I have a feeling, and my feelings are very good, that you are the key to finding that out."

This caused Ainsley to feel a warm fuzzy sensation fill her entire being. For the first time in perhaps her entire life, she felt filled to the brim with a sense of purpose. Even before when Artie and the Voice tried to explain all this, she felt stupid and crazy for believing any of it. But when Leonardo spoke of it, in his cracked accent, and overwhelming confidence in what he said, Ainsley knew that all of it was true, that she wasn't crazy for believing it, for seeing it. She was a Sevardinal, and it was her job, nay, and her privilege to be part of a rare few of individuals who got to see and experience the world's last great mystery. Ainsley can't help but smile.

Letting out a drawn out yawn, Leonardo drops down from his stool, and approaches Ainsley, cane in hand. "Now my dear, it has been wonderful meeting you and chatting with you, but I am knackered, I need some rest." Standing, Ainsley follows him toward the identical hole in the wall. Placing his cane in it once more, the walls creak open. Too curious to leave without knowing, Ainsley asks, "How did you do that?" laughing torpidly, Leonardo turns to Ainsley. "My dear, being around 7000 years garners you a few perks. That's one of them, another is being able to recognize my own…"

This caught Ainsley off guard. "What do you mean?"

Smiling, Leonardo turns to the passage and makes his way out. Wanting answers, Ainsley quickly follows. Upon exiting, Leonardo keeps up his exceptional speed, though Ainsley notes, much slower than when heading the other way earlier. Seeing he was playing coy, or refusing to answer, Ainsley forces the issue; rushing ahead of the stout immortal, Ainsley blocks his way. "Leonardo, what did you mean?"

Sighing, once more, brandishing his initial condescending tone once more. Ainsley could see Leonardo was tiring of the questions, and more importantly, the company. "What I meant kid was I know a Sevardinal when I see one, I mean, I was one, once upon a time…" This surprises Ainsley, even though, given what Leonardo has told her, it really shouldn't. "How though?"

Removing a platinum lighter from his vest pocket, clearly the newest item he owned, Leonardo coldly grabs Ainsley's hand and holds it above the lighter as it ignites. "Do you see?" he asks. Ainsley isn't sure what he's meaning until she sees it. Something she thought impossible in in this world. White glow, pulsating out from the epicenter, positioned directly above the flame, the same white glow that Ainsley giddily mused herself with 3 years ago in the deserts of the other world. "I see it!" she says excitedly, glad to see, it, thinking of it as more proof she wasn't dreaming any of this up. "Do you know what that is?"

Ainsley then realized that the Voice never really explained it that well. So playing dumb Ainsley just shakes her head. "That, my child, is the sole factor that differentiates us from everyone else. It's our lifeline, our bloodline, brimming with power, and magic's that even after all this time, we have only just begun to fathom. What you see there child is proof, to me, to anyone else who catches it, that you are without a doubt, a Sevardinal."

Ainsley was amazed, looking down at the pulsing white plasma like substance as it rimmed away from the heat, Ainsley could only think to herself, giving into her immaturity for just a moment, 'Cool'.

Releasing her, and killing the flame, Leonardo moved onward towards the door. Leaving Ainsley to try and catch up.

"So does that mean I can open up doorways that aren't there?" excitedly asked Ainsley, to which Leonardo bored replies "Yes, that and much, much more."

Reaching the glass door, Ainsley stops, hand on the handle, and looks back. Standing there, somewhat impatiently, Ainsley can see she has time for only one more question before he goes ballistic. Carefully considering the millions she still possess, she settles on perhaps one of the simplest...

"I, I may not be here for much longer, yet I have so many questions... I guess what I'm trying to ask is this... Will I get to see you again?"

Breaking out of his scowl for just a moment, Leonardo steps forward and clasps his tiny hands over Ainsley's and looks up. "Not here now, no, but perhaps, someway down the line... Don't fret, I'm not the only one that knows these things, you will meet others, others who know more than either of us could ever possibly hope to learn alone. Just trust your urges, they are there to protect you. Just do that, and you'll be fine. Now go. Its late."

Feeling sedated with that remark, Ainsley sighs and turns to the door once more and opens it. As she walks through it, she hears over her shoulder Leonardo saying, "I'm sorry for your loss of your friend, he was taken to the morgue if you wish to see him still…" Ainsley only then realized how unbelievable she must've seemed, coming here to see her friend, and instead forgetting entirely about him. She hated herself immensely and promised she would go see him.

Turning to watch the glass door slowly air shut, Ainsley could see deep thought on Leonardo's face. Confused, Ainsley was about to say something when he shouts, "Look in 37 C and 37 G!" Shut. The door closes, and Ainsley can hear a vacuuming blur occur, and a latch lock. It occurred then and there that whatever occurred in that warehouse, in that cave, was on the good graces of someone unseen. Someone let her in. And now that she had left, someone was keeping her out.

XXXI. Last Days

It was breaking dawn by the time Ainsley emerged from the elevator, none had risen, and the hallways were blissfully, if not suspiciously vacant. Silently walking down the cold tiles, Ainsley felt a certain rush of hypersensitivity. All around her she heard and felt things most would over look. The humming of the fluorescent bulbs above, the low whish of the fans as they lazily drifted back and forth on their perches on several of the columns in the common room. A fly as it brashly banged against the outside of the window, trying desperately to get it in. And all Ainsley could think was, 'you don't want in here fly.'

Wasting no time in crossing the open space of the ward, Ainsley couldn't help but glance at taped off remains of Patrick's cell. And as she did, she couldn't help but feel almost responsible for its destruction. She didn't know why, she knew it wasn't her fault, nothing she said, or did could have prevented what occurred. But for whatever the reason, whether it was her guilt for completely forgetting about him once meeting Leonardo, or perhaps just the fact that she was the last person he ever met, and all she did was ask questions about his horrid history, a subject no one wants to have as their last conversation. But he did.

Exhaling a breath, Ainsley barges through the double doors of the sleeping quarters, not caring if she woke any of the patients still desperately clinging to whatever dreamless slumber they held. Flopping down on her spring-loaded bunk, Ainsley quickly wraps herself in her sheets and falls off to sleep.

She knew this was against the rules, she knew it would look suspicious, but she didn't care, all she wished for was the night to come, so she may once more wander off into the *infirmary* where Patrick was supposed to be, but wasn't... As she lay there, listening to the rustling from the bunks near her, knowing they would all soon rise and she'd be alone in the quarter, Ainsley couldn't help but go over all that Leonardo said.

'What does it all mean? So what if I'm actually what he and Artie say I am? Some mythical writer who documents some long forgotten lands history? God, why does it sound retarded when I say it but, so elegant when they speak of it? Okay, calm down Ainsley, you've decided to believe them; truth is stranger than fiction right? Right, so then what does it all mean? Ah! Why can't I make sense of this?' exclaimed Ainsley frustrated with her garbled hindsight on the matter.

Breaking it down she centered on a few core things that she deemed the most fascinating. The first was the fact that Leonardo was seven thousand years old, even if he greatly exaggerated that; Ainsley knew he was still inhumanely old, probably having lived through every war ever fought in recent history; seen things that she couldn't even possibly imagine. She thought that this above all others was proof enough that she should trust him, how could he know the things he does unless he's lived them? The second fact that Ainsley found interesting was how she had never EVER heard of the SLC, and yet, just 8 floors down, they held but one, of hundreds of historical and cultural works. Some Ainsley was sure people had never seen, or had thought destroyed. She wondered why the SLC felt stockpiling them was so necessary; why not show them? Surely being a business they could make money out of it? That suggested that something sinister was indeed at that places core. Why else would the keep Leonardo captive? Though thinking back, Ainsley saw no cameras, no guards, much unlike when she and Lia ventured down there years before. So was he really captive?

There where too many unanswered questions, too many holes that could easily destroy the whole myth. Ainsley needed to know, she needed Rhapsody to arrive, and soon. But alas, he was still 2 nights away…

The final thing that Ainsley thought about incessantly, beating herself up for having not mentioned it to Leonardo, was the fact that she was in possession of yet another volume of the *Sevio Dionisus*, Patrick's edition. The edition, that Ainsley could only assume didn't belong to him personally, something his father must've inherited or bought. Ainsley was now in hands of the book, that only Ainsley knew brought demise to Patrick's father, and perhaps Patrick himself.

Because as the day slipped away, and rolled into the dawn of the next, all while Ainsley lay there contemplating all that was dropped onto her consciousness, Ainsley found herself, ending up in the morgue, alone. She wasn't sure how she did it, sweet-talking the nurses perhaps? Making up a sap story of needing to say good-bye to Patrick perhaps? She couldn't be sure, all she knew was she was alone standing in front of the meat locker labeled in insignificant type *Cadaver M.P. 31.*

Ainsley's every developing temper flared at the sight of this. The cold, heartlessness of it, to treat a persons body so casually. It must've been criminal. But it wasn't, it was medical. The campus nearby needed cadavers for the students to practice and study from. And given Patrick's deformed, mangled remains, she couldn't imagine a worse choice for examination. Though she didn't know him very well, she could tell that he above all others wouldn't want to be gawked at, especially after he was gone.

Trying to calm her breathing, Ainsley noticed below the label, a clipboard fitted magnetically to the lid. Not caring if she was allowed to read it, Ainsley swiped it off the lid and carried it over to a gurney nearby where she sat reading the clipboard's contents.

It was a police report... Signed by Detective Fredrick Mallory...

Ainsley found herself incapable of taking in a breath without sniffling. She didn't realize it till just now, how scarred her mind was from her encounter with Mallory and his mutt of a partner Charles. But she was, even just seeing his name, caused her heart to accelerate to unhealthy speeds, cold sweat to break out on her forehead, and a slight pang of pain pinching at her neck near where the knife that Charles had was tightly held. Letting a tear fall freely onto the paper, Ainsley quickly dried the document, not wanting the ink to run. Then realizing it would be pointless unless she stopped herself from crying, Ainsley wiped her scrub sleeve across her eyes, sating the stream.

Focusing through her blurred eyes, Ainsley forced her way through the document. Despite all the police jargon, one thing was precisely clear, hinted at in the subtext... Mallory was looking for the book... The book from which Patrick had taken from his father, who must've taken it from right under the SLC's nose; the book which Ainsley now had hidden away, squished between a leather cushion. Once again, Ainsley had thwarted the SLC. Only this time, they didn't know that.

Skipping all the pages of useless fingerprints lifted from varying nurses, and doctors and firemen; used to rule out their presence at the crime scene at the time of the accident. Ainsley came across something that held her gaze. Something she had since given up on finding out about...

It was the breakdown of Patrick's father's death.

'Must need it for reference to prove Patrick as a suicide case' thought Ainsley, which as of now he was strongly being considered for.

Carefully reading the text, Ainsley skipped the bits she knew. How Patrick found his father face down on the table in his study. How when pulling his father back, he was shocked to see he had no face. This Ainsley knew, but what she didn't know was that it was Patrick who led him to his final form. So terrified at what he had seen, Patrick turned to run for help but instead tripped over a slightly protruding part of the carpet and tripped whacking his head hard on the edge of the table, knocking him out cold. But what it also did was cause a candle that was peacefully sitting on the table to lose balance and topple over. Turning it into a frenzy of heat and flame.

Waking to the smell of burning paper, Patrick saw that his father's entire library was up in flames, his father included, charred to the bone, with just a few scraps of clothing relentlessly remaining. Slowly rising, blood gushing out of a giant gash on his tempo, Patrick, not thinking clearly, grabbed the slightly torched volume his father had been reading and made a run for the exit, only to have himself blown backward by a backdraft of flames that had built up from the other side of the door.

Poor Patrick didn't stand a chance; he lit up like a log of dry wood. But for whatever reason, whether he secretly knew its significance to his late father, or the world. Or more likely his body, and his nerves locked up causing him to tightly curl his body around the book, keeping it safe, more or less. Meanwhile he fell into numbness, caused only by nerves dying. Patrick would have died had it not been for the fire department to arrive at just that moment and quickly douse the flames, and get him to ER as quickly as they could. They saved his life, he saved the book, but in the end, it was the book that killed Patrick.

Reading over the report several more times, Ainsley didn't buy for a second that Patrick intentionally lit his cell on fire in hopes of killing himself. It was preposterous. But what concerned Ainsley the most, what frightened her beyond all measure was just why Patrick was transferred to here, hundreds of miles away from New York, and why, anyone in their right minds would give a suicidal, hell even physically disabled person an open flame.

Unless they wanted him to kill himself.

Hearing voices coming down the hall, Ainsley, flying at speeds fast even for her, replaced the clipboard and dove undercover behind a medical cabinet in the near corner. Listening, as the voices grew louder, she relaxed a bit when she could hear the youthful and naïve voices of university interns fill the room.

Not taking in their surroundings, the pair of young female nurse interns, chatting about some new reality dating show, that had then drooling over some hot and amazingly sweet guy, went straight for the gurney where Ainsley sat just seconds before. As they went on and on about all the guys they liked, all Ainsley could think of was 'why don't I talk like that? Because dummy, you've spent your entire puberty in an insane asylum!'

Pulling the gurney over to the meat lockers, they open up Patrick's and for the first time since they met, Ainsley gets to see his remains. They would have been kinder to cremate him. A few scattered bones, and flesh still clinging here and there, his face somewhat in tact, though charred black, any fat that he had on him flared away, leaving a paper thin veil of a corpse in its wake. The nurses stopped talking, as they struggled to keep Patricks' body bag from tipping any of his ashes or bones onto the floor as they moved it the short distance to gurney. Then resuming their conversation as if nothing had every disrupted it, the couple of oblivious nurses, retreated down the hall, leaving Ainsley alone once more.

Ainsley didn't return to the wards, not yet, she had one last bit of business to before her reunion with Rick. She had to know what Leonardo was referencing when he said 'Look in 37 C and 37 G!'

Making the quick bolt across the main floor of Singing Loons, keeping an paranoid watch for anyone, though knowing at this time of day all either were doing their morning routines in their respective wards or eating breakfast in the staff lounge upstairs.

Seeing that the coast was clear, Ainsley sprinted down the steps taking her down into the basement, a route she had never taken before.

Emerging moments later, she saw that she was already in the mess of doorways in the seemingly never-ending hallway. She didn't know how she missed it last time she was here.

Getting herself situated, reading the door number in front of her as *2R*, Ainsley could tell she had a ways to go down the hall before she found what she was looking for.

She ran, feeling for reasons only the Voice knew for sure, that she was running out of time. Arriving at the doors, two doors apart from one another, Ainsley took a moment to catch her breath as she took in her surroundings making sure she was indeed in the right spot.

The doors didn't look anything out of the ordinary for this place, same dreary color, same lack of maintenance, water logged and presumably rotted, the only thing that separated these doors from the rest, as far as Ainsley could tell, was that the featured gold plated door handles.

Thinking nothing of it, coming to accept bizarre as a common occurrence in her life by now, Ainsley approached the door labeled *37C*, the first door. Placing her hand on the knob, she noticed it had the similar effect the flame had on her flesh, admiring for a moment as the white subtle glow emanated out from her contact with the door. Then focusing her attention back on the door, Ainsley opened it, revealing something Ainsley had not expected... Bars.

Blackened steel bars, just as waterlogged as the door that encased it, guarding a blackened room that Ainsley couldn't see any further into than the bars that prevented her from entering. Confused, Ainsley set her hands down on the bars, anticipating them to hold her weight, only to find them swinging forward, letting Ainsley fall to the floor.

Feeling humiliated and vulnerable, Ainsley quickly scrambled to her feet as she threw her hands up in guard, expecting something to attack her, but nothing did, all that she heard was a faint breathing far off into the back of the room.

Dropping her hands, Ainsley feeling more than creeped out by the ominous room, wanted to leave, to investigate the other door. But something that had not occurred in many years occurred just then. The Voice took hold of Ainsley and forced her inside the cell.

Ainsley focused on the sweat collecting in the palms of her hands, feeling exposed, yet knowing nothing, not even nocturnal creatures could make her out in this. Listening to her feat pat down hard on the cobblestone surface of this apparent dungeon of sorts, Ainsley felt almost as if being flung back in time. And this fact was realized with to the right of Ainsley, came the faintest of voices, but undeniable. It was Lia.

XXXII. Escape

In the dim light emitting from the doorway, fingertips emerged from the darkness, mere silhouettes of their true selves, seeking comfort from Ainsley's. Not sure whether or not to believe it to be possible, Ainsley lightly raised her hands to meet the fragile, ghostly ones of Lia.

Linking them together, she could only notice how cold they felt to her touch. Ice felt warmer. Slightly tugging back, Ainsley pulled Lia into the twilight of the room. Her face sunken and deathly, looking nothing like the sole friend she had in this place. The person sitting before her was undoubtedly tortured. "My god Lia what have they done to you?" asked Ainsley, pleading almost, as if she'd hoped saying so would bring her friend back from beyond, bring her back from this shell of her once friend.

Lia opened her mouth, cracked and dried, bite marks noticeable on her lips, scars from where she bit down during moments of extreme pain. Nothing but high pitched gags came out. Instead of words, words for which she couldn't bare to say, Ainsley took Lia in embrace, holding her firmly yet gently, trying her best to not hurt her further. Warm droplets fell on Ainsley's shoulder, Lia was crying. Ainsley couldn't blame her, if this indeed was where she was taken after the last time they saw each other, then Lia has surely endured a lifetime of pain. Ainsley couldn't keep it together; she too joined her friend in tears. Then it came, "You've grown so much…" spoke Lia, voice cracked and raspy, sounding as if it were Ainsley's grandma talking to her now.

Smiling, and breaking the hug, Ainsley pulled back and looked at her friend, her, for all intensive purposes, sister and was relieved to see that she too had stopped crying and was now doing something Ainsley was sure she hadn't done in years, she was smiling.

"Thanks," spoke Ainsley, trying to indulge Lia in her casual compliment. But beyond that, Ainsley couldn't bare to not ask what was plaguing her mind. "What happened to you? Why are you down here?"

Fear rushed through Lia's eyes, paranoia followed. Looking left and right rapidly, Lia started to breath faster, still labored. "I, we, I can't speak of it, they could be watching" whispered Lia. "Who Lia, whose watching?"

CLANK, CLANK

The sound echoed repeatedly as it came down the hallway. "They are coming, you have to get out of here Ains its not safe here!" begged Lia as she unevenly pushed Ainsley to the doorway, but with little success, Ainsley wasn't going anywhere. "I'm not going anywhere without you!" "You must, they are almost upon us!"

"Lia? My pet it is time for your meeting…" came a weasely voice from down the hall, not far off. "Pet" whispered Ainsley to no response; Lia was far too worried. Shoving Ainsley away into the darkness of the far wall, leaving her and her alone standing in the light of the door. And just in time.

"What the?!" came the same voice now appearing in the door way confused and angered, examining the opened cell. It was the guard, the one that fended both Lia and Ainsley off those years ago. "How did you? Who did this!" Demanded the guard, storming into the room and grabbing a now hysterical Lia by the arm and dragging her into the light. "It wasn't me! I, I would never run away, I like it here!" lied Lia, trying desperately to convince the guard. He wasn't convinced.

"You lying bitch!" screamed the guard as he let his hand fly across Lia's face, sending her to the floor. Then, instinctively, he removed his thick black leather belt and began to welt on the now terrified Lia, screaming in agony as the deep red welts began to appear under her tattered white blouse; presumably the only thing she's worn since being in here.

Ainsley couldn't bare it, but catching a fleeting glance from Lia, she knew not to move, to wait it out, despite how badly she wished to help her friend; now was not the time.

"Tell me who opened your cell, or I'll have to do it again, do you want that bitch?" warned the guard ominously, looming overtop Lia who could barely speak let alone prevent herself from shivering in fear. "I, I don't know who it was, by, by the time I came to the light they ran off..." lied Lia, hoping her genuine fear of the man would convince him. "They?" he asked.

Not realizing she said they, Lia quickly improvised. "Yes they, two of them, they looked young, maybe from one of the wards?" presumed Lia, this got the man looking around wildly, backing slightly out of the cell to look up and down the hall, of course not seeing the phantom perpetrators. Looking back down at the whimpering Lia, he raised his belt made whip in warning at the woman. "I tell you now woman, if your lying to me, so help me, this belt will be a welcome treat by the time I'm done with you... When did they flee?" he asked, "A while ago, I'm sure they are long gone by now" spoke Lia hoping this would convince the man not to go looking and thus not return empty handed.

Kneeling down over Lia, the guard began to smirk slightly, and then extending his muscular forearm, he gently parted her matted blonde hair as he examined her face. "I'm sure your right, I guess that means I'll have to punish you then doesn't it?"

215

This brought on even more tears as Lia began to wiggle wildly on the cold floor, as if she were having an epileptic attack. It was then that Ainsley realized that she too was running a tap of tears from her eyes; she didn't know how long she'd been crying, but if she had to guess, it wasn't too long, when she realized what was taking place in front of her.

The guard was going to rape Lia.

And the way he spoke of it, Ainsley shuttered to think that this might not be the first time.

Ainsley wanted nothing more than to help her friend, she slowly began to slop her way toward the incident at hand but a shooting, intense gaze unexpected in this time of sorrow, froze Ainsley in place, in the darkness.

"Don't fret love, it won't hurt much, surely you're used to it by now?" sadistically ployed the guard, enjoying the power he held over the frail Lia. She didn't respond, just shut her eyes, blocking out the sight, but sadly listening to the sound of the zipper of his fly slowly being undone.

The pants fell to an abrupt thud to the ground, sending several oblong things out into the darkness, all being ignored by the guard, more interested in his prized below him. Among the items were his keys, presumably to Singing Loons, a flashlight, and something Ainsley knew she had to take from him; a gun.

Pulling her gaze from the cold lifeless steel of the firearm, Ainsley caught the steely eyes of Lia as they slowly gave way to dismay, as after years of rape and torture, she no longer could hold out. Ainsley then knew, that regardless if the guard did it or not, Lia would not survive the night…

Not if she didn't do something to stop him.

Falling silent, not having realized her own rapid breathing, thankfully presumed an echo of Lia's, Ainsley stood from her crouched pose,

216

gracefully walked to the edge of the twilight where the gun rested and thinking not of the death she now could inflict, but about the hate growing in her heart for this place, this room, this man, this life that had been unfairly thrust upon her in her most innocent of years. She thought about these things, then, not even knowing she could. Pulled the trigger.

The sound was beyond deafening; Ainsley fleetingly thought 'movies lie so bad!' as she dropped the gun carelessly and clasped her ears protectively, desperately trying to shield them from the already past shock.

In the panic of the moment, and the momentary hearing loss incurred, Ainsley forgot to open her eyes to see the carnage she unleashed. And as she realized this, she also realized, she didn't want to. No good could possibly come of it, she either hit her target, and a man was now wounded or dead on the floor, which wasn't all bad, considering what he's done to her friend, but nonetheless, Ainsley never thought much of violence. If not that, then she misfired, after all she barely was able to lift the weapon, which was odd given her fairly well toned arms. For all Ainsley knew, she hit Lia, which would be something Ainsley was sure she couldn't live with, and she knew, that if that were the case, a gun would be a dangerous thing to leave in her care. The only other possibility would be that she missed everyone entirely, which seemed the more likely, as she heard nothing, but the sound of someone rising, and walking toward her.

Ainsley couldn't help but to begin to weep, she hated herself, she funneled all her hate at her life thus far into that single solitary bullet, and it was something that she never thought possible of her own action. But here she was, firing a gun to kill. And the thing that upset Ainsley the most above all other feelings of guilt or fear, the single thing Ainsley really couldn't live with was… she liked it.

Then, as she recoiled in her own twisted sadistic insecurities, soft hands came to her wrists, still wired shut over her ears. And as they did, she relaxed instantly, almost miraculously, all thoughts flushed from her mind and she was left with nothing but the urge to sigh a sigh of relief. Because, those hands could not be that of some masochistic rapist guard, no they had to belong to someone kind, and caring, someone Ainsley never doubted as her closest thing to a friend since her arrival here. Ainsley knew those hands belonged to Lia.

And sure enough, as she pulled away it revealed just the person Ainsley wished most to see, her still shaky, but none the less kind friend Lia. Doing something Ainsley knew she wouldn't be able to do if put through the same agony. She was smiling.

"Thank you... I can't seem to think of something more suiting than that." Awkwardly spoke Lia, trying desperately to clear her throat, and failing miserably. This brought a slight smile to Ainsley, "Your welcome... I can't think of anything more suiting than that."

And without warning, Lia leapt onto Ainsley slightly suffocating her as she hugged the life out of her, seemingly trying to sap some of Ainsley's life back into her weakened one.

Toppling back a few steps, Ainsley recovered and gently patted her friend on the back, feeling something protruding against her hands, unable to tell exactly what it was, Ainsley felt with her hands up and down Lia's back, and only then did she realize what it was, it was Lia's ribcage. Lia was starving to death.

Ainsley had to hold back a gasp, but let out a slight one anyways, which Lia wrote off as a sigh of relief as she released her death grip on Ainsley. It all made sense now, why Lia didn't fight back, why he voice seemed so groggy. It was so wrong, so inhuman, beyond all the equally disturbing factors that made up this hell house of an asylum, Ainsley thought of nothing worse than starving someone.

Living where she did, on such a limited, if not non-existent budget for most of her life, Ainsley on several occasions spent weeks sickly fighting off the sickly feeling that takes you over after weeks of skimped foodstuffs. She could only imagine what 2 years would do.

Resuming her smile, as to not draw attention to her unintentional staring, Ainsley reassuringly took Lia's hands once more. "Lets get out of here!" she happily, soothingly spoke. Lia said nothing but nodded graciously and turned to follow Ainsley's hands as she pulled her away from the darkness that was her life.

But it didn't last long, as Ainsley stopped dead in her tracks, staring down at the one thing she feared, and now remembered why she refused to open her eyes.

Splayed out on the floor, contorted into an irregular pose, lay the still twitching corpse of the once guard, now headless, gushing blood out onto the cold stone cobble, and just a sip onto the white tile of the horizon hall.

Ainsley felt nothing, heard nothing, not the encouraging tugs or whispers from Lia, not her heartbeat, not her own thoughts, just the faintest sound of blood exploring alien territory as it filled the deep crevasses of tile.

It was then that Ainsley knew something had been taken from her that moment, maybe it had been there all along; Ainsley lost her care for this world, all except the few people she now cherished, the rest of the world, was nothing but pure, monopolistic, sadistic, ignorant evil. The SLC, Singing Loons, Cops, Doctors, Drugs, her mom; she felt nothing for any of them, where once she'd feel something, anger perhaps, betrayal, sadness, nothing, maybe pity. For that was what she felt for the dead body she had made. Pity.

Feeling slightly calmed by her apathy for the world. Ainsley gently pulled Lia beyond the cadaver and into the hall, being careful to avoid the ever-ambitious blood flow.

Stopping a few paces along, Ainsley released Lia's grip. "What is it?" gently asked Lia. "Go on ahead, I have something I must check first…" vaguely responded Ainsley as she silently turned back towards the open doorway, looking beyond it, remembering there in the hall, the other room. 37G.

Being too week to argue with Ainsley, Lia staggered on down the long hallway toward the elevator. Being left alone, truly alone. Ainsley casually approached the doorway, identical to the previously opened counterpart.

Hoping not to see another friend, or worse family member inside, Ainsley quickly opened it, holding her breath as she did. But was relieved to see just another room filled with books.

Carefully entering, Ainsley was happily surprised to see that this room had motion detected lights, which flickered slowly to life low over her head, cast vibrant blue glow. Looking round the slightly larger room obviously designed just like Lia's cell, but fashioned into storage instead, Ainsley couldn't figure why Leonardo would send her here. It contained no reference to anything she'd find of use or interest.

The room was set up, in a much more structured fashion, clean cobblestone beneath, walls lined with bookshelves, filled to the brim. A center console of filing cabinets made up of six cells. Making a sort of circular path between the books. Walking apace, Ainsley generally glanced at the books lining the shelves, so many to examine, all sure to be chalk full of fascinating historical and cultural facts. But alas, none that Ainsley expected Leonardo wished her to find.

Turning her attention away from the bookshelves, Ainsley focused on the six storage cabinets filling out the center of the room. They seemed ordinary enough, not unlike something you'd see in any corporate office. But then, and only then, as Ainsley circled the cabinets, did she get the strongest urge of her life. The feeling was overwhelming. It blanked her vision with white light at its most intense, her chest tightened, it felt like a stroke or heart attack, but Ainsley knew, it was a sign. She was near whatever she was sent here to retrieve. Circling faster, Ainsley slowly began to pin point her destination. It was the middle console on the far side. Identical to the rest save for a padlock on the lowest drawer. An unusual thing for sure, considering the fact that the key was suspiciously left dangling inside, and the lock open.

Leaning down, fighting through the madness that was her urges, Ainsley took the key from its place and looked it over, and saw that whatever it was for, it wasn't meant for the lock she pulled it from. It had another purpose. Turning back to the drawer, Ainsley slowly opened it, relishing the reveal.

But as she opened, it she was shocked and disheartened to see nothing inside, nothing but a scrape of paper. Curious, Ainsley took hold of the paper and read what was clearly written upon it in fine aristocratic font.

Look Up

Unconsciously following the instruction, Ainsley's eyes required a double take as she adjusted to staring directly into the light. But as they did, she saw it, nestled between the square grid of lights. Something that no one, no matter how sane, or insane for that matter would bother to look; what Ainsley saw… was a safe.

Carefully sunk into the low ceiling of the room. The filing cabinets now made sense so did the suspicious key. Because as Ainsley climbed onto the series of cabinets, she stood just tall enough to reach the safe, and, thanks to her urges, and Leonardo's guidance, Ainsley now held the key that slipped happily into the built in lock of the cavalier safe. It clicked open.

Ducking instinctively, Ainsley narrowly dodged the heavy safe door as it fell open overhead. Giving it a moment to come to rest, Ainsley looked up, expecting the contents to hastily follow suit. Nothing did. Which as Ainsley curiously looked up, thought 'its empty.' She thought wrong.

Hovering, almost as if by magic but actually being held in place by heavy magnets placed underneath it that attracted to the deep end of the vault, floated the notebook. The one from so long ago, the one that Lia gave to her, the one she long since thought she'd never see again. But there it was, in the last place anyone could possibly imagine, hovering in a ceiling safe in an anonymous room attached to a huge hallway, belonging to some rare book collectors who have homicidal tenancies.

Ainsley didn't understand it, why it was here, but if there ever was a time to trust her urges it was right now, because every second she lingered wondering, was another that caused her to feel weaker and weaker. Reaching up, Ainsley roughly pushed the magnets away one at a time, listening as they smacked against their oppositely charged wall.

Taking it down once more, Ainsley looked it over carefully, still in disbelief of its presence, but relieved that the urges and be sedated.

"Ainsley?" came a whisper from the hall.

It was then that Ainsley remembered about poor Lia, who must've been worried sick waiting and came back to check on her savior.

Wasting not a minute more, Ainsley leapt down from her perch on the cabinets and ran out of 37G.

Almost colliding with Lia, Ainsley eased herself and apologized to the weakened Lia and then together, they took off down the hall.

It took them longer than usual, given Lia's state, but at long last, they reached the old elevator. Entering, Lia reached for *M*, but was stopped by Ainsley who instead reached for *7*. Quizzingly looking to Ainsley for answers, Ainsley bluntly said… "Forgot something."

As the doors opened to Ward 7, it was night time already, which shocked Ainsley, and only her, which confused her for a second but then remembered the Lia would have no idea what time of day it was down there. Though for Ainsley it seemed odd that twice now, the basement had affected her time management severely. 'Perhaps, something strange is going on down there…' thought Ainsley, before brashly dismissing the thought. 'Of course something was going on down there.'

Exiting the elevator, walking swiftly to her only solace outside of Lia, the chair in the corner, Ainsley sat down in it once more.

Caressing the broken in leather, feeling it as if it were a feeling she'd been denied for years. Ainsley sighed welling up inside for the sentimentality that this chair brought. Finishing her medial goodbyes with her favorite place, Ainsley stuffed her hand deep into the cushion of the chair and pulled from it Patrick's volume. Clenching it under her arm with the notebook. Ainsley took one last look round the place she unfortunately called home for the last 3 years of her life, and retreated to the elevator once more.

They walked quietly, not making a whisper to one another, nothing to say of this place that both hated for similar and varying reasons. They quietly unlocked the white grated door that separated the main intake area and the rest of the hospital and crossed the room. Looking up as she walked, Ainsley recalled how she always loved the view from this particular spot, looking up and out through the glass domed roof. Smiling slightly, Ainsley held the door open for Lia who struggled outward. Ainsley soon followed.

It was fall, the air at this time of night was nippy at best, and all Ainsley could think of, despite all the shit that had occurred in the last 4 years of her life, was how good the night air felt, and how this was the first time since she entered, that she breathed fresh air.

It almost made her last four years worth it.

Walking briskly, along the driveway, careful as they went, realizing they should have gotten more whilst on 7, prepared more, Ainsley extended her arm, assisting her friend as she shivered violently.

Pulling the thick black bars of the Iron Gate apart, Ainsley led the way as they stepped of the premises of Singing Loons.

Neither looked back.

Part Three

XXXIII. Reunions

All eyes were on them as they made their humble exit out of Singing Loons. They knew not of their surveillance, how could they, the sheer efforts that went into it were staggering. Walnut sized cameras, dozens of FTC initiates, Jackals and Ferrymen all keeping close watch of every possible angle of the aging institution, it was impossible for them to leave unnoticed as they presumed they had.

Rick sat in the driver's seat of his classic Royal's Royce several blocks down, just far enough to not appear suspicious, but close enough to keep watch.

Ever since being promoted from Jackal to Head of Western District, Rick had essentially revolutionized the purpose of the FTC, and for good reason. More and more Sevardinal were going MIA, and in such a well-structured guardianship, that was not supposed to happen. Ever.

Suspecting the SLC to be behind the disappearances, Rick made short work of the 'college club' image that his district had become known for. Scowls of young and bright minds would join not so much to learn about the mysteries of this hidden continent, but moreover to study under the late Lawrence Henderson, the scholarly cofounder of the FTC and mentor to Rhapsody. But after his passing, both he and his beliefs about how the FTC should be run went away. It was time to act.

It started out small, little things here and there; name changes for the varying factions spread out through the west, and then came the more radical motives. People replaced, memories wiped; a necessity for those higher up who knew too much. Personnel trained in hand-to-hand and short-range firearms. Less and less people given access to what they referred to as *The*

Gift, which was the knowledge of the *Sevio Dionisus*, a privileged only few now were deemed worthy of.

Rick knew his late mentor would not approve of any of these changes, and on any other day, Rick would agree, but these were desperate times. And measures needed to be taken. War times are not without regret. And they were indeed a war.

It wasn't spoken from either side, both just quietly hating the other for decades. But as time went on, and both of their respective networks of influence and knowledge grew, it was inevitability. For the FTC stood in the way of the one thing the SLC now craved, the one thing they did not possess. *The Sevio Dionisus.*

Even now, as Ainsley, dutifully holding onto Lia giving her as much support as she could give, were walking down the street away from their former prison, more eyes than just the FTC were upon them. Enemies were afoot.

The FTC long since knew of the hidden purpose behind the seminal institution; a prison, for those that knew too much, but meant something more too both the SLC and FTC alive, rather than dead. And of course the suspected lower levels. Only assumed, as no proof could be had as of yet. Filled with rooms upon rooms of stolen and illicitly gotten items, mostly books. Withheld from the world, for the sole purpose to fuel the SLC's greed. For them quantity, not quality of knowledge was power.

The pair of frail girls were getting ever closer to Rick and the numerous other Jackals he had in circulation on the nearer blocks. As she came close enough to make out more clearly her defining features; Rick couldn't hold back a gasp at how rapidly she changed in the three years since they last saw one another, where once was a naïve little girl, now walked an assured,

227

confidant, albeit scorned woman. She was gorgeous, and much to Rick's dismay, she looked more and more like him as the years went on.

Rick always regretted his time with Abigail… But he never regretted his part in creating Ainsley. She was without a doubt his single greatest achievement, and the tragedy of it all was that she knew not of his relation to her. A protector, that is what she thought of him. He should have been so much more.

Rick knew, that soon, he'd be able to explain it all to Ainsley, beg for her forgiveness for his abandonment, leaving her to fend for her self, and bare the burden of looking after his former half of a whole. Abi.

As a crack came from his walkie-talkie, Rick realized he lost himself in thought, and had indeed missed his mark; his time to 'obtain the target' as both he and most military ops would describe the situation. But all he could think about was 'time to obtain my daughter…'

Knowing he was late, but thinking it better to risk it rather than run the risk of one of the numerous SLC operatives to snatch her and take her somewhere far more diabolical than Singing Loons, Rick unlatched the handled to his door and stepped casually out. Dressed in a fine dark suit and an equally fine dark trench coat and fedora, Rick brushed his wrinkles away, and stared longingly at the backs of the two girls, both too exhausted to fear him, or notice.

"Ehem, may I be of assistance ladies?" he spoke, albeit apprehensively.

Ainsley froze first, signaling to the weaker Lia to stop as well, though weariness was written all over her face as she locked eyes with Rick. *She doesn't trust me, and why should she?* Thought Rick. *After the hell they both must've endured, I wouldn't trust a stranger let alone my best friend.*

Then slowly, almost as if not wishing to be let down, Ainsley turned, and her brilliant green eyes, always stunningly vibrant, locked with his. There was silence, neither spoke; Rick could tell he was cracking a friendly smile, trying to ease the tension, and remind her he was a friend.

Oh god, she has no clue who I am! Thought Rick, *perhaps they confiscated the letter I wrote, oh dear, what she must have endured not knowing I was going to come for her...*

Dropping his smile, Rick coughed uncomfortably, feeling more scrutinized now than he ever had by any of his superiors. Ainsley, aware of it or not, knew how to destroy Ricks strong sense of confidence.

What if she did get the message, and is mad that I took so long in coming for her... Yes that must be it. I would have come sooner, but Henderson wouldn't have it. It's not my fault... thought Rick panicked.

Then after what felt like an eternity of blank stares from his estranged daughter, came the wave, recognition. She knew him, and from the winning smile that crept across her face, she knew him on good terms. Very good.

Because to both Lia, who lost her balance and toppled over, and Rick's who did not expect this in the slightest, Ainsley ran over to him and jumped onto him wrapping her whole body around his, arms, suffocating his head into her bosom, and her legs, locked around his torso. Rick required every bit of self-control to hold back even the sight of watery eyes that so desperately wished to appear.

"You came!" excitedly proclaimed Ainsley, speaking more for her own needs of validating the reality of the situation rather than needing an answer. "Of course I did, I promised didn't I?" happily replied Rick, feeling for a fleeting moment what it must be like for a father to embrace his daughter after her first dance recital, or wishing her good luck as she takes off to her first day of school. Memories, things Rick guarded, yet had none of his own.

Climbing down and beaming a smile at Rick, one that Rick knew melted not just his heart but anyone's who saw it. Ainsley turned to introduce her friend, only to find her still struggling to stand up. "Oh my god, I'm sorry!" apologized Ainsley running back to Lia's side and picking her up and staggering her over to Rick. Holding out a hand to Lia, Rick for the first time really took in the girl; she was not well by any means. "I would shake your hand sir, but I'm having trouble keeping my eyes open long enough to see it…" weakly exclaimed Lia to Rick, who politely retracted his hand. "No worries, too formal anyways. My name is Rickard Rhapsody, you can call me Rick."

Looking Rick over in a new light, and seeing how her friend took to him, Lia relaxed her gaze and broke a small smile. "It's a pleasure to meet you, I'm Amelia Hamilton, and you may call me Lia." Spoke Lia.

"Lia, very well then. Now I don't mean to be pushy you two but, I have to get you both to safety, right now." Cautiously explained Rick. This worried Ainsley, "What's wrong?"

Looking from Lia, to Ainsley's concerned face, Rick glanced round swiftly then leaned in between both their heads, whispering to them ever so gently, "We are not alone."

XXXIV. Returning to the Abode

Though the foreboding mention of not being alone, the drive away from Singing Loons was an uneventful one. The city was dead, not a whisper to be uttered as they drove silently, with so much to say, but all knowing it could wait. Rick in particular was anxious to confess his long held truth to Ainsley. Glancing over to her as he drove, admiring at how after being through so much anguish, she could still look so innocent, so peaceful.

Lia, laying down in the back seat, had long since past out, too exhausted from years of abuse and malnutrition. Rick knew she needed to be cared for soon, she was in terrible health.

Behind the trio, drove three other cars, all vans, plain as any other, white, unlabeled, perhaps not the most inconspicuous of vehicles, but at this point, the FTC had made a stance, they had put there necks out on the line to rescue Ainsley, luckily it had paid off.

It was mid day before anyone uttered anything and they were long into the countryside by now; Ainsley had napped here and there; not wanting to be the first to break the comfortable silence that had developed. But alas, her curiosity got the better of her. "Where are we going?"

Glancing over to Ainsley, holding her eyes probably longer than he should have, Rick couldn't help but smile, as he happily said. "Home."

Rick should have known that this would have brought on more questions, given Ainsley's naturally curious nature, but he didn't, and then spent the next half of the trip explaining to Ainsley, and the now conscious, and even more so confused Lia.

He told them that they were going to Ainsley's home, or what should have been her home of the last 3 years. What was once Artie's home;

Ainsley's great grandfather. The narrow mansion sitting atop and in between 72nd and 74th Westmont St. Something that Rickard described as *A Narrow Abode*.

He explained how each and every Sevardinal had such a place, spread out all across the globe. A sort of safe haven for Their kind, a place that fended off *evil spirits*, people who by nature were deemed immoral or unethical, or worse… unnatural.

"Unnatural?" asked Lia, confused of the out of context information she was being barraged with. Tossing a look over his shoulder, it was evident that Rick had forgotten Lia was there, or perhaps thought she still be sleeping. "Yes… well. I don't know exactly what they mean by that… You have to understand, Sevardinal's are very peculiar people, they don't generally talk in slang, and everything they do is very archaic." Said Rick. "But I don't talk like that?" quipped Ainsley, causing the evermore confused Lia to interrupt Rick's potential response. "Wait, you're one of those Sevey thingy's?"

This caused Ainsley to laugh at her friends justified, yet amusing bewilderment. "Yes, I am, apparently." It was then that Ainsley recalled something that Artie told her long ago about Sevardinals. Something that she originally thought odd, but didn't probe deeper while she had the chance; turning back to Rick, she asked, "Rick… Arthur told me Sevardinals were only born in the other world… yet I was born here… How is that possible?"

Rick turned to look at Ainsley, caught off guard by the off tangent question, and how difficult it was to answer. "Uh, well, Ainsley, that's a very good question… I don't know to be honest… But whatever the reason, that is why you above all other Sevardinal, are unique."

This satisfied Ainsley, for the time being, she felt bad for asking all these things around Lia, who already was delirious from lack of food, water and rest, but on top of that, had no clue what they were talking about. So accepting that for now she would let the matter rest, Ainsley turned once more back to the window, and admired the decaying cereal of the Great Plains.

"Hey you two, wake up, we're here." Spoke Rick, shaking both Lia and Ainsley away. She didn't know how long she had been out, but it must've been a while, because it was nighttime once more; she never realized she was this tired before. All she wanted to do was go back to sleep. But as she slowly rose from the car seat and stood in the frosty night air, Ainsley's urge kicked in once more, not in a sickening way, but in a more smooth happy sense, and Ainsley looked up.

And once more, almost as if in a dream long forgotten, through the high ceiling of the fog, the dim glow of the *Narrow Abode* could be seen fleeing through. Ainsley smiled, not for sure why, perhaps just happy to see a familiar place, a place that didn't bring with it sadness and betrayal.

Ainsley went ahead, almost bounding up the fire escape, looking back she saw Rhapsody, struggle to maneuver Lia through the mesh of rusted metal as he carried her over his shoulder.

Arriving at the top, Ainsley was surprised to see not the blank rooftops that once sat before her years ago. Instead there was an infestation of life squirming about. Illuminated tents spread out all over, some big, most small bringing silhouettes of anonymous figures within.

Ainsley must've been staring for a while as Rick and Lia soon joined her. "What is all this?" asked Ainsley. "Impressive isn't it?" proudly stated

Rick as he rested his one free hand on the small of Ainsley's back as he guided her forward. "Welcome to the FTC's new Western Headquarters".

"This?" comically asked Ainsley, slightly disappointed, having expected grand halls and mass quantities of technology. Much like what she saw in the SLC basement.

Slightly offended by this, Rick shot a look at Ainsley. "Come now, don't be harsh, we aren't anywhere near as well funded as the SLC, but what we lack in finances, we make up for in tactic, and quantity; our personnel alone outnumber the SLC's 20 to 1!" proudly, albeit desperately defended Rick as he pressed the pair of them through the tent city toward the dominating backdrop.

Ahead, just stepping out of perhaps the biggest of tents, in a heated discussion with someone still hidden inside, was a woman, strikingly beautiful, though obviously stressed. Black hair pulled back into a tight ponytail, stretching her skin back into an uncomfortable tension. Wearing oddly short cargo pants, almost as if in attempt to make them into capris, but failing. And on top she wore the opposite, an overlarge cargo vest, draped off her body and a skimpy white tank top, dirty, appearing almost grey. It was as if upon exiting that tent, she exited the Australian Outback.

Spotting her, Ricks, slightly hurt demeanor changed and he joyfully picked up pace. "Joyce!" he happily shouted. Turning from whomever she was arguing with, she quickly waved a hand dismissing the mystery co-argueant and walked toward the trio. Happy.

"Rick! Oh my god! You're back!" she yelled equally as loud as she jogged over to him. Setting down Lia who made do by leaning against both Ainsley and a nearby tent pole, Rick jogged ahead and met Joyce halfway and picked her up and swirled her round in his arms, this sight reminded

Ainsley of those old World War 2 movies where a soldier had returned from war, getting off the train and running to his sweetheart, twirling her in delight. It was just as adorable then as it was now.

Out of earshot, Ainsley couldn't make out what the pair were saying to one another, but by the way Rick adoringly placed his hands on the small of Joyce's back and they way she lovingly caressed his stubble ridden face, it was clear they were lovers.

Waiting patiently, Ainsley and Lia were finally remembered by the good Rick Rhapsody, who double took them and then enthusiastically dragged Joyce over to them. "Joyce, I'd like you to meet Ainsley and her friend Amelia." Proudly spoke Rick. "Its just Lia." Weakly spoke Lia, ever so defiant of her given name. "Oh right, I'm terribly sorry, Lia."

With her smile just as big as Ricks, Joyce first extended her long sultry hand to Lia who, having gained some strength since the past night, shook it briefly. "And this must be your," "charge, yes this is our Sevardinal that we must look after..." interjected Rick, cutting off Joyce's almost ecstatic proclamation. Ainsley didn't note the hint of emphasis made in Rick's statement. Only that he was giving deathly stares toward Joyce, who finally figured out what he was going for. "Oh, right of course, well it is most definitely a pleasure to meet you."

Looking over at Lia, who was about to pass out, Rick quietly spoke to Joyce. "Could you be so kind to take Ainsley's friend to the Infirmary, she's in dire need of R and R." Smiling in response, Joyce quickly gave an unannounced kiss on Rick's lips, and extended her hand to Lia, who took it without comment.

Both watching their friends disappear into the same tent that Joyce emerged from, they finally turned back to one another. Still smiling, Rick extended his arm, much in the way a gentlemen from Victorian times would to a dance partner as they enter the floor. Giggling slightly by this light gesture, Ainsley locked her arm around his and let him guide her toward *The Narrow Abode*.

As they walked the short distance, Ainsley couldn't help but ask, "So… was that your girlfriend?"

Stiffening a bit, but remaining composed, Rick replied, "My wife actually, we've been together for 17 years now."

"She seems like a lovely woman?" asked Ainsley, feeling a slight trepidation in Rhapsody's voice. "She is, make no mistake, I couldn't ask for a better mother of my child…"

Ainsley couldn't help but contain her girly excitement. "She's pregnant! Congratulations! You must be so excited! The both of you!"

Arriving at the front door, Rick paused, causing Ainsley to pause before entering the still pungent first floor. Trying desperately to keep his composure, Rick coughed to cover up a slight whimper that escaped him. "We, are very excited… only she isn't pregnant." Said Rick. "So you guys have kids then?" asked Ainsley growing more concerned by Ricks apprehensive behavior.

Putting his hand on the knob, Rick let out one last deep sigh. "Just one, a girl…" then opening the door inward, Rick started in saying as he went.

"We named her Ainsley."

XXXV. Family Meeting

The door hung wide, black as she remembered it once long ago. Still reeking of soiled lumber and drywall. Only now no amount of foulness, or darkness could distract what Ainsley just heard, what she still was struggling to compute.

"We named her Ainsley." He said.

He's my father? Thought Ainsley seeing if it made any sense. She never knew her father, he left before she was born, or at least that's what her mom told her. *My mom isn't my mom!* Realized Ainsley, Abigail wasn't her mother, or at least according to Rick she wasn't. And given the truly un-motherly behavior she presented to Ainsley the last few times she saw her Ainsley could only assume what he just told her was true.

This was amazing, terrifying, and wonderful depressing all wrapped up into one. Undoubtedly overwhelming, it seemed Ainsley was never allowed to not be in a constant state of shock and awe.

Knowing she needed confirmation of this new reality, Ainsley snapped out of her daze and entered into the darkened floor. Not wasting any time to marvel or rejoice in visiting her *home*, she quickly made her way to the steep stairs and climbed rapidly upward. Peering round to look down the hall, she saw no sign of Rick. Figuring he must've gone at least as high as the 4 floor; mainly to escape the stench of the lower levels, Ainsley proceeded upward. And indeed she was correct, because as she warily arrived at the fourth floor, she found him; standing beside the half visible dining table, leaning against it, almost as if he were to faint at the sight of her. He was out of breath; running must've been the cause. *He's scared of me...* thought Ainsley.

Timidly approaching, not sure how to respond to Rick's confession, Ainsley arrived at the opposite end of the table. And there they stood, silent; knowing what was about to occur wouldn't be simple to explain away.

Growing more anxious by the minute, Ainsley went to speak. But Rick beat her to it.

"I always loved the name Ainsley, ever since I was a boy, I would always be fascinated by the written word. My parents they, they gave me an Oxford Dictionary when I was little, told me that *there was nothing more powerful than knowledge.* At the time, I thought they were just being silly, making up useless significance. But as time went on, and the more I read, the more I realized, they were indeed correct..." spoke Rick, then turning his attention to the table, he gestured toward the half chair sticking out in front of Ainsley.

"Please sit," he calmly instructed. Causing confusion within Ainsley. "But I, there isn't any..." rambled Ainsley trying her best to explain. "Please, just trust me..." pleaded Rick reemphasizing the chair.

Looking down at it, Ainsley sighed then gently extended her free hand, and with the lightest of touch, ignited the room into life.

Much like her great grand father before her, she animated the chair and table into action, and watched in marvel as they widened out from the wall. Coming to fill the space. But it was much more than that it kept going. The walls expanded, widening beyond impossible measures, turning the hall into a large open space, wide enough to walk around in, much like Ainsley originally envisioned her great grand father's house when her *mom* told her to go to his mansion.

"This is what you thought isn't it?" quietly asked Rick.

Surprised that he guessed her present thought, Ainsley let out a slight gasp as she slowly descended into the already parted chair. Setting her duo of books onto its spotless surface.

"How did you know that?" Rightfully asked Ainsley.

Shrugging slightly, Rick simply replied "Its my job, I have to know everything about you, your fears, your desires, your ambitions, thoughts, you name it, I know it. I even know what you dream about…"

Ainsley couldn't help but be defiant at such a cocky statement. "Oh yeah, prove it. What am I thinking about right now?" slyly asked Ainsley as she fell into thought about everything that had occurred and settled on what she thought would throw him, something she had been wondering about viciously since he picked her up…

Smiling slightly, Rick said, "You are thinking about why I haven't asked about your books."

Ainsley's jaw dropped. That was exactly what she was thinking about. It seemed odd that her supposed protector, and bodyguard of her and the book, wouldn't ask to see or take into protective custody.

"That's because its not our job to take them into protective custody Ainsley, we are supposed to protect you, first and foremost, we only protect the book should anything happen to you." Mind read Rick. Ainsley ignored his mystical telepathy and let slip her slight resentment of him, and of the FTC.

"Like getting sent to an insane asylum for 3 years?" this caused Rick to sigh, knowing this would come eventually. "Ains, I had not choice in the matter, my superior at the time forbid me from helping you, me giving you that letter alone was treasonous by the FTC's standards." Explained Rick.

"But why was it forbidden!" demanded Ainsley, "I mean, I was a kid! I still am! And my god you're my dad! And yet you let me stay in that hellhole for that long?!"

Rick remained silent. He deserved all of this and much more. He should have been there for her, he should have rescued her long ago, taken her far away from danger, from pain, from all this forced responsibility that was now thrust upon her. In ways she was still unaware of.

Ainsley didn't wait for any response. "And now you come after 3 years and tell me that I'm your daughter! And that woman, that woman IS my mom! Not Abigail, my mom my entire life but her?! All my Uncles, Grandparents, they aren't even related to me!"

"I know, all you say is true, and I cannot even begin to explain the sorrow that has befallen me from putting you through all this. You deserved none of it. At all. This life was not meant for you. We didn't intend any of this for you. We wanted nothing more than for you to have a happy normal life." Gloomily explained Rhapsody.

"So that's why you two abandoned me and led me to believe that Abi was my mom?" demanded Ainsley, coming off harsher and harsher as more and more of the situation sunk in.

"No, see, well it's very difficult to explain Ainsley… We had no choice. You were chosen. We couldn't deny that, it would have jeopardized the whole *world*!" pleaded Rick, trying his best to keep his deep voice from cracking.

"Oh, so you served me up to be a sacrifice for a place I've been only twice, a place that any doctor would tell you isn't real, that I'm crazy! That you are crazy!"

"I know that must be how it looks. But you don't understand. WE didn't have a choice! We didn't give you up…"

"You were taken from us…" came the soft-spoken voice of Joyce as she appeared far down the long and now wide hall, dimly light in the twilight of the numerous lamps.

Ceasing the argument, they waited as Joyce approached.

"What do you mean… taken?" asked Ainsley, still brimming with pent up emotion. Arriving at the table, Joyce moved to the center of it, acting as mediator between the arguents; extending his hand, Joyce supportively took hold and held it firm.

"She means that you were taken from us, without our permission, no not by the FTC, but by someone else… Your *mom*"

At the mention of her now ex-mom, Ainsley's tension broke, and she went limp as tears now freely fell down her face. The lovers, Ainsley's parents, didn't seek to interrupt; instead Joyce vanished for a moment then returned with a glass of water. Which Ainsley graciously drank. "I, I don't understand, if you didn't give me away, how did *mom* get me?"

Pulling up a chair from the now far wall, Joyce sat down right beside Ainsley, gripping her hand gently, offering support Ainsley never knew before, and was undoubtedly comforted by. Moving closer also, Rick cleared his throat. "Well to answer that Ains, we need to explain some things about when you were born."

XXXVI. Birthday

The days were very much like they were now. Frosted in the morning, leaving a whitish, crystallized tinge to everything the new day touched. Withered leaves, once vibrant with glamorous colors both in auburn and gold, fell to their seasonal death giving way for the onslaught of winter.

Joyce felt the kick at 3:33 am on October 3rd, a Sunday. She and her new husband Rick were quick to the gun and feverishly packed all the necessities for the short couple nights stay in the hospital during the laborious hours to come.

Constantly swearing under his breath at his stupidity to forget this and that as he drove, Joyce, always the calmer, more collected of the two gently soothed him, encouraging him to focus on the road, rather than on toothbrushes.

Luckily for them, they lived not far from the nearest hospital, inexplicably named after some anonymous donor who did some charity at some point in his life that deemed him to have a place of life and death named in his honor. Illegally parking in the handicapped parking space, Rick ran like a limo driver on his first day driving a celebrity, speeding too and from one side of the car to the other; rapidly opening it for his beloved(s).

The rest proceeded as it did with every new set of parents-to-be; triage – waiting. Emergency, waiting. Extreme bouts of pain. Waiting. Movement to a maternity room. Waiting. Pain. Panicked impatience of father. Waiting. Doctors occasional visits; and disappointing admittance that there was indeed more dilation to be had. Waiting. Finally, after what must've been roughly 7 hours of bitter labor, *Ainsley* was born.

Weighing in at 7 pounds, 3 ounces, Joyce was denied the right to hold her child, due to a *complication* that neither she nor Rick, learned the cause or diagnosis of. Whisked away from the room, and away from her parents. The fragile and undoubtedly innocent Ainsley wailed her still slimy little head off, as the nurse briskly walked down the hall. It was a truly bizarre sight, especially considering the bizarre occurrences that happened daily at such an establishment.

Walking further down the hall, painted a muted green, intended to calm tension with its paleness, instead evoked a sense of sickness to all that sat dying or ill looking at it. As she went, Ainsley in hand, the cross-traffic became less and less, and soon enough, she was alone with the newborn as they turned a corner and, with her back pushing gently against the heavy door, entered the *abandoned wing.*

All was silent now, no clamoring of agony from patients in varying rooms, no hushed discussions from doctors to patients. No hysteria from grieving family members having lost a loved one. Only the somewhat softer yelps of Ainsley, who having been alive only for minutes, was already succumbing to a world that she, would never fully understand.

Turning a final corner, sounds once more could be heard from the end of the hall, weakened by a thick construction plastic wrap that draped down in strips from the ceiling, mimicking a door. However, amongst the noise emanating from Ainsley, none could discern what the alternative sounds were.

Brushing back the thick plastic strips, paying close attention to avoid any whacking Ainsley, the Nurse looked up to see that she was indeed the last to have arrived with her *package.*

Inside the room sterilized and looking unlike the decaying surrounding of the wing, was seven maternity grade NICU cradles. Or so it would first appear...

Nodding to the fellow nurses all proudly standing about happy with their discoveries, rejoicing, Ainsley's nurse carried her forward the short distance and quickly glanced over the cradles. Five were filled with newborns, all now cleaned and properly wrapped, preventing hypothermia and any other benign toxins that wouldn't affect us, but would prove fatal to infants.

Five

"Am I not the last to arrive?" worriedly asked Ainsley's nurse, as she quickly handed her off and watched as she was cleaned and wrapped in her traditional pink blanket, and then gently placed in the third NICU cradle.

As it snapped shut, a tiny LED light on swapped from monotone red to light green, signifying only to those in the room something they already suspected.

"Its her alright..." trepidatiously spoke one of the older male nurses, standing diligently overhead of Ainsley's cradle.

"Excuse me?" forced Ainsley's nurse, with a slight temper of being ignored by her subordinates.

Snapping out of his gaze, the male nurse looked up to Ainsley's nurse.

"Sorry Abi, err I mean madam..." he said; now looking down respectively, especially after letting slip *Madam's* true name. Abigail.

Slightly annoyed, but not bothering to punish, Abigail glanced to a young redheaded nurse standing idly to the side, obviously hoping not to be called upon. "Well, where are the others?" demanding Ainsley, speaking directly to the redheaded nurse, but also loud enough for it to be addressing

244

the rest of the nurses. "There were… complications Madam…" confessed the redhead, scrunching her eyes, almost as if expecting a blow from the long and sensuous Abigail, looking glorious in her prime, with just a slight hint of dis-jointment deep in her eyes.

"Complications?" sniped Abigail, eyeing down the poor redheaded nurse, clearly a guilty component to the *complication*. Manning up, the male nurse stepped forward, drawing Abi's gaze. "It wasn't her fault, it was no one's they were stillborn" explained the male nurse.

Giving a slight upward nod, completely unimpressed, implying if she were there that wouldn't have been the case. "I see," pondered Abi, glancing round the room once more, making the rest look down in cowardice. "Well, no matter, you lucked out, I was the one that birthed the child, as you can so see here." Said Abi, pointing toward the green LED light steadfast on top of Ainsley's NICU.

"Let me see!" demanded a small cracked voice.

Startled, Abigail quickly turned to reveal Leonardo Sevardina standing there, looking no different than when Ainsley would re-meet him years later.

"Sir!" squeaked Abi, beyond holding up her tough façade around such a legendary face. Appearing from behind Leonardo, standing tall, having no need for his wheelchair yet, was Lawrence Henderson, smiling at Abi's fright of seeing a Sevardinal present.

"Abi, I do believe you've met Leonardo Sevardina, Sevardinal and *Withardina* to boot." Chuckled Lawrence as he patted the cranky Leo on the shoulder and pushed past him into the gleaming white, yet dim room of the 6 children.

Quietly approaching Lawrence, Abi quietly spoke into his hear, out of earshot of both Leo and the rest of the *nurses*. "Sir, may I ask what his purpose is here?"

Looking surprised, Lawrence simply blinked at Abi then turned to the room at large, clearly defying Abi's hope of confidentiality. "Well he's here to help in the authorization of such a monumental occasion, I mean surely you did not think we were going to let just the 7 of you Jackals do the authentication yourself did you?" chuckled Lawrence once more, only in a slightly condescending tone, one that hurt Abigail's feelings more than she cared to admit.

"Now, if you would be so kind as to assist me ladies and gentlemen, I would like to inspect the first child please, Leo?" signaled Lawrence to Leo, who clearly had zoned out for a moment, but quickly recovered and moved into position beside Lawrence at the far left cradle.

"But sir, we already have a confirmation from the NICU, it's the third one, the one I birthed!" exclaimed Ainsley, hopeful to garner some attention from both Lawrence, her superior, and Leo, her idol of sorts. But instead all she got was an annoyed strong arm from Lawrence, signaling her to silence herself. And so she did.

As the first lid cracked open, a decompressed sound could be heard, as the recycled high percentage O2 was released from with in the cradles confines. And as soon as it did, the wailing began. Crunching his wrinkled hands over his droopy ears, Leo was clearly aggravated with having to be here. "Lets get on with it already!" demanded Leo.

And so, carefully lifting up the newborn boy, the male nurse, the head honcho of the bunch below Abi of course, held the child mid air, and waited, watching for Leo's actions. But all he saw was his disgust at something.

Then realizing Leonardo's short stature, and his brooding hold of the child overhead, he quickly lowered him down to Leo's level.

"That's more like it... now lets see..." said Leo, as he carefully scrutinized everything about the newborn boy, from his fingernails, to the tiny tuft of Jet-black hair narrowly scalped to his head. Finally, in perhaps the more bizarre of acts to the bewildered lower level Jackals, Leo withdrew from his grew tweed vest his platinum lighter and held it underneath the newborn's forearm. And as quickly as he did, he snapped it shut and walked away. "Nope, not one of us!" he declared and quickly moved onto the next child, a girl, with a glorious golden tone of skin, but with no hair to speak of.

Spending no time at all on her, he quickly dismissed her, not even bothering with his usual once over, and simply jumping to the flame test. Almost as if he knew what he was looking for, and she wasn't it.

As he arrived at Ainsley's cradle, where she lay, a small blondish (for the time) tuft of hair, doing playful swirls upon her head, he slowly, up on his tip toes, eyed the girl, waiting for the lid to be lifted for him. As the red headed nurse, who happened to be closest at the time, did the honors of lifting off the lid, it took Leo but a millisecond to declare, "She is one of us!!!!" he excitedly proclaimed, almost shocked at his own words. All were shocked and awed, all except Abi, who already knew that was the case.

Leaning down over her, Lawrence examined her more closely. "Are you sure Leo? You have to be sure?" cautiously asked Lawrence, obviously not convinced. "I'm sure of it, we can tell each other apart you know."

"Smiling down at his old friend, Lawrence looked once more down at Ainsley, fast asleep amongst all the commotion, and gently shut the lid once more. The LED went green, validating what both Abi and Leo knew in an instant.

Despite being overlooked and disregarded, Abi couldn't help but be pleased she was the one that birthed the girl; it was sure to advance her position. But as she thought of all the places she'd get to go, being upped from a low level Jackal to a high class one, she did not realize the break of happiness that occurred thanks to Leo as he reached the final cradle, empty.

"WHERE IS HE!!!" hysterically asked Leonardo, beyond distraught at the absent child, as if it were his own.

All looked to him confused, especially Abi, having only just tuned back in. "I'm sorry where is who?" asked one of the female nurses, confused. Annoyed, and unable to contain his anger, Leo raised his short cane and bashed at the nurses chin causing her to gasp in pain and limp back away toward a gurney in the back of the room.

Trying to remedy the situation, Lawrence approached carefully. "My friend, what ever do you mean, we were only here to find the one child, we were told there was to be only one…"

"Who told you that crap? Edmondus wasn't it! Figures you'd trust that quack of a *Sevi*." Raged Leo, mumbling under his breath. This did not ease the group's confusion. "I'm sorry but I still don't understand friend." Admitted Lawrence, chuckling slightly, trying his best to lighten the mood, especially in front of his subordinates, showing he was still in control.

Flicking his finger, gesturing for Lawrence to lean down to his level, Lawrence did as he was told.

The room was deafly quiet, and yet as Leo spoke softly into Lawrence's ear, not a sound could be registered.

As Lawrence rose from his hunched position, his back turned to everyone; Abi could tell by his tensed upper body that he had heard dreadful

248

news. Sighing, Lawrence turned, with a gracious smile back to his group. "Alright guys, you have all done splendidly, if you would all be so kind as to deliver these five children back to their respective parents, and also be sure to apologize for the delay." Spoke Lawrence, keeping his leadership unwearied by the news. They all nodded and left, all but Abi, Leonardo and Lawrence. After the group had left, the two gentlemen quickly, but still quietly broke out into argument, only to have Leo end it abruptly and storm off out of the room.

Confused, and wishing for some sort of insight into the obvious issue at hand, Abi quietly, approached Lawrence who had settled, hands on both sides, of Ainsley's cradle.

"Larry, what's going on?" asked Abi. She got no reply, approaching the other side of the cradle, Abi, briefly looked down that Ainsley, the new Sevardinal. Then back to Lawrence, who was now staring intensely at her? "Larry?" started Abi, "you will be her guardian, her mom for all intensive purposes, you *birthed* her, its only fair you raise her, she'll need a Jackal at hand to fend off from SLC agents." Bluntly ordered Lawrence.

Abi nodded to this, "but what about her parents, how can we do this Her parents won't allow us...", "Don't worry about her parents Abi, I'll think of something... tell them the child died perhaps..." proposed Lawrence, much to Abi's dismay.

"Oh no, don't do that..." started Abi, getting emotional at saying such things, for she was once destined to be the mother of a Sevardinal, however, it wasn't meant to be, for her womb was deemed *hostile*, and as such, she couldn't reproduce. Abi couldn't imagine what it must be like to lose a child, and she was certainly not going to be the cause of such a tall tale. However she also wasn't cool with stealing a child either, despite how desperately she wanted one. That's when the idea hit her. "I got it! Recruit them!"

This caused Lawrence to gawk in disbelief, "You can't be serious Abi?" "I'm deadly serious, recruit them, that way they won't be completely cut off from their kid, and we can keep an even closer watch over the girl. Plus, when they rank high enough we could even let them take over?" countered Abi.

Lawrence thought for a moment, considering the idea. "If we did this, I would hold you responsible for any issues that arise, do you understand?" warned Lawrence, almost accepting Abi's offer.

Abigail happily nods. Then smiling, the pair of them shook their hands and carted out Ainsley from the room. Strolling down the hall, they pause, allowing Lawrence to dawn a doctor's coat and badge, giving him the impression of working at said hospital. "Well, I guess I'll go ahead and start the recruitment process," said Lawrence smiling. It was at this though that Abi recalled her initial question.

"Sir... what was it that Leo told you, if you don't mind me asking?"

Breaking his smile, obviously pained at confessing this, Lawrence leaned in quietly, and whispered two words, vague if you didn't have the context. Lawrence whispered:

Another one...

XXXVII. Its good to be with Family

"Another one?" repeated Ainsley, confused for a moment. Both Joyce and Rick dropped their gaze, disappointed they'd have to go into further detail on the subject. "Yes, cause Ainsley, you see, you weren't supposed to be alone, at least according to both Leo and the *Natal*, you were supposed to have a sort of twin that night." Explained Rick, "Twin?" quirked Ainsley, "Yes, a Sevardinal sibling... of sorts..." explained Joyce further, which pushed Ainsley over the edge.

"Huh? Look guys you have completely lost me, I thought you were telling me how I ended up with Abigail, not some phantom Sevardinal kid who died... what does this have to do with anything?!" shouted Ainsley, growing angry with feeling so overwhelmingly uninformed.

Joyce squeezed her grip tighter around Ainsley's hand, trying her best to calm her estranged daughter. "I know, I am sorry about all this being so confusing, it's not an easy thing to explain." Joyce teared up slightly at thinking back. "Why'd you give me up?" coldly asked Ainsley.

It was then that Joyce broke down and started to weep openly, which brought Rick's arms around her caressing her back soothingly. Then turning back to Ainsley, who felt no sympathy for her new mother, "Look Ainsley you have to see what kind of situation we were put in... We were both only in our early twenties at the time; we didn't know a thing about the world. All we knew is we wanted to keep you. But then this man, this; Lawrence comes and tells us that we don't have a choice in the matter, he starts spouting all these terrible accusations at us, about how there were numerous reports from friends and family alike telling him that we were unfit parents. That we wouldn't be able to raise you properly... And the sad thing is... he was probably right, we were a mess back then, we didn't know what we were doing. But then he tells us the only way we may stay in your life is by joining this 'society'; he described it at the time as an organization for unfit parents, a sort of place to *train* us and make us better. He wasn't totally wrong."

This caused Rick to fall into deep thought, still automatically rubbing his wife's back slowly. Staring at them, trying to digest and understand their predicament, Ainsley came to only one sad realization, completely unrelated to her parents. *The FTC aren't always good...*

"Fine, okay, so why didn't you guys sue him, flip him off curse his name, tell him he had no right to say such things, why didn't you fight for me?" argued Ainsley. "We tried to, of course we tried to, but you don't understand Ainsley, the FTC is everywhere, with the flick of a pen, they can change your whole life, they can rewrite your history, literally, claim you were a child rapist, and there isn't anything you can do about it, its either join them, or go into hiding. We only saw one option that gave us any possibility of seeing you again." Told Rick, smiling only briefly seeing the look on Ainsley's face, recognizing in her the sense of understanding.

He was right, Ainsley did understand, if it were her child, and a powerful essence came in and blackmailed you into taking your child, and there wasn't anything you could do about it, Ainsley could see herself doing the same thing. But one thing remained odd.

"Okay, I understand, but why did you stay with them, what now, that I'm here, are you going to leave the FTC? Your reasons for being here are over. Aren't they?" asked Ainsley.

Taking deep breaths, calming herself and wiping away her tears, Joyce resumed the conversation. "We stay now, because despite there truly

252

despicable ways, despite them taking you away from us, something I'll never forgive them for, never forgive Abi for letting happen, they do offer one very important service. They look after you. They love you, just as much as us granted for differing reasons. You are their treasure; their secret. Even if we did leave, they still would be here, there, everywhere, watching us, we'd never truly be apart of them."

Ainsley thought about this for a moment, and decided she agreed. *Joyce, my mom… she's pretty smart..* Ainsley mused happily to herself, liking her parents more and more, each and every moment she spent with them. "I see," offered Ainsley, biding for more time to think and let all this new information sink in.

However, her parents took this as a distressing sign. "We really do love you Ainsley, we only did what we thought was best given the circumstances we were put in." desperately explained Rick.

Ainsley, though no longer mad at her parents, did think it odd that if they loved her so much, why then they never tried to contact her before. But given the situation, with both the FTC and SLC constantly watching and listening, it made sense. *They didn't because they couldn't.* And it was then that Ainsley instantly switched over from blaming her parents to sympathizing for them. *I couldn't imagine being torn away from my child and told you weren't allowed to contact them.* Thought Ainsley, depressing herself at the thought.

Breaking her comatose gaze, Ainsley made eye contact with her emotional parents. And sensing their ever-observant gazes, smiled warmly, hoping that would sate their worries. It did. They smiled right back. Just as warm, just as lovingly. And it was at this thought, this feeling of love, that

Ainsley suddenly realized that for all those 13 years she spent with Abigail, she never, not once, said: I love you.

Did she care for me at all? Thought Ainsley.

Reading her thoughts like he so skillfully showed earlier, Rick replied though retorted, "More than she'll ever want to admit."

Not even flinching at Rick's telepathy, Ainsley, much like Joyce, took in a deep breath and calmed herself not noticing till that moment how she was holding her breath.

Rising from the table, Ainsley paused for a moment, not sure how to leave the conversation, one so loaded with information. Picking up her books, she looked once more at her parents, both expectantly looking at their child. Opening her mouth, she wanted to tell them that she was glad they were her parents, glad that they finally found her. Tell them that she was happy for the first time in as long as she could remember. But instead, all she could muster was, "I'm tired... I think I'm going to go to bed..."

Slouching slightly, clearly deflated at the anticlimactic remark, both Joyce and Rick rose as well and walked round the table toward Ainsley, and without her permission, gave her the biggest group hug the duo could manage. It was heaven. Ainsley didn't want it to end. Neither did Rick or Joyce. But it did, and carrying her books with her, Ainsley disappeared from the fourth floor of the Narrow Abode, up to bed. Ainsley knew things were going to be different now. And as she lay there on the mystically expanded bed out of the wall, she fell asleep, smiling.

XXXVIII. Reading at the Table

Ainsley had one of the best night sleeps she could have remembered, filled with dreams of a life she may have once had, had she not been born into Sevardinal. But though it never happened, in a way, it glazed over all the years of absence that Rick and Joyce been.

Picking up her books, Ainsley noticed that she was plus one. Sometime during the night, Rick or Joyce, or whoever had returned to her *The Sevardinal*, a book she was sure she'd never see again just a month ago, was now sitting atop her other mystical, and quirky texts. Ainsley couldn't contain her happiness at seeing it. She jumped down the steps and saw no one in the *dining room*. However the faintest of familiar odors could be detected, perhaps an odor is not the right word, aroma. Following her nose, Ainsley descended two flights, only to come to the sight of Rick and Joyce, somehow, given the still have-sunk stature of the appliances, and the stagnant smell emanating from the floors below, had made breakfast, or were rather still making breakfast.

Joyce noticed Ainsley first. "Oh damn! We were going to surprise you with breakfast in bed!" confessed Joyce happily, Ainsley could only think *you already did.* Carrying over a plate with a full palate of scrambled eggs mixed with cheese, sausage, hash browns, and a tall glass of orange juice. Ainsley had never seen such a scrumptious meal.

Backing up to the mini table Ainsley bumped into it accidently, causing the room to expand much like last night, causing the table to fully reveal itself. Sitting down, Ainsley was speechless at the hospitality that Joyce was giving her, something she was never used to. Grey gruel and stale bread at

Singing Loons, and multi grain cereal at Abigail's; Ainsley never had a good meal in her life. She did that day.

"Thank you so much! That was amazing!" exclaimed Ainsley, unable to keep her containment about the meal she just ingested. Her parents, both just finishing off their eggs, and making their way to the sausage, simply smiled and let out appreciated giggles, making Ainsley feel accepted. "No problem sweetie." Said Joyce, which broke right through Ainsley, causing her to drop her gushing about the meal, and everything else, and all she could think about was *its not fair, why didn't I get her, them for 16 years?*

Rick sensed what she thought, but didn't probe; he could feel it was rhetorical. Letting out a sigh, Ainsley cleansed her thoughts once more, promising she'd no longer feel sorry for herself, or her parents. She was going to take charge.

"Rr... Dad" Ainsley awkwardly started, to which both Rick and especially Joyce gave a winning smile. "Yes dear?" he replied. "I was just wondering some things.." continued Ainsley, "yeah what is that?", "so I'm sort of the reason for all this feuding and secrecy, me and the other Sevardinal right?" asked Ainsley.

"You got it, exactly. Why do you ask?" replied Rick. "Its just, everyone has been lecturing me about this and that, giving me all this information that I'm not ready to handle, but am forced too. I don't like it. I want to be in charge of what I know and don't know, you know?" casually said Ainsley to both Rick and Joyce, who were slightly confused. "I'm not sure I'm following honey." Confessed Joyce.

Rolling her eyes, Ainsley picked up her books, and set them down hard on the table, causing some of the lighter items to leap this way and that. "Oh my, you have so many books." Said Joyce surprised; having given the recent events hadn't even noticed them.

"I know I do... Don't you want to know how I got them? Do you want to know what they are?" proudly asked Ainsley, happy for once that she knew something the FTC, didn't.

Rick who, was usually very good at figuring this, was stumped, having only recognized one book. "Well, that one is *The Sevardinal*, your volume. That much I am sure, but as for the others... I can't be sure, any idea sweetheart?" asked Rick looking to his wife for guidance. She just shrugged her shoulders. Then both of them looked to Ainsley.

"Well dad, you are right, this is *The Sevardinal*, third volume of the *Sevio Dionisus*. And these two, I think you'll both want to take a closer look at..." pushing the equally large mystery volume and the dwarfed notebook toward the couple, Ainsley sat back smugly and sipped at her dwindling orange juice.

Having given Rick the large volume, he looked it over carefully, much like a paleontologist examining a fossil. Rolling it over in his hands, his face got closer and closer to it, examining each and ever marking it possessed. Meanwhile his wife, Joyce, took a much more relaxed approach, merely flipping through it here and there.

Ainsley was quite proud of herself, she conceived this plan late last night, just before she fell asleep, she desperately wanted to know more about these books, having not gotten a chance to ask Leonardo about them, but she was sick and tired of being told everything, so she concocted this scheme in which she played up knowing and made them figure it out. It was awesome. Especially their equally exponential faces, growing full of excitement.

257

Then quite to the surprise of everyone at the table, they all came to a shocking discovery, all except Ainsley, who once again was just confused. Saying in unison, both Rick and Joyce said, "Oh my god!!!"

Turning to one another they quickly compared notes, and showed each other their discoveries, then turned back to Ainsley. "Ains do you know what these are??" Asked Joyce, excited, not remembering Ainsley had claimed she did. Being stubborn though, Ainsley lied, "Of course I do!" but then chickened out. "What are they?"

"This is amazing! I can't believe it survived!" Said Rick now holding the little notebook. Which Ainsley thought odd considering it was just something Lia gave her long ago, just a journal she inherited from someone even longer ago.

"What survived? Could you please fill me in on what's so amazing about all this?" demanded Ainsley; disappointed she lost control of the situation again.

Calming herself, Joyce excitedly laid down the large volume she held and looked adoringly at Ainsley. "These are two very special books, that one in particular, if we were to pick one being more special than the other, that would be it." Said Joyce, pointing to the notebook. Ainsley only responded with a twisted face of not understanding. So Joyce continued, "These books Ainsley, they are BOTH part of the set, the *Sevio Dionisus*, this big one, which I figure you must've guessed or knew was a volume, is actually *Conratbadna* or how we pronounce it *Contraband*, the seventh and final volume in the set. Inside that book is all the final answers, to this world, it's the end of days, perhaps the single most important timeframe, undoubtedly the most unknown." Explained Joyce. "How come?" asked Ainsley.

"Well simple Ains, all the Sevardinal that are put in charge of it, somehow all seem to end up dying somehow. That little baby, the *twin*, you were supposed to have, he would have been in charge of this book, had he lived. Since then, none have managed to live long…" explained Joyce, in perhaps the clearest she's ever done. This appalled Ainsley, she didn't know she was carrying around a death trap, though given what happened to both, Patrick, his dad, and that infant, it now seemed to make sense.

Joyce didn't stop her gushing at that though. "But Ainsley, this right here, this is truly remarkable." Said Joyce holding up the notebook. Taking it from her hands, Rick gave it back to Ainsley. "Can you guess what that is?" he playfully asked, to which Ainsley just shrugged, having no clue.

"This is something, that everyone, and I mean everyone, FTC, SLC, history, would have thought destroyed, and yet, somehow you have it… Ainsley, this is the *Natal*.

Ainsley just stared blankly for a moment. "It is?" was all she could get out, not understanding at all, how she came to have, it how Lia came to have it, how anyone came to have it that somehow ended up in that place. That's when she recalled the one person in that place who could have brought it with him. *Leonardo*.

"This book, was destroyed 30 years ago, or at least it was thought to be, burned down in a fire. In a historical museum in Zurich, many great works went up in flames that day… How'd you get it?" asked Rick, to which Joyce joined in at looking at Ainsley curiously.

Ainsley didn't wait time in reciting her experiences in the Singing Loon's basement, in the SLC sect, where she met Leonardo, what he told her, about how that's where she found Lia, and the book. She also told about the curious case of Patrick, how he arrived, the strange old man, the book, the burns, and how he somehow was allowed to have a candle in his room, the night he died.

"I can answer that, at least I think, I can guess at least… If the SLC thought he had the book, that would explain why they moved them to Singing Loons, it would also explain the candle, they would know from their agents in the NYM that he was suicidal, prone to fire, given his history. So they probably intentionally gave him the flame hoping he'd act out of his depression and take his life, thus letting them swoop in and claim the book for themselves. Stick it in one of their ghastly sects, much like the one you saw Ainsley. Just a guess." Said Rick, still in deep though, contemplating all the possible conspiracies.

Joyce just shook her head at him. "Rick my darling you really are paranoid, that's just crazy. However, for the sake of not knowing any other alternatives, we'll believe you, the bit that concerns me is that they have Leonardo." Said Joyce concerned. "Why is that a concern? Besides the obvious of him being in a giant prison, he seemed happy enough…" said Ainsley, thinking back and realizing that wasn't necessarily true. He seemed very impatient with Ainsley, almost as if he was afraid the ax was to fall on them at any moment, *may that be why he forced me out so soon?*

"That's a concern Ainsley because Leonardo Sevardina is the oldest and most wise retired Sevardinal we have, he also happens to be Witherney, which doesn't help." Explained Rick. "What's a *Witherney*? I thought that was just the fourth book?" Asked Ainsley.

"It is, but the reason it was named *The Witherney*, is because of Leonardo, at least originally it was, now it refers to all his followers as well. Basically Ains, a Witherney, is a Sevardinal, who is capable of entering and

260

exiting any volume of the *Sevio Dionisus*, he is the overseer of the other Sevardinal, the keeper if you will. It goes like this, he runs his course as a Sevardinal, then based on that, he is *elected* to Witherney, you yourself could be one, only time will tell. But once you are one, you are in charge, you stand above the seven Sevardinal, as your own entity, you can rewrite any part history, to an extent, you can't bring back dinosaurs or anything, but you can prevent certain events from happening, hell you can even rearrange things. Everything you saw in there, was somewhat influenced by Leonardo. Out here, given time, he can even rearrange things here, like the wall, in the Sect Ainsley. But most importantly, and what's most relative to this conversation is, out here, he's in charge of the *Natal* he is its keeper.

Suddenly it all made sense, Leo had mentioned he'd been down there for a while, at least 10 years, and perhaps, 10 years ago, Lia came to visit him, and he gave her the book, and she took it, not knowing why, but because of his power and influence, he convinced her to, knowing that some day, she would meet me… *Wow.*

Ainsley couldn't believe it; what's more, knowing what she knew now, she knew it was bad news that he was trapped there. Ainsley didn't even bother to ask why he couldn't break out, given how high tech that room was; Ainsley suspected it was built just to accommodate him. "We gotta get him out of there!" shouted Ainsley, a little louder than she intended. Gladly, her parents didn't say anything.

"I agree, but now's not the time, nor the place, Leo can wait, he more than anyone despises the SLC, he won't tell them anything. I suspect they are keeping him there mainly to suppress his knowledge. Didn't manage to keep it from you though did they?" smugly asked Rick knowing the answer.

Though Ainsley did recall how the door automatically snapped shut and locked after she left, perhaps they intended to let her in.

"No they didn't… Okay, well what's the plan then?" assertively asked Ainsley.

And at this, her parents jumped to life running round the room, cleaning things off, Joyce briefly disappeared upstairs only to return with books and maps galore. Splaying them out over the table, clearly organizing a war room of sorts.

Standing now, Rick looked down at papers that meant nothing to Ainsley, "well first, we need to get you back in there" said Rick. To which Ainsley only said, "huh? What about Leo?"

Then walking peevishly by Joyce said, "we'll take care of him, our Jackals are forming right now. We'll get him out of there don't worry. But right now, this instant we need to get you in THERE!"

"Where?"

And at that moment, both Rick and Joyce pointed to the front most maps. A map of a place Ainsley had never seen before, looking somewhat like the United Kingdom, and Australia, but clearly not either, with names and places and mountain ridges she'd never heard of. None of it was clear until she spotted one place on the map that did. The Maltyrn Woods.

They wanted her to go back there, to the land beyond, the other world, the inland island, call it what you will, they wanted her to fulfill her duty as a Sevardinal. And the only thought that occurred was, *but we only just met…*

Sadness was clearly written on Ainsley's face, but rather than Rick taking note, Joyce did this time, and came round and gave Ainsley the biggest most loving hug she could. "You won't be gone a moment in our time. You'll be back before you know it. Then you and I can go shopping, as you can see, I could use a girlfriend to straighten out my fashion sense." Joked Joyce, making light of her mismatched safari get up that she constantly wore it seemed. This break of tension helped, and Ainsley relaxed enough, to accept it. "Alright, but only because you said so m-mom." If Joyce was squeezing tight before, it was pale in comparison to how hard she was squeezing after hearing herself be called mom.

Seeing that Ainsley was turning blue from lack of oxygen, Rick stepped in and pried Joyce away. "Oh I'm so sorry dear." Said Joyce apologetically to which Ainsley just waved her hand considerately.

Stepping in between them, Rick offered up his elbow once more, just like when he walked her to the door last night. Smiling just like she did last night Ainsley accepted it and let Rick guide her, it was only then that she noticed he was carrying the books.

Arriving on the sixth floor, Rick pulled down the hidden stairway without a hitch, and Ainsley was relieved to see that no skeletons were left in the attic, no was the gaping hole. The FTC must've repaired it during her absence. And instead of the grody tweed chair that sat there last time, instead what sat there, Ainsley had to double take. It was her chair! From Singing Loons!

"How did you??" started Ainsley to which Rick answered, "Well you didn't think we were just not going to make an appearance there just cause we picked you up a little early, we had to, and we offered to dispose of that chair, seeing as no one ever used it, so we took it. It arrived early this morning we lifted it over your head, I was amazed you didn't wake." Joked Rick. But Ainsley wasn't in the mood to joke; instead, she tightly wrapped her hands around Rick's waist and gave him a big hug, seeing as he had no idea how much that meant to her.

"Thank you."

Releasing, she looked up and smiled then sat down in the chair, relishing in its familiar shape and feel; the cracked leather, soothing her right wise. Sighing happily, Ainsley didn't even notice as Rick turned on the overhead lamp, also new, not the cracked, bankers lamp Artie used, but a stainless steel, floor lamp with a long twisting arm.

Plopping the trio of books down on the table near them Rick pulled *The Sevardinal*, away from the stack and set it down in Ainsley's lap, then, he handed her the key, something she was sure was long since lost, but was indeed like he said in his letter, safe.

Taking it, she looked at it briefly and then set it in the lock. Looking up to Rick, he simply smiled, and said, "Don't worry we aren't going anywhere, we'll be right here when you get back."

This soothed Ainsley a little, "But where am I going when I get there?" anxiously asked Ainsley. Rick just chuckled. "How am I to know, just listen to your heart, it'll tell you." Ainsley assumed he meant the Voice, so she would do that; she let it guide her, no questions.

Nodding, Ainsley hugged her dad once more, and then before she chickened out, twisted the lock.

XXXIX. Reaching the Coast

The ground was cold and moist, smelling of recently fallen rain. Ainsley suspected this is what a rainforest would smell like, if she ever had been to one. Above her, high above, were the ceiling that she had once known, long ago, she was back in the woods of Maltyrn. Only this time, she was utterly alone.

Not a sole around her, no animals either, no soft buzzing of a wilderness filled with life. It was silent.

Rising slowly, Ainsley looked round, noticing, if she wasn't mistaken, that she was in the exact same spot she was before, when she collapsed, falling face first from the young gawn.

Standing, she looked deep into the distance, seeing if she could see any sign of Eye or the gawn, or anyone really. She saw nothing, only the deep maroon of the trees, as the sun set in the trees, long after the real one had.

Ainsley didn't know what to do, she was alone, in perhaps one of the most dangerous places in the world, and she didn't have a clue where she was going. Eye was supposed to be guiding her, but he was nowhere to be found. Granted, Ainsley also didn't know how long she had been gone, a few minutes, a day, and a year? A week? A year? A few years? Ainsley suspected the latter. If that were indeed the case, Eye would have long given up on her, and her silly little quest north.

Knowing what she knew now about this place, she knew being alone and without a guide was not what she wanted, she needed protection, especially since she was probably the most uniformed Sevardinal ever to live. She figured most Sevardinal were indoctrinated in the art of observing undetected, keeping just enough of a distance, to be safe, but not enough to not be involved. But here Ainsley was, her third time back, and she already had been almost trampled by giant deer, killed by a cannibalistic tribesman, and gouged by and angry mother deer. Ainsley did not like being back. And chose to ignore the warm satisfied sensation that continually rushed through her, making her get that absent feeling that she refused to admit, a feeling of having missed the place, a feeling of being home.

Deciding that standing still would be the worst option available to her, Ainsley moved in the general direction that she and Eye were fleeing.

Welcome back Ainsley. Politely and disinterestedly said the Voice, which as it always did, caught Ainsley off guard, causing her to topple sideways flailing her hands wildly to prevent the perpetrator from nabbing her.

Relax, I'm not going to hurt, that would be the worst thing I could do, if you die, I have no purpose in life I cease to exist! Explained the Voice, to Ainsley whom was only half listening, still recovering from the shock. "You scared the shit out of me! I'm going to have to teach you some manners sometime!" grouchily retorted Ainsley. *That would be most inappropriate, I'm not human, I'm just part of you, and you don't have any manners, so any attempts you made wouldn't be proper manners in the first place.* Argued the Voice, proving it wasn't human by taking no pleasure in proving Ainsley wrong. It didn't stop Ainsley from feeling annoyed.

"You aren't doing a good job of reminding me why I should even stay here and not just throw up my hands and wait till I get yanked back out again you know." *I'm sorry about that, I don't mean to be a smartass, its just facts.* Apologetically spoke the Voice. "Whatever." Was all that Ainsley deemed necessary to that apology.

I detect that you've grown bitter since I've been with you last… cautiously dared the Voice. And caution was the right idea, because Ainsley flipped. "Bitter? I've grown bitter have I! I thought you were still with me out of here just unable to talk?!" yelled Ainsley forgetting the need for silence for a moment. *This is true, I can hear and see everything you do.* "Then why in the world do I need to explain to you why I'm bitter!" screamed Ainsley.

You don't, I was merely offering me as a good person to talk to if you need a good listener. Calmly informed the Voice, to which Ainsley just scoffed. "You, a good listener? You are me! You basically just told me I should talk about my shit to myself! Wow, I really did need to be in that place." *That's not true Ainsley; I detect no signs of brain deformation or malignance. You were a prisoner, nothing more.*

Instead of listening to what the Voice was saying, Ainsley couldn't help but notice how it was saying it. "Is it just me or have you gotten more… intellectual since we last talked, you talked pretty much just like me last time, now you seem to be almost like a cyborg or something." *I'm not just some cybertronic organism, I'm the same voice you spoke to last time, and only thing that's changed is I've gotten smarter. Much smarter.* Explained the Voice, "How so? Why? I mean, I'm not smarter." Asked Ainsley. *Oh but Ainsley you are, you just deny it to yourself, you are incredibly smart, and its because of this that I am even more so. For you see, because I am a 'dual consciousness' as some refer to it, that means that anything you learn, I learn everything there is to know about it. I'm basically a carbon copy of you, but only on extreme doses of steroids.* Explained the voice. "So let me get this straight, anything I know a little about you, you know everything there is about?" inquired Ainsley. *Yes, you understand perfectly.* Ainsley wasn't convinced. "So, if I said I wanted to know more about the *Sevio Dionisus*, what could you tell me?" If the voice could sigh, it would have then. *I'm afraid that subject and anything to do with the origin of this world, is beyond my capacity. I can only know things I see with you, either here or else where, if we were to say be in the first volume, 'The Fools Wish' then I could tell you all about it, but unfortunately we aren't. I can tell you what little is available from this time frame?* Offered up the Voice. Ainsley was delighted to hear this. *Very well, what little information I have obtained is that whatever created those books, and birthed this new world, was from long ago, before your European settlers landed on North America, even before the Vikings before them. And even before the great tribesmen of the Asian Plains crossed the icy passage to the Place you now call Canada. They came and discovered this land. Who they were, is uncertain, at least to me, where they went, or how made these living time capsules of their history is a mystery, at least to me for now.* Explained the voice, soundly a little frustrated that it couldn't give a full answer, Ainsley didn't mind though, she was beyond happy with that answer.

And so it went, they walked for hours on end, each and every day, some times in silence, others in full conversation, Q and A about this and that, the proper name of those Giant Deer's; *Megaloceros giganteus*; what plants and fruits were delectable and which were lethal. How the Maltyrn trees obtained their illusionary everlasting skies, the list of questions never ended.

One day however, the questions abruptly stopped, for the skyrocketed trees overhead, suddenly ceased their outward battle, and gave way to rolling hills, green and lush, rising and falling hundreds of feet, obscuring their road; a common occurrence here. This sight struck Ainsley. "Is this still Maltyrn?" she asked. *Yes,*

but only just, just a few more miles, and we'll be onto Sevardinal country.
Explained the Voice. "Wait! I have my own country!" excitedly exclaimed
Ainsley, the Voice laughed. *No, you don't, that would defeat the point of you and
your brethren needing to keep hidden now wouldn't it?* Jokingly asked the Voice.
Ainsley just lowered her head in foolishness. *No, I guess I should have explained
this earlier. Sevardinal, at least here, holds multiple meanings. Its not exclusive to
you and your others, it also refers to any group of 7 or more people who are
highly influential or powerful. So when I speak of 'Sevardinal country' I'm in fact
referring to the Seven Queens of Galesport.*

Ainsley couldn't help but ask, "and who are they?"

*The Seven Sisters, Queens of Galesport, they are Galena, Treysta, Luvia,
Lolati, Flantia, Renavive, and Belle. Decedents of a long since fallen nation are
the last remaining royal bloodline in this world. All other provinces, or war states
more like, are ruled over by tyrants and sadists. Galesport remains the last free
nation. And event that is at risk. For once the forces of Maltyrn and Gaste finish
their feud of the Barren Wastes, where we first met. They will turn their sights on
Galesport.* Told the Voice with as much an authority as a voice could have. "But
why, what's so special about Galesport?" logically asked Ainsley, knowing there
was sure to be an answer.

*You must first understand this place Ainsley, every coast East, South
and West is a rocky maze of horror, no ship, despite the skill of their
captains, can traverse it, and most of the coast for that matter is sharp cliffs,
falling off for hundreds of feet, making for a perilous climb and even more
risky decent, that's partially why this place has never been discovered,
whomever arrived always either stayed, or died trying to escape. The answer
to your question is this, Galesport, as its basis for a nation, is a bay, a gulf,
with a respectably wide coast along the inner rim that is nothing but lush*

beaches; a most desirable location indeed for ambitious tyrants. Ainsley now understood. "Because if they claimed it, they could leave this place, they could, go out into the real world…" guessed Ainsley. *Precisely, luckily the Sevardinal of Galesport is the most cunning and industrious of peoples, as you will soon see.* Teased the Voice.

And sure enough early that following morning, having not stopped for the night being so near civilization, Ainsley saw exactly what was so amazing.

There, from their vantage point, high up on a steep cliff looking over the entire of the bay, lay their scene of Galesport, a brimming society indeed. Along every inch of the glorious white beach, was a massive chain of a city, stretching all around the bay. Never ending it seemed. Shops, ports, docks, castles, straw thatched houses, and all was there, all surrounding the crystal blue waters of the bay. But as Ainsley's view panned across the panorama of the splendor, her eyes finally fell upon perhaps the most immaculate structure ever created by man anywhere.

The Voice read Ainsley's mind. *Behold, the Bridge of Treysta!*

A bridge was an understatement, one wouldn't be able to tell it were one save for the three large noticeable arches along the base, and seven on the other side, making entering and exiting the bay tricky, but doable still. The structure, was very much like what Ainsley had once read about in a sleazy old tabloid whilst she was in Singing Loons; she had read about how the London Bridge had only just been moved from London to Arizona of all places, and along with the immense effort of moving the bridge, came a brief but potent backstory, including one of the first incarnations of the bridge, which supported a teeming village along its length. The Bridge of Treysta was like that, only ten fold.

Where the London Bridge rose only but as high as the royal houses did, which at most was three floors, the Treysta Bridge rose several, it was hard to tell, it had at least 7 decipherable 'levels' to it, each probably making up 3 floors, which given this places nature would make sense. The higher it rose the more Ainsley was impressed, though all she could really see was grey brick quarried from who knows where, the immense size of the bridge alone deserved awe. It scaled so high that there even was a bridge on top for those travellers coming from the cliffs up above needing to get to the other side of the city in a hurry. What it reminded Ainsley the most of was a… wall.

Precisely, for you see Ainsley, travellers have accidently or otherwise ventured as far as the gape of the Galesport, and it was decided rather than risking one slipping by undetected, they'd build a wall, a defense mechanism that would shut out unwanted eyes, and limit traffic into the bay, it also helped that they were planning on building a bridge anyways so a fortified fortress is what they got. It alone is a city. Explained the Voice rather unexpectedly.

Ainsley was speechless. She wanted nothing more than to go to that bridge, and sure enough, that was exactly where they needed to go. But it wasn't until the following morning that they reached their current destination, *the gates of Treysta.*

XL. The Citerary

Standing flush with the bridge, Ainsley couldn't get over its immense size and grandeur. The large entrance alone, though at a distance appeared but the size of a keyhole, up close lay enormous.

Hundreds of people all minding their own business, consistently went to and frow from the massive mouth of the bridge. Amongst them Ainsley felt more insignificant than ever before, which if any of the ignorant peoples knew, wasn't the case.

"I can't believe the size of this place! I mean the city, the bridge, the bay, its... gorgeous." Exclaimed Ainsley. *Yes it is, however you are incorrect about one thing...* said the Voice. Looking up, thinking that would be the best way to 'look' at the voice in her head, Ainsley furrowed her brow in confusion. "How do you mean?" she asked. *You are incorrect in thinking of it as a 'city' when in fact it is many cities, 6 to be precise, well 7 if you include the bridge. Which most people do.* Spoke the Voice, then forcibly taking control of Ainsley's limbs, the Voice spun Ainsley round stopping about face looking at the deepest part of the gulf. Then raising her arm, the Voice pointed to a particularly large cluster of buildings. *That is Gale, the Capitol of Galesport, founded by the eldest of the Sevardinal, Galen; it is mostly used as a governing headquarters, made up mostly of political offices, and dignitaries. However it also houses many important trading posts, due to the large and relatively straight passage it carves through the mountainous terrain behind it. However that has ceased due to the wars south.* Then the voice slightly turned Ainsley and her pointing finger the right.

There, though smaller than Gale, lay Luveir; nothing more than a residential quadrant, home to most citizens who commute to and from Galen and Lola. The voice then directed Ainsley to the rather tall set of buildings being erected near the quaint series of buildings that made up Luveir. *Those that live in Lola are almost all architects and stoneworkers, most escaping the Stone Quarries of Terra-Mal, they are all responsible for the splendor that makes up the structures of Galesport, they just recently finished the Bridge of Treysta in fact. And are now working on expanding both Lola and if you see there...* said the voice turning Ainsley's head to the barren patch of beach with a white cliff closely behind it, the only spot in the chain of cities unindustrialized, was littered with scaffolding and the faintest of noises could be heard from the melody that was up of made chisels and hammers, busy at work.

They are scaling the back that cliff, succeeding doubly in both clearing space for the expansion of the cities, but also in obtaining stone for the upward expansion of Lola. Explained the voice.

"I see, how long must it have taken to finish all of this?" asked Ainsley truly curious given the size of Treysta Bridge alone would have taken centuries by Ainsley's figuring.

Each city was erected in the celebration of the birth of one of the late King's daughters. The Sevardinal I speak of. They were all commanded to finish them in time for the 30th birthdays of each daughter for which they are named. So if you will see Beau-vity over there.. Guided the Voice pointing across the bay to the only city across the way, still very small and sparse, spread out over a great spread of land, a large structure was visible, and Ainsley assumed that made up the castle of one of the seven Queens.

*That is for the youngest of Queens, Belle, she is currently only 17,
meaning it is far from being completed. It goes for Renat and Flaure as well.*
Said the voice then pointing to a pair of cities, nearest to Ainsley, both
brimming with life and buildings, though a few construction projects could
be seen. *Twin sisters, twin cities, only 3 years till completion.* Said the
Voice, to which Ainsley quickly figured out that the twin sisters of Flantia
and Renavive, must've been 27 then. "So why then is Belle so young?"
asked Ainsley.

*Alas, I do not know, all I know is the Sevardinal were forced out of
their father's Kingdom and fled to their incomplete sanctuary of Galesport,
still part of their father's Kingdom at the time. As far as what happened, I
cannot tell you that occurred in the last Trinity Year, so I am unable to
recall. However that was only 10 years ago, perhaps there are some here
that would know?* Ventured the Voice, to which Ainsley nodded in
agreement, not wanting to talk anymore having gotten some stares at her
bizarre behavior over the last few minutes, the Voice figured the same.

*Come, we mustn't linger any longer, the last thing we want right now is
to be recognized for what we are.* Cautioned the voice, now more subtly
turning Ainsley back to the gate lying before them. From there Ainsley took
over and moved forward into the basement of the Bridge of Treysta.

He was panting heavily, and the pain in his ankle constantly reminded
him of his past, a past he wished to forget. Eye, as he decidedly chose to
stick with after Ainsley's inexplicable vanishing, had eventually managed to
escape the woods of Maltyrn and made his way north, figuring if it was good
enough for a Sevardinal, it was good enough for him. He had wished to stay
there, and wait to see if whatever mystics were at work, would cease and she

274

would return to him, however, as the night fell and his ankle worsened, Eye had to move on, it also did not help that cracks of branches and rustling of leaves could be heard from a distance.

Upon discovering Galesport, Eye quickly, and without comment, did his best to blend into the mass of humanity there. It was difficult, many were fascinated with him; its not every day that a dark skinned man in tribal wear, with a broken ankle and riding a gawn wandered into town. However he eventually managed to get a housing, many were available, after all it was the grand opening of the Bridge of Treysta and very few had made the transition to it. And seeing as all housing is free, depending only on your reliability as contributing citizen, Eye managed to slip right into a decent 3rd level apartment, overlooking the bay. Upon accomplishing this, Eye spent the next week's bed ridden, healing his ankle as best he could. He knew he couldn't inform a doctor of his infliction, he'd have to explain how he got it, and one thing he knew about visiting places foreign to him, you never tell people your past. Especially when you are from territories such as Maltyrn, or the equally odious Gaste.

Eye had no interest in the ambitions and wrongdoings of these provinces. Why would he, he never was privy to it, all he was a cowardly excommunicated tribesman who failed twice. Once to his tribe, and again to Ainsley, he didn't protect her, he let her vanish. It was his entire fault.

To say he was depressed was an understatement. He loathed everything about himself, and the only solace he could garner was when he managed at long last to get a job as a runner for the *Citerary*, the name given for the union between each of the seven cities making up Galesport.

It had always been one of his great joys to run, he loved the feeling it gave him running further each day, pushing beyond his limits, beyond limits even he thought impossible. And in this, Eye found peace.

And so, 3 years later, still performing his task of running to and frow from each local Government to the Citerary Head Quarters in Gale, Eye came across information that he thought would never hear.

It was mid afternoon, and Eye had been hard at work already for several hours. He was almost always out of breath whenever he arrived at his location and would often take some time before he took off to his next location. It was during one of these rests, that Eye heard the news. He had just arrived at the Citerary HQ, and took no time to admire the spectacle that was the lobby. Made of creamy white marble, and having an atrium scaling up to the highest floor of the building, allowing one to view the lobby from any floor. Taking to the steps, Eye quickly ascended them, making way for dignitaries occasionally. He went round and round, as the spiral stairway, attached to walls went round and round, plateauing occasionally at each floor, opening to let individuals off. His destination however was the very top, the seventh floor, the Royal Palace of Galen.

It had taken some time, but eventually Eye, thoroughly exhausted, and always hating messaging to the Royals, casually walked from the stairway to the sole mahogany doors that lay not far.

Pausing, Eye finished catching his breath, then gently knocked, and waited. He heard the slow walk of a Royal guard as he approached. And sure enough, the door swung open revealing the guard. Dressed in a flamboyant white garb, with crimson red striped indentations along the poufy shoulders and hips, a fashion statement separating them from traditional soldiers or guards, who simply wore flattened out tunics and leggings. Of course it simply made them look ridiculous.

"Speak your business." Demanded the guard, doing his best to seem intimidating, but failing miserably in comparison to Eye whom over the past 3 years had spurted to a significant height of 6 feet, but only weight 160 pounds, making him particularly skinny for his size.

"I have a message for Queen Galen from Queen Treysta." Explained Eye in a formal tone. Saying no more the guard moved aside and Eye swiftly entered the inner chambers of Galen's palace.

Adorned in the same marvelous white marble of the rest of the building, Galen's penthouse like palace was draped in similar crimson red fabrics, the drapes, the furniture, even the decadent stonework in the marble flooring, carved into such designs, depicting epic battles from centuries past.

Quickly moving through what must be the living room, Eye, knowing perfectly well where he was going, having been here many times, burst through the double doors at the end of the room and quickly, ignoring the study found there, turned right and came to a smaller single door. Then waiting patiently, he knocked once more.

"Come." Came a familiar voice. Entering, Eye's eyes quickly located Galen standing over her desk pointing down distractedly at a map on the desk. A couple of her political advisers were huddled around on the other side, patiently listening as she spoke.

"This cannot wait any longer, the wars in the Barren Wastes have ended, they will soon turn their eyes north, and we must fortify the south. Gentlemen it is paramount that a wall equivalent to that of Treysta must be built. We do not have the means to uphold them by numbers alone, together their forces make up 17 times that of ours. We must abate their push." Spoke

Galen passionate, yet frustrated to the advisors. "We understand Sister Gale, but we don't have the time or money to make such a wall in such a short amount of time. After all, the forces of Maltyrn have the speed and strength of the Great Deer at their disposal, and Gaste has the phenomenal archers of the West now under their thumb, a wall would only do so much." Argued the taller of the two advisors, while the other, clearly nowhere near as experienced in war or such judgments, remained silent. As did Eye, who knew from past situations like this, that it was best to not speak until spoken too. Besides he needed the moment to catch his breath, which almost always was short.

Galen wasn't pleased with her advisors wise point and sighed deeply, looking back down to map of her realm. "Very well, I will think on it more and discuss it with you and the rest of my sistren at the summit on the morrow. Good day gentlemen." Dismissed Galen, to which they deeply bowed and expectantly whispered 'Sister' as they turned and left out of the door from which Eye entered.

Sighing once more, Galen looked up finally to see Eye awkwardly waiting. "Eye, please do come and sit." She politely spoke whist offering an inviting hand. Eye didn't argue, and proceeded to sit down in the luxurious leather bound, cushioned chair.

"What news does my sistren bring?" she casually asked, doing her best to distract her from her more pressing issue.

"Well, not much really, no news from Belle, she is still debating on the drapes of her castle. Luvia is busy at work on expanding the residences in Luveir. Lola asks when the next shipment of marble will be arriving for her tower's inner walls. Flantia wants you to visit as soon as you have the time, other than that, Renee was the only one that had anything to say," spoke Eye

278

trepidatiously. This however wasn't noted as Galen only sighed. "No word from Treysta?" she asked hopefully. Eye could only give Galen a disappointed shake of his head. Galen was clearly saddened by this, but said nothing more on the matter "What was that then what Renee said?" she asked.

With this, Eye looked round then pulled his chair closer, causing slight alarm for Galen. Then leaning forward, and looking her dead in the eye he said, "She says she's found them."

Galen's eyes went wide, flushing with excitement. "She, she has?" she asked, seeking validation. To which Eye only nodded, having no clue the context in which his words meant so much, for he wasn't the messenger for the early relay of conversation between the two queens. Then remembering the other part of the job, Eye quickly pulled out from his inner vest, a letter, sealed shut.

"She also gave me this, told me it was of the utmost importance with regards to the first part of the message," explained Eye, still having no clue what the conversation was or what the letter spoke of. He then handed off the letter to Galen who quickly snatched it up, appearing more excited than she intended to be when in company. "Thank you Eye, your services are no longer required, you may go, take the day off, full pay, I insist!" excitedly spoke Galen, offering charity for which she was NEVER known for.

Eye played up his happiness about it, for he was, but still he down played his suspicions with it. And nodding and saying the typical good bye, he turned and left the office of Galen. But rather than doubled back through the palace like he usually did, Eye stopped just outside the door, feeling somewhat compelled to not leave just yet. He didn't know why this delivery bugged him so much, but it did, it felt, mischievous. And made Eye feel like a pawn in a greater game, a feeling he had no taste for ever since his abandonment of his tribe, and their manifest destinies for their kin.

Turning his head to the right he spotted a wide window, bubbled texture, still primitive for the sake of window making but revolutionary for the age in which it was conceived. And as such, windows were extremely rare in the world. But this window, this lone window in Galen's study, it was ajar. Going to it, he tested it and found it pushed open without a hitch. And then, beyond Eye's better instincts, he climbed out onto the ledge.

Eye had never been one for heights, his people were all ground dwellers, fearful of heights and what horrors they contained, like the Black Hand. Just being this high made him feel queasy and clumsy. But still, Eye did not stop, he stood there and, closing the window behind him, looked right once more and found, as if on purpose, Galen's office window fully open, and her balcony barren. Side stepping to it, Eye as silent as an insect, held onto the rail of the balcony for dear life, and looked gently into the room he previously was in.

There he saw Galen, hanging low on the desk reading intently the letter for which he delivered. Her smile couldn't be matched, and was uncommon for a woman of her stature and stress level. But whatever that letter contained, it was the best news she heard in ages. And before Eye knew it, she began to laugh as she exited the room, from the same doorway he and as it seemed, everyone else did, surely to go tell someone the good news.

Eye had to know he had to see what could make the most powerful woman in the world so pleased. Pulling himself up and over the railing, he silently crept into the room, keeping apace not sure how long he had, or where exactly in the palace Galen was. Arriving at the desk he quickly whipped round to the inner side of it, and leaned over the desk, and looked down at the opened letter.

And so it was, that Eye saw what he thought impossible, the words that both exhilarated and scared him. It read:

The one known as Ainsley, newest Sevardinal to be birthed, has again arrived in this land, and is as we speak descending the cliffs toward Renat with a destination of Treysta, we suspect Treysta Bridge is not her final destination, but merely a layover on her way to meet with the rest of the Seven. We MUST intercept her in order to reach said Final destination.

Every effort will be taken to apprehend her in accordance with your arrival.

Very best,

Seth Goldwin

Associate Intelligence Officor

Ainsley was alive, and they were after her.

XLI. Racing to Ainsley

Two minutes inside the gates of Treysta, and Ainsley knew that her imagination was not responsible for such magnificence. Though being relatively darkened and gloomy, the first level or *block* as locals seemed to call it, was entirely dedicated to shops, the whole length of it, up and down both sides, off into the far off other side of the bay. Bakeries, chocolataries, perfume shops, butchers, fisheries, tailors, blacksmiths, doctor stands, messenger posts, even public restrooms. It was all there, a thriving slice of capitalism.

However as Ainsley walked and looked round, she quickly noticed that none of these people were carrying any form of currency. *There is no such thing here.* Interjected the Voice, "How come, what's the purpose of stores if not to buy anything?" asked Ainsley. *Where else is a population this vast ever to collect what they need to live? And as for the shopkeepers, what better a way to spend your time than doing something you enjoy?* Knowingly explained the Voice to a surprised Ainsley. "So you mean to tell me that these people work for nothing and do it only because they want to? That sounds awful? All I'd do would be lay around and do nothing at all."

But really would you? Perhaps from where you come from that has become an option, what with dawn of the technological age, but here those marvels of the new millennium are somewhat a rarity around here. Books are only available to the educated, which is in itself, difficult to obtain, being the waitlist is generations long; you'd have to apply for your great grandson to stand a chance. Furthermore, if it weren't for work, nothing would work, the society, in fact all society would collapse. These people don't do it for nothing, they do it knowing that they are keeping the world turning, and that is enough for them.

"I see, wow, I'm so out of touch with this place aren't I?" awed Ainsley, slightly ashamed at her love of monetary gains. *You are just young, just wait till we reach our destination Ainsley, all will be explained, don't worry; you will be a laymen no longer.* Reassured the Voice, which strangely comforted Ainsley, for she had no real reason to be ashamed of not knowing everything, but promised herself quietly that when the opportunity came, she would learn everything that there was to know.

Reaching halfway along the bridge, Ainsley felt urged to stop. A cold chill ran down her back. Looking down at her hands, she admired momentarily the fluid orange glow that played across it as the *Teardrops* above emitted their fiery glow down upon her. Looking every so subtly over her shoulder, Ainsley could feel eyes upon her. She was being watched...

Treysta was on the opposite side of Galesport, and not an easy run through the 4 cities that stood between Gale and Treysta, him and Ainsley. After a few minutes of weaving in and out of narrow streets, and side passages, occasionally bumping into onlookers and commuters, Eye committed to the beach, figuring it would indeed be the fastest route to Treysta.

Bursting onto the beach, Eye was dismayed to see it scattered with thousands of people all minding their own business, having fun in the bay, fishing, jogging, and quarreling with on another. Indeed in a society where fun was a hard thing to come by, the beach was a most reputable spot of entertainment.

Fearing his time was running short, and seeing the great Treysta Bridge in the distance, Eye took off with all might in its direction.

His general build allotted him a fairly broad pace, leaping bounds across the pearly beach, knowingly avoiding masses of people here and there, and predicting cross traffic, allowing him to avoid a collision.

He should have been thinking more about how incredible it was that Ainsley had returned, that he hadn't lost her, that he could redeem himself for his past failings, which he could atone for failing Ainsley. Instead however, all Eye could focus on was the fire in his chest as he heaved and puffed his way to Treysta. A half-day of running this place and that had indeed weakened his initial resolve of speediness. Especially since his last location, Renat was right next to Treysta, meaning he'd run this course once before today, and it was indeed an unwelcome one.

On average, Eye could deliver anywhere between 3 and 7 messages, depending on distance between them, and he currently held the record for most delivered in a day with 21, a number which he regularly played down being that most of them were in the same city or nearby. However, it indeed gave rise to his fame and eventually garnered him a place in the Citerary. A place that he now cherished for it allotting him the chance to learn this most important of news.

In front of him the wall that was Treysta Bridge was growing bigger in his sight, and soon, he found himself engulfed by the gate.

Eye was very familiar with Treysta, seeing as he still held a residence here despite working regularly for the Citerary. His apartment was located 2 blocks up from where he was now, the main floor, the most frequented by patrons and commuters, whilst the second block was dedicated to local authority, the stocks were held there, as well as a primitive fire brigade, basically a bunch of men with barrels of seawater that they would dump onto flames, not very effective but impressive none the less for the effort and dedication. Also on this block was the homes of the workers of these important trades, as well as lower level dignitaries, for these weren't apartments but buildings dedicated entirely as homes for them.

The 3rd through 6th blocks, were all residential housing, varying in size, but generally and ultimately all equal in filth and stench. Despite being enlightened about financial obsolvation, they knew little about cleanliness; all save for the *Educates*, none of which lived in Treysta.

The mob inhabiting the first block was as always chaos, and almost impossible to pick someone out in, walking space was scarce, making it almost impossible for Eye to not bump into someone.

His urgency was rising, and his heart rate, despite the slow pace at which he kept, was still dangerously high.

Picking up his pace, using his agile body type, tall and skinny, Eye elegantly avoided the crowds, and, spotting a tall Herald podium, Eye hopped up onto it, and then jumped up onto the overhanging arm for the small Teardrop that hung extinct.

Squinting his eyes narrowly, attempting to make out any discerning characteristics that he recalled of Ainsley, Eye suddenly remembered that 3 years had passed and chances were most likely that Ainsley had changed drastically since then, after all, she was just a little girl back then, perhaps he wouldn't recognize her… That is to say until he did.

Her figure unmistakable, taller, obviously, but no less than gorgeous, she stood not too far off, stopped in thought, or conversation, Eye couldn't quite make out which from his viewpoint.

She then slowly turned her head, looking behind her, and for a moment, Eye was sure she was looking to him. But it wasn't true, her eyes suggested otherwise, she was looking directly back, and sure enough, as Eye followed her gaze back, he found what her eyes could not, for they weren't supposed to find him. An *Officor*. An agent for the Intelligence department of the Citerary, or as it was more commonly called the ID. Officor's were legendary for their swift and efficient actions toward targets, as well as their keen, almost superhuman capability to go undetected, despite their most distinguished apparel. Dressed entirely in black, in a most rugged material similar to canvas, only coarser, Officor's wore only black stockings for footwear, silencing their footsteps but causing great discomfort and callous sores on their feet. But perhaps their most recognizable mark was their masks. Masks in general were only granted to upper class citizens, who often wore them as a fashion statement, or for more political reasons. In fact even in the *Citerary House of Peoples*, a sort of parliament of Galesport, only much more primitive, people would gather and show their approval or disapproval all depending on what mask they dawned after the turn of the query is put upon them. However, in the lower, uneducated, trades-society of Galesport, Masks were seldom seen and often mocked.

Which makes and Officor ever more impressive, for their masks though basic, consisting of just a black, finely polished clay, with tiny white tears painted upon them, still stood out sorely in the commerce. And yet they were never detected.

This Eye knew, because many a time, his delivery would be to and or from an Officor, and never did he see them arrive or leave the meeting place. No one ever saw them, until Eye did.

Not thinking clearly, Eye brashly dropped down from the arm, and leapt into the crow, making a beeline directly for the incredibly fast Officor. He wasn't sure what he was going to do exactly, Officor's though rarely used, were trained in several ways of hand to hand combat as well as weaponry, given some missions required assassinations or hostage taking. These people were trained spies capable of immoral and unsympathetic death, and Eye was charging right at one.

He collided heavily with the Officor, who together fell to the floor, drawing a small circle around them from the surprised crowd. Ainsley turned fully now seeing that her suspicions were correct and that she was indeed being followed, however she was shocked to see Eye, and not thinking or knowing for that matter of what acknowledging him would do, Ainsley said, "Eye? Is that you?"

The Officor's actions were swift, withdrawing a small *splinter blade* from his bag, he grasped it firmly and lifted Eye up and wrapped the blade around his throat, death but a tug away.

Ainsley gasped at the sudden turn of events. Calling into memory her most traumatic experience with Mallory and Mr. Charles in the police station.

"You are to come with us *Trinity Yearling*" coldly, and detachedly spoke the Officor, slowly inching toward Ainsley with Eye in his grasp.

"Us?" nervously asked Ainsley, hoping beyond hope that it was just a mis-saying. But as two more Officor's appeared left and right of her, she knew it not to be.

"It appears we have no choice." Spoke Ainsley defeated.

XLII. The Plea

They walked a short distance to the primitive, and all together impressive elevators that had been erected at the center of the long bridge. Spanning a large portion of either side of the bridge, the twin elevators sat wide and ever moving. Based on a simplistic pulley system that pulled the elevator on the left upward as the elevator opposite descended. Similar in design to a pair of waits tied on opposite ends of a piece of string being dangled on a longwise pole. Only apparent downside of this innovative system was of course that only one could go upward at one time and the other downward. Also, unlike our elevators, you couldn't choose to go directly to a floor. You had to wait through each floor, and then exit.

As it was now, the elevator on the left was just arriving on the main floor noting that it would indeed rise soon. Picking up pace, the trio of Officor's carried Ainsley and Eye into the opening of the elevator.

Ainsley now took this time to take in her once travel companion. He hadn't aged well, the soft supple features that Ainsley admired and, even though young lusted after, were even now three years later wrinkling and coarse. It looked as if Eye had been through hell and back, and sadly lived to tell the tale.

"What are you doing here?" asked Ainsley hushed, trying not to draw the attention of the Officor's. "No what are you doing here? Where the hell did you go?!" Whisped Eye obviously annoyed with the situation both he and Ainsley were now in. He had clearly become more jaded since the last met, and as such dropped the nice guy protector for frustrated boy. A regression.

"I didn't choose to leave! I was forced to! Its not my fault!" spoke Ainsley now angered with Eye, still not sure why, he had a right to feel upset about her vanishing act. After all, he was injured, in the middle of some of the most notorious woods in the world, riding an untrained gawn, with no home to return to. Ainsley now only argued fearing she couldn't openly admit an apology.

Eye just shook his head in dismissal, looking up as the slow moving elevator finally arrived at the top floor. The Seventh floor of the Bridge of Treysta designated solely for Treysta's palace. The largest of the seven, was almost always empty, as Treysta never stayed in one place for long, in fact few have ever seen Treysta's face; for it was her, in her younger years that brought on the obsessive fad that had overtaken Galesport, vis-à-vis the masks.

Masks had been unheard of in the northern lands. Historically they had varying levels of significance, dependent entirely on what place you called home. The most obvious and significant use of masks would be that of the Stoneworkers of Terra-Mal. Whose young children at the age of 7 would be outfitted with whole-head masks, nothing fancy, simple iron enveloping their entire head. And they would wear these for the rest of their lives.

However, Galesport did not take their fancy until Treysta turned 15, a day which held no real significance except for the tragic accident that occurred. An accident that left poor Treysta, long considered the jewel of the Sevardinal, horribly scarred across her gorgeous face. And as such she took refuge in her father's palace in Dorsan, and a few years later, emerged to the public a changed woman. Gone were her long flowing red locks, cropped to her scalp, and gone was her pleasant demeanor, instead now a jaded, and aggressive, hot headed tomboy who enjoyed nothing more than to isolate herself and take long walks in the woods. But the most prominent change in her was the pure silver mask that was glued to her face, disguising her horrific scars, and in that simple fact, changing Treysta.

How the masks became such an Phenomena in Galesport isn't quite clear, but is most likely associated entirely with how proudly Treysta wore hers when she made her limited public appearances, and to put it bluntly, how cool she looked. However the method, the mask slowly began to emerge in the upper class of society and soon enough, was uncommon to see anyone, save for those who could not acquire the rare quantities manufactured every trimester.

Upon exiting the elevator, which awkwardly popped up from the ground in the middle of the large, cathedral like hall that made up Treysta's palace. Ainsley's jaw dropped. The sight was breathtaking, nothing but milky crystal for pillars and black marble for the floor. It was dark, and ominous, but undoubtedly gorgeous. Ainsley turned to look at Eye's reaction, he gave none, unbeknownst to Ainsley, Eye had been there many times before, however he never saw farther than this, the *Chalice*, as it was called, why no one knows. Eye often was there at the request of his unofficial boss, Gale, who often sent him to deliver a letter, the same one every time, for the past 3 years, chances it being much longer than that even. Same result every time, Eye returning to Gale with the exact same letter.

Moving along the bridge-sized hall, Ainsley wondered the purpose of such a hall, when suddenly at the far end it became clear why. Resting there, eternal, were 10 thrones, 7 looked new and Ainsley could figure their purpose, the halls purpose, a ceremonial gathering of sorts for important occasions, like marriage or trial. Made of the same glorious crystal and black marble, the thrones sat evenly spread out on an slightly elevated floor just a few meters higher than the ground. The real question of the thrones was the significance of the three resting ever higher on and elevated perch with no apparent way up to them. They looked very much out of place in this hall, and clearly were not built for it. Made out of simple wood, carved very much in the tradition on many monarchal thrones, the looked worse for wear and on the one on the left even slightly mended.

Ainsley didn't have time to quietly ask Eye their purpose, as they were quietly torn away from the *Chalice* and taken beyond the thrones to a back room.

Inside it was darkened, no form of natural light present making it extremely difficult to orient to. However the Officor's had no issue, and quickly sat Ainsley and Eye down in a pair of chairs. They then released them and vanished from Ainsley's senses.

All was silent in the room, all Ainsley could hear was her quickened breathing, and that off Eye's calm breathing.

A door opened then, where in the room Ainsley couldn't be sure, where ever the door opened from, the room it joined also had no light. The door shut, and then Ainsley felt a presence in the room, and knew that she and Eye weren't alone.

"What is this place?" quietly asked Ainsley to Eye, hoping he still wasn't mad, he wasn't. "I'm not sure, if it is what I suspect it to be, we are in trouble…" quietly warned Eye. "What do you think it is?" asked Ainsley wanting to know, but also not wanting to.

"This is a *Dark Room*." Came a voice from the darkness, deeply feminine with a hint of masculinity but muffled. Both Ainsley and Eye blindly jumped. "Whose there?!" demanded Eye standing up only to have hands emerge from behind and seat him once more.

"Please don't get up." Coyly spoke the voice, closer now than before, perhaps even as close as the table at which they were seated. "Seth, if you would be so kind as to escort our young messenger out." Came the voice, which instantly triggered the identity for Eye, Queen Treysta. However it took a little longer for Ainsley to cue in.

Grabbing hold of Eye, the Officor known as Seth picked up and Eye and removed him from the room, if Eye put up a fight, it wasn't heard.

"Who are you?" asked Ainsley, feeling handled and not liking it. "The real question is not who I am but who you are," countered the voice. A saying that Ainsley was growing sick of hearing, and that being the case took stand. "Yes, I know I'm a fricken Sevardinal! You don't have to lecture me on it again!"

This brought out a chuckle from Treysta, "I see, well that's very convenient, because I too am Sevardinal, only of a different brand."

This finally clued Ainsley in, the darkened room, the Chalice, it all le to one conclusion. "Treysta!" exclaimed Ainsley.

"I'm glad to see we know each other, that will quicken things greatly. Seth lights." Directed Treysta to Seth who quietly entered the room once more. And after a few moments, a warm glow from the large teardrop above ignited and filled the tiny room. And in this light, Ainsley looked upon the second eldest daughter of the forgotten king; hair short as always, just barely registering on her scalp. Wearing clothing similar to that of the Officor's, Ainsley wondered then why that was. *She's the head of the Intelligence Office* spoke the Voice, to which Ainsley gave no reply. Staring deeply into the piercing blue eyes visible only through the small slits in the strikingly beautiful silver mask adorning Treysta's face, Ainsley instantly felt small.

"That's better, now, I'm not one for talking much, you know who I am, and what I represent in this place, so having said that, I need a favor from you." Asked Treysta.

This was peculiar, Queen Treysta was notorious for never asking favors, and hating owing anyone anything, and yet here she was, asking something of Ainsley. Not knowing what else to do, Ainsley said, "Sure, what do you need?"

Though not directly visible to Ainsley, Treysta smiled broadly to herself, glad at the ease of this difficult process. "I require that when you reach your destination, you give your Witherney, this." Said Treysta as she handed Ainsley a sealed envelope. Taking it, Ainsley looked it over, and then looked to Treysta, slightly disappointed. "That's it?"

"No." said Treysta, leaning forward now, emphasizing what she was about to say. "I require that you fight for what it says, defend it. At all costs, we need your elder to agree, do you understand, it's of the utmost importance. You cannot fail me." With this, Treysta leaned across the table and grabbed a hold of Ainsley's shoulders. Startling Ainsley.

"And, and what if I don't?" asked Ainsley, "Then my wrath will the be the least of your worries. Please, I'm not accustomed to begging, but we need your help." Begged Treysta; Ainsley couldn't help but be unhinged by Treysta's uncharacteristic showing of vulnerability. And knowing this was rare, and a sign that what ever was in that envelope was important; Ainsley stared deep into Treysta's eyes, and nodded.

XLIII. The Door

The trip up the long spiral stairwell hidden deep behind the Chalice's brooding walls; beyond even the Dark Rooms, used as a form of torture and interrogation, was a relatively short one, being them on the top block of the bridge, it wasn't long till they emerged on the outer side of the bridge's wall and climbed a small utility ladder to the topside.

Ainsley had agreed to deliver Treysta's message on one condition, that Eye accompany her. Why in that instant she decided upon that, she wasn't exactly sure, an urge took over her. She didn't really know the man well, but regardless, one fact was true, she did owe him for abandoning him three years prior. And a thought kept running through her head, one that she felt like she had before, but knew she didn't. *He'll save my life someday*...

Treysta didn't follow Ainsley and Eye to the surface; instead she slipped out the door from whence she came. Leaving Ainsley and Eye with the three Officor's who originally picked them up.

They walked them the short distance to the end of the bridge. And that is where they stopped, releasing their hold on the pair and looking blankly at them behind their similar black marble masks.

Taking the hint, Ainsley grabbed a hold of Eye and carried him off forcibly down the well-beaten path.

The sun was setting overhead as Eye and Ainsley walked further and further from the boarders of Galesport and into the uncharted jungle ahead. All was silent between them, an awkwardness had grow between them since they last met, both having faced hardship in that time, and both not wishing to talk about it, but wanting to know more about the other. However neither could come to an appropriate starting point. So silence remained. And it stayed that way late into the night when finally Eye, resuming his guide of sorts, grabbed a hold of Ainsley's shoulder. "I think we should camp soon, we'll be reaching *Gapestom* soon."

Turning to Eye, Ainsley with no passion left for curiosity bluntly asked, "What's that? Another city?" "Huh? No not at all, well no that's not true, it used to be, a glorious city somewhere in time, but now its just barely a ruin, its been repurposed as a dumpsite. You know for Galesport's wasted materials and matter." Explained Eye to which Ainsley couldn't help but be disgusted with. It wasn't really that bizarre, back home she lived not far from a dump, but still it was slightly disheartening that they did that here too, and on ruins to boot. "Charming." Scoffed Ainsley who tugged her arm away from Eye's grasp rather harshly, "What's your problem with me!" he demanded, annoyed with her cold nature towards him.

Turning away from him she went and sat on a rock nearby. "Nothings wrong, its me, its, its been a rough few years…" spoke Ainsley as tears, unbeknownst to her, began to fall and wet her flowing white dress provided to her by Treysta. Taking sympathy on poor Ainsley, Eye sat down beside her and wrapped his arm around her and hugged her tightly. "I know same here, it'll be better now, just so long as we stick together. I can protect you, I swore it, I haven't forgotten, I won't let anything happen to you, I promise."

Though short, Eye's words soothed Ainsley and she eased her tense state and relaxed into a calm embrace with Eye, not even denying how good he smelled despite having been walking for several hours. And together, they fell asleep, still hugging one another, laying on the large flat rock beside the road.

Hoofs could be heard, quietly and slowly approaching, then the deep snorting of some majestic creature. Ainsley was the first to open her eyes, dawn had not yet broken, and the way she laid, the sounds rested behind her.

Fearing the worst, Ainsley slowly turned, at first she saw nothing, just a starry night sky starting to blend with a vibrant morning light. But as she finished turning, in came in to sight, an epic stag, not of her recollection, not like deer from her world, no this was definitely one of the Giant Deer she had been told about and had experienced quite unfortunately. However this one was different, its antlers weren't as long and were aimed directly back over its long back. Its size too was much smaller than the mother Deer Ainsley and Eye experienced in Maltyrn. Something about it gave the sense that this Giant Deer wasn't here to cause bodily harm.

Get up said the Voice, to which Ainsley dutifully did, gently removing Eye's loving arm from her back she stood. The deer stood staring straight at Ainsley and then gave a curtsey bow of sorts, as best as a deer could, to which Ainsley awkwardly returned. Then without notice the deer turned and started off down the path.

Follow it. Now. What about Eye? Shouldn't I wake—*Follow it, NOW!* Ainsley didn't have a choice, the Voice claimed her bodily functions and carried Ainsley off down the path after the deer.

It wasn't long till the deer and Ainsley reached what must've been the beginnings of the Ruins of Gapestom. Large half destroyed, half eroded pillars stood opposite one another leading into a massive pile of waste, sky high, and yet, oddly, no smell was present. Ainsley didn't even have to ask. *Industrial grade perfume*, "Ah, that makes sense, where are we going?" asked Ainsley never actually having asked the exact location of this journey, just 'North'.

Suddenly however, the deer stopped, and its antlers began to glow softly as if they were heating up. *Where are we going Ainsley, we are here.* Explained the Voice. "Huh?" *Get on the Deer* Ainsley slowly approached the deer and carefully climbed on top of it, finding that she fit eerily well on its back. *Grab a hold of its antlers*, Ainsley didn't immediately do so, the sight of them were slightly alarming. *Do it!*

Without saying more, Ainsley shut her eyes and reached out to touch the antlers. Only her grasp returned nothing, in fact before she could comprehend that fact she was rubbing her behind which was now sore from rudely hitting the ground.

Opening her eyes, she found several things shocking, first the deer had vanished, second all color had faded from the lush jungle leaving just her in color. However all this was miniscule compared to the grand city that had popped up instantaneously around her. It was as if Gapestom rebuilt itself in the blink of an eye.

Rising from the soft dirt, Ainsley looked round the immense stony city, it was beautiful, a thriving labyrinth of castles, and primitive high rise towers, dancing in and around one another as far as the eye could see.

Forgetting entirely about the vanished Deer, Ainsley began to walk along the deserted street of Gapestom. It was clear to her that this indeed wasn't a reality that in fact she was probably wandering through piles of rotting meat, and moldy bread. But that didn't stop her, her urge to move forward down the main street of this lost capital was of the utmost importance.

Looking down the long seemingly endless street, Ainsley saw something in the far off square that she recognized, as if it were from a dream. It was humongous, round, taking up a majority of the large space made available for the square. It was a Follisenwit, portals of the Sevardinal. And as she approached, Ainsley knew, at long last, after countless hours, day's… years, of travelling through this mystical land, Ainsley had finally reached her destination.

Entering the square, Ainsley looked round at the ghostly shops and homes that littered the rim of the square, it was very sad to know that all this beauty was just a mystical figment of the Follisenwit, that in fact all of it had long since perished.

Turning her attention back to the Follisenwit, Ainsley admired the structure altogether, not very impressive, this particular Follisenwit wasn't smooth or as round as the one she came from, it was cobbled with jagged stone, that gave a faint outline of a circular structure. And also, unlike Ainsley's Follisenwit, this one had no clear stairway up to the Chamber that sat up top, just large layers of stone, similar to the Pyramids of Egypt.

Knowing that she had to climb to the top, Ainsley sighed to her self and began to climb, using the uneven cobble of the lower levels to get both foot and hand holds.

As she clawed her way up to the first ring of stone, Ainsley couldn't help but feel bad now for leaving Eye behind once more, he most definitely would have loved to see this, but something told Ainsley that it wasn't meant to be, that, even though she liked him, there were things that he wasn't privy to.

Frowning at this, Ainsley started up the second ring. As she did she noticed, not really to her surprise, that this Follisenwit had seven rings in total, getting smaller as they got higher.

Unlike the Follisenwit in the desert, or *Barren Wastes* as they were locally known, Ainsley did not find it difficult to scale up the tall structure, other than the physical exertion. Again proving that this Follisenwit was older and perhaps not as well endowed in magical properties. How wrong she was.

Upon reaching the top of the tall structure, Ainsley was exhausted, she now stood high above the city square and could see now just how vast this city once was, stretching as far as the horizon in each direction, now the fact it was gone was even more sad.

Turning to the large opening in the chamber, Ainsley hesitated just for a moment, but then, calming herself, walked into the black void.

Ainsley took tentative steps deeper into the darkness, and as each step passed, Ainsley noticed that she was far beyond the end of the physical space available for such a chamber. Wherever she was, it wasn't in that chamber.

As she walked in the distance of the void, came a small speck of something, Ainsley couldn't be sure what, it looked like a white dot, but as she came closer, it grew in size, and complexion. No longer looking like a dot, or white, but a square, and then a rectangle, windows could be made out, dim light shining through them, then a wide double door at the center. Until finally, Ainsley could clearly see, it was a house. More like a mansion by the size, seven stories. But this mansion wasn't just any mansion. Arriving at the front door, Ainsley paused, and reached for the knocker. And there, she had the greatest sense of déjà vu in her life. The knocker was one and the same the one from Artie's Narrow mansion. A deer head, with the handle connected between the antlers.

That's when it finally hit Ainsley, this building, was this world's version of Artie's home. Former home. And as Ainsley was lost in memories of yesteryear, a familiar face opened the door.

"Ah Ainsley, we've been expecting you."

Ainsley looked up to see her great grandfather Arthur standing in the doorway smiling wide. Ainsley returned the smile, and without saying more, gave Arthur a big hug, not realizing how much she missed him.

The foyer of the Mansion was excessive to say the least, if this was indeed the doppelganger of Artie's Earthly home, it bared it no similarities on the inside. Dressed with fine silk draping's of several different colors, the vast size of the room was dominated by a set of 7 identical curved staircases all laying side by side running up into the ceiling as one, separated by their respective railings. It was a truly odd sight, Ainsley knew mansions by design were meant to be flamboyant, but such a wide expanse of stairway seemed pretentious. And yet, as she followed Artie, she saw that indeed the stairway was indeed where they were heading.

As they approached, Ainsley casually took her first few steps up the stairway to the far right. "Oh, no not that way child, here." Spoke Arthur as he doubled back down the stairs to come and fetch her. Then gently grasping her arms, Arthur made a wide birth round the stairway to the middle-most steps. "This is it, after you." Warmly spoke Arthur encouraging Ainsley upward. Looking up the stairway as it disappeared into the ceiling, Ainsley's sense of wonder took hold and she quickly raced up into the opening.

It was dark, no light coming in from above as far as she could see, only the dimming light from below lit her way. Below her she could make out Arthur's footfalls as he brought up the rear, but somehow that didn't seem to matter, all that mattered was what was the end of this tunnel.

It wasn't long till they reached the opening, and the first thing that Ainsley realized, was that their staircase was the only one that stopped here.

Looking round, she could see the enclosed staircases on her right still proceeding up, whilst the two that *were* on her left were no where to be seen.

Arriving beside her at the top of the stairs, Artie rested his hand on her shoulder and leaned heavily on her, panting. "Come on now, we must not keep them waiting, they've been doing enough of that recently." Ainsley looked to Artie and then looked forward, at the wide expanse of the floor, adorned wall to wall with portraits of figures Ainsley had no clue were, and places Ainsley could only assume were from here, not home.

Peering to the far size of the room, Ainsley saw a lone set of double doors alone on the far wall, wedged between two great banners, with symbols Ainsley couldn't place.

Turning to Artie, she looked at him, wanting to ask him so many questions, but for whatever reason, the words wouldn't come out. And in a seemingly immaculate moment of telepathy, Artie said, "don't worry child, soon everything will become clear, you'll see."

Turning back to the door, Ainsley tentatively took her first few steps toward the far side of the room. She looked round at the portraits on the walls, seeing these majestic people in backdrops of great battles long since gone, cities long since destroyed. It then dawned on Ainsley that not matter what she thought she knew, she still knew nothing. *What more do I have to learn?*

With every step Ainsley took towards the door, the more she missed home, miss her old life, before all this came to pass, when she was just a silly little kid who wanted a knew mp3 player, whose only worry was forgetting to brush her teeth. Those days were gone, and never to be seen again. *Times change... Everything's changed...*

Arriving at the large doors, much larger up close than at the distance from whence she saw them, Ainsley let out a trepid sigh.

Fingers entwined themselves into her left hand, and Ainsley looked down to see Artie's hand holding hers. "Don't worry, it was scary for me too. But you have nothing to fear, honestly, these doors don't hold anything bad for you. Only your birthright..." spoke Artie reassuringly, trying his best to calm her down for what was to come. Ainsley looked up at him and finally mustered up something to say. "What's my birthright?" she asked timidly, feeling foolish for needing to ask. Artie didn't ridicule her, he just smiled down warmly at her and squeezed her hand, then placing his other on the doors before them, and he pushed them open, and said, "everything."

Then he quickly carried Ainsley forward into the room beyond. And consequently with this simple action, carried her into the next stage of her life.

What will become of me? Thought Ainsley, as the doors silently swung closed behind them.

End of Book One...

Printed by
Schaltungsdienst Lange o.H.G., Berlin